Reclaiming Herself

By

DJ Martin

CHAPTER ONE

My head throbbed as I fitted my key into the lock. I didn't usually get horrible headaches, but that day was, obviously, an exception. I'd had to leave work just a half hour after my lunch break, although I hadn't eaten a bite.

As I opened the door, I was hit by the reek of an unknown perfume. Then familiar and unfamiliar sounds assaulted me. The familiar was my husband's voice in the throes of ecstasy. The unfamiliar was a female voice, exhibiting the same emotions.

The headache immediately got worse, almost blinding me. I'd had my suspicions for a couple of months but now? My worst fears were confirmed. And in *our* bed! I pulled my cell phone out of my pants pocket, hit the camera function (perhaps a little hard), and headed to the bedroom.

"Both of you get the fuck out of my house!" I yelled as I held the phone up and started clicking away. I was certain I'd gotten at least one shot of both of them looking at me from the bed in all their naked glory.

"Oh, shit," Rob said, fumbling for the bedclothes to cover himself. The girl simply stared, making no effort to hide any part of her body.

I took a deep breath and looked Rob straight in the eyes. "You have until seven o'clock tomorrow morning to get all your shit out of this condo. After that, I'll be changing the locks."

In a daze, I stumbled out the door, back to the elevator, and got myself out of the building. I turned left, oblivious to my path or destination, and started walking. My fingers were tingling as if their blood supply had been cut off. All the blood in my body had probably migrated to my head, which was throbbing. Several steps away from the door, I lost what little I had in my stomach. I sank to my haunches, leaning against the building's wall. This was Midtown Atlanta. Passersby didn't even look at me.

As I squatted on the sidewalk, the feeling returned to my hands. I grabbed a tissue from my purse and cleaned my face. I sat there, in full view of the public, waiting for the tears. They didn't come, and my head hurt even worse. I knew they would, though. I always cried when I was angry, and this definitely qualified. With still-shaking hands, I texted two of the best pictures to my boss, the divorce lawyer. THAT'S HIS SECRETARY IN MY BED, I said. I WANT EVERYTHING.

Thirty seconds later, my phone rang. "Holy shit, Jo," Burke said. "Are you okay? Where are you? What can I do?"

"Of course I'm not okay," I snapped back. "I just found my husband banging his secretary; my head hurts like hell; I'm too keyed up to even lie down, much less sleep to get rid of the headache; and

I have no fucking idea what I'm going to do now. I'm sitting on the sidewalk outside the building next to ours."

I had worked for Burke for almost twenty-two years as his personal secretary after he pulled me out of the firm's typing pool. We knew almost everything there was to know about each other, and he was used to my coarse language.

He sighed. "Okay. Today's Thursday. Call Denise and go get a bender on, taking tomorrow off. You've already retained me…you can do all the paperwork on Monday. By the way, did you say anything to them?"

"I told them to get the fuck out of my house. Then I told Rob he had until seven tomorrow morning to get all his shit out before I changed the locks. He'd better. I'm going to need a change of clothes, and I don't want to see him again until the arbitration meeting."

"That may or may not fly. Depends on how well he's thinking at this point, and what attorney he gets. It's his condo, too. Can you stay with Denise and Abby for a couple of days?"

Denise was my best friend. We'd known each other since grade school, been tight since middle school, and if I swung that way, we'd probably be together. But her wife, Abby, was awesome. I didn't lose a friend when they got married but gained another BFF.

"Probably. And Abby's clothes will fit me. Thank God we don't have any pets. I don't want to go back there right now and wouldn't trust him to remember to feed anyone."

"Okay. Like I said, call Denise. I'll do what I can to start proceedings on my end and will see you Monday morning. Don't worry, Jo. We've got this. Call if you need me. Any time of day or night. Okay?"

The waterworks finally started. "Okay. Thank you." I sniffled hard as I disconnected and immediately called Denise.

"Denny?" I burst into uncontrollable tears as I said, "I need you!"

An hour later, I was sitting on the sofa in Denise and Abby's Virginia-Highlands house. Both my friends had taken the afternoon off; Denise had come to get me while Abby rushed home to prepare a headache tisane for me. She was even better with herbs than I was…my headache was gone in about fifteen minutes. After I felt better, despite the early hour, Abby poured me a double gin and tonic.

My tears had dried on the ride, but they came in a fresh wave. "That asshole!" I yelled. "I know guys sometimes cheat but in *my* bed? They couldn't even go to a hotel or her place? Now I'm going to need a new mattress, too. I'll never want to sleep on that one again."

Denise already had her arm around me. Abby moved from the chair to my other side and stroked my hair. I started calming.

"Did you have any inkling he was cheating on you?" Denise asked.

"Sort of, yes," I sniffled. "A couple of times in the last month or so I'd called his office to remind him about a dinner engagement or ask a question after he didn't respond to a text message. He was out of the office, and it wasn't Camilla that answered the phone but someone else.

"Then last week, he came home smelling of the same perfume permeating the condo today. I sort of shrugged it off…maybe a client had hugged him or something. But I had that niggling suspicion, you know?"

The more I thought about catching them in the act, the angrier I became. My secretarial job had put that asshole through graduate school, keeping a roof over our heads and food in our stomachs while he studied full time. That was the only reason he was now a bank vice president instead of a teller or loan officer. My fingers started tingling again, and as I looked down, I saw sparks coming off them. I stared in a combination of amazement and fear.

"What the hell is happening to me now?" I cried, waving my hands around. They looked like Fourth of July sparklers.

Denise grabbed my hands to keep me from scattering the sparks. As she did, Abby chuckled and said, "Looks like it took this amount of anger to waken your latent abilities. No, don't pick up your drink right now. That's electrical fire, and it won't get along with the condensation on the glass. I'd prefer you not burn our house down."

I turned to Abby, eyes wide. "What the hell are you talking about?"

Abby made a pushing motion with her hands, and I felt all the anger drain out of me. The sparklers on my fingertips winked out. "Go in the bedroom and change into comfortable clothes. My stuff's on the left side of the closet and in the highboy dresser.

"After you're out of your work clothes, we'll explain."

Denise pushed me off the sofa with a "go," and I stumbled into their bedroom to find clothes. In a daze, I pulled a pair of lounge pants and a T-shirt out of her dresser, leaving my suit on their bed for the time being.

I plopped back down onto the sofa. "Can I have my drink now?"

This time, Denise guffawed. "You're not sparking, so you're safe. Yeah, go ahead and slug it. We have more, and you'll probably need it."

I took a huge gulp of my gin and tonic, feeling the burn of the alcohol down my throat. I didn't normally drink doubles, but this time, I was glad of the extra booze.

Abby took a sip of her wine, inhaled deeply, then said, "That fire coming off your fingertips? The way you're so good with herbs without doing much in the way of studying? You're a witch, just like we are."

I choked on my next gulp. Denise thumped my back. "I'm…you're a…what?" I coughed out.

Abby smiled. "A witch. You know, like in stories. But real. You've always had power, but for some reason you suppressed it."

I stared, first at her, then Denise, who nodded. "Don't you remember when we first got our periods? Shit started happening to both of us, and my mom explained it all."

I thought back. I had a vague recollection of some emotional discomfort back then but shook my head. "You're going to have to remind me. I just don't remember much."

"Man, you really did repress. Okay. I got my period two days before you did. I was in a lot of pain from cramping. The second day when I finally stopped cramping and started flowing good, I got pissed when my pad leaked on the way home from school, and Jarrod Walker's teasing didn't help. I kicked a rock and instead of just dribbling down the sidewalk, it flew into his groin. He chased us all the way home."

I remembered that day. I also remembered Jarrod Walker. He was a bully. Large even for a twelve-year-old boy, he lorded it over the neighborhood, forcing kids to do his homework or run errands for him. He couldn't steal lunch money because none of us had it. We were all on the free lunch program at school. Otherwise, I'm sure he would have. Those who didn't comply were beaten soundly. He also leered at girls, exposing himself when no adults were around. He was, to put it bluntly, a disgusting child. He was arrested when we were fifteen for running drugs. I never saw him again – thankfully.

"I thought you aimed that rock and was impressed. That stuck. But…?"

Denise sighed. "When you started the day after that, all the grass and weeds along our route home from school grew at an alarming rate. Like something out of *Little Shop of Horrors*. It wasn't until we got into the house stuff stopped sprouting. It was *so weird!*

"That was my mother's week to make sure she didn't work overtime. When Mom arrived, we told her what had happened, both with Jarrod and the green stuff. Instead of fainting or taking us to the nearest exorcist, she laughed, hugged us, explained what was happening, and how to keep the magic from spiraling out of control.

"I thought it was the coolest thing. You got scared. I'm really not sure what was going through your mind because you refused to talk about it. The next day, when Mom asked if we wanted magic lessons, you clammed up and made some excuse. I didn't want to upset you any further, so I never talked about it or the lessons Mom gave me.

"And we come to now. Whether you like it or not, your magic just erupted, and you're going to *have* to deal with it."

Well, shit. I finished my drink and just held the empty glass up. Abby took it and less than a minute later, handed me a refill. I drank almost half of it before saying, "What else is going to be dumped on me today? First, I find Asshole cheating, then you tell me I'm some character out of fairy tales? What next?"

Denise hugged me again. "Nothing more today. We'll get you good and liquored up, feed you, then pour you into bed. You can stay here tomorrow, and we'll talk more tomorrow night, okay?"

I shook my head. "No, Burke's taking care of the asshole for the moment. Since I, as you say, *have* to deal with it, I want to know all about this witch stuff now."

"You always phrase things better than I do," Denise said to Abby. "You tell her while I figure out dinner." She rose from the sofa and went into the kitchen.

"Okay." Abby blew out a breath. "All the creatures from fairy tales exist. Werewolves, well actually, were-beings because there are those who transform into creatures other than wolves, vampires, fairies, witches…they're all real. Magic keeps them hidden from plain ol' human eyes.

"Witches not only can control the elements like the wind and that fire coming off your fingertips, but we also have special affinities. Like Denise is good with animals and I'm good with herbs and healing."

Denise was a veterinarian, and a damned good one. Her partners always transferred difficult cases to her. She had an inexplicable way with animals, able to calm the most agitated, or figure out what was wrong when no one else could. Abby was an herbalist. The State of Georgia frowns on remedies that aren't pharmaceutical, so she worked in an office with an acupuncturist and a chiropractor. She determined what was needed, and one of the guys who had a license did the "prescribing" to keep it all legal. I knew she was good at her job…she had clients who'd come to her for a decade or more.

They had met at a natural medicine conference in Colorado fifteen years previous. To hear Denise tell it, it was love at first sight. Abby had been living in California, and it took two years of a long-distance relationship for her to establish professional connections in Atlanta and make the move to Denise's house. Then they had to contend with one neighbor who didn't like having a pair of lesbians, one of whom was Black, living next door. He said unkind things within their hearing but, thankfully, that was all. Denise and Abby simply ignored him. Two years after Abby moved in, he moved out. The couple who bought his house had become friends.

"The power we have hits at puberty, but just like our bodies, we grow into it," Abby continued. "Most of us have a parent who's magical, and they teach us to control the magic, as well as help us find what we're good at. Just like regular parents do.

"Apparently, you have magic in your blood from somewhere, but from what D's told me, it wasn't your mother, so it was probably a grandparent or great-grandparent, or maybe it came from your father. *Something* scared you about magic, and instead of embracing it as D did, you repressed it. That can happen. Sometimes repressed magic never manifests again; sometimes it comes out with a bang, like yours just did.

"So, I don't know about the healing part, but I do know you're good with herbs. You have an instinctive knowledge of which herb to use for what but as far as I know, you never studied, right?"

"No. I have a few books I've picked up over the years but no formal schooling like you."

I'd always liked plants, and even had a couple of monstrous pothos in the bedroom I shared with Denny when we were kids. We lived in an apartment so I couldn't have a garden but when I had the chance, I weeded around shrubs and flower beds in a nearby park. That sometimes garnered odd stares from walkers and cyclists along the path, but I didn't care. It felt good to take care of the plants.

When Rob and I bought the condo, I filled the balcony and kitchen window with pots of herbs. That afternoon I had intended to head straight to the balcony to pinch a few leaves of feverfew when I got home, knowing eating them plus an hour's nap would get rid of the headache. Of course, that had been horribly interrupted, but I could taste feverfew and lemon balm in Abby's tisane.

"Your tisane worked better than eating fresh feverfew leaves. Why?"

"Magic!" She grinned. "I pushed a little healing energy into it as it was brewing. Not sure, but I think you'll be able to do that, too."

"Can I curse Asshole? Maybe make his dick fall off or something? It'd serve him right."

"We're already working on that," Denise called from the kitchen. "We don't keep baneful herbs in stock, so I had to call a friend. She'll drop off what we need on Saturday."

I finished my second double G&T and handed my glass back to Abby. "After dinner," she said, pushing my hand down. "Let's get some food in you. My hangover remedies are da bomb, but you'll still feel better if your stomach is full, especially since you didn't eat lunch."

Denise set a plate of pasta with marinara sauce and a couple slices of French bread on the table in front of me. "Eat," she ordered, returning to the kitchen for two more of the same. I picked at the food, not feeling very hungry.

"Seriously, girl, put the food in your mouth, chew, and swallow," she commanded.

"Not hungry, Denny," I said. "And why am I not ranting and raving or at the least, wailing and weeping? Instead, I just feel numb."

"Emotional shock," they said in unison.

"I gave you some calming energy a bit ago, but that's worn off. You've shut down…for now. It'll all come back full force after another drink or two when the alcohol has relaxed you enough," Abby said. "That's why we're staying up with you until you pass out. We don't need a repeat of the fire fingertips. But yeah, eat. I'll force-feed you if you don't."

I dutifully ate the food on my plate, forcing myself to swallow every bite. It tasted like cardboard, even though I knew Denise's homemade marinara sauce was delicious on a normal basis. It took me twice as long as the others to clean my plate, but once I had (and drunk a full glass of water at Abby's insistence), they gave me another G&T.

"I have an early surgery tomorrow," Denise told me. "But Abby will go with you to the condo to get some clothes. You're staying here until you're ready to go back by yourself."

The waterworks started again. "Thanks. You two are the best. Burke said not to go back to work until Monday, but I think I'm going in tomorrow. I can't just sit here all day and wallow."

"You're not going to," Abby told me. "I always have Fridays off unless there's an emergency. Tomorrow is a school day. After we go get you a few changes of clothes, I'm going to teach you about your magic…and more about herbs."

Denise turned on our favorite movie, *Practical Magic*, and both kept me plied with alcohol until halfway through the movie – and halfway through my fourth double gin and tonic, I passed out. Although I'd cried until the front of my shirt was wet, there had been no more fireworks. I'm sure they were both grateful.

CHAPTER TWO

I woke with a moan the next morning. I was no lightweight when it came to consuming booze, but the equivalent of seven drinks was more than I could handle. My head was pounding (again), my mouth felt like the Sahara, and my stomach rolled with even the thought of sitting upright. Then I noticed I was in the bed in the guest room and wearing a granny nightgown – the kind Abby favored.

"Mornin'." Abby appeared in the doorway holding two glasses. She approached the bed, holding out one that looked as if it was filled with green sludge. "Drink this one first. It tastes like shit and will be tough to get down, but you'll be glad you did."

I slowly moved myself into a sitting position, took the glass in shaking hands, and nearly spit out the first sip. "What in the hell is in this? It's awful!"

"Warned you. Hold your nose and slug it."

I obeyed, nearly choking on the consistency, even though I couldn't taste much when not breathing. When I'd emptied the glass, she exchanged it for a glass of clear liquid.

"This is plain water. Sip it while you're waiting for the potion to work. Should take about ten minutes or so."

I took a sip. The water felt wonderful on my parched mouth and started washing away some of the aftertaste of her concoction. "How'd you two get me in here last night? And is this one of your granny nightgowns I'm wearing?"

She gingerly sat on the edge of the bed, knowing any movement would probably have me upchucking what I'd just forced down. "Man, you really *were* out of it. We got you woken up enough to guide you in here after the movie ended. D helped you change clothes. You know she sleeps in the nude, so all we had was mine. It was that or a T-shirt and your panties."

We'd had this conversation multiple times. Rather than a granny gown, I'd argued, why not just wear a cotton jersey nightshirt? We weren't grannies – yet – and one of those would be more age-appropriate. She liked wearing what she'd worn as a kid and there was no budging her.

Slowly, her potion started to work. My headache subsided, and my stomach was feeling more normal. I continued sipping the water and finally felt good enough to get out of bed. I pushed her off and swung my legs over the side.

Her eyes twinkled. "Told ya. Change back into your outside clothes. Coffee's ready when you are."

My suit was on a hanger in the closet with my blouse next to it. I went into the bathroom, washed my face, and using a spare toothbrush I knew they kept in the medicine cabinet, brushed my teeth. After dressing, I felt more human.

Abby handed me a cup of coffee as I entered the kitchen. "You feeling up to a trip to the condo today? You can always continue wearing my stuff if you want."

After a couple sips of eye-opener, I sighed. "No, I have to go. While I appreciate you letting me wear your clothes, I'd prefer mine, as well as my own toiletries. And I want to make sure Asshole is gone."

Through last night's tears, I'd decided I'd only use his given name in an emergency – or in legal proceedings. Otherwise, I'd just capitalize his personality.

"Fine. I'm ready to zap if he's there and gives you any shit. Come to think of it, you could do it yourself."

"Beg pardon?" I didn't think the coffee had quite kicked in. Zapping someone?

"You know your sparkly fingers? Use the anger I'm sure you'll feel, let the sparkles come, then fling them at him. It's like a mild Taser."

She was quiet for a moment. "On second thought, let me. Your sparks would probably set his clothes on fire, burning him, and then there'd be an even nastier lawsuit. But let's hope he's not there at all."

While I really wasn't averse to making him a real Burning Man, she was right in that I didn't need a personal injury lawsuit.

"Want breakfast? I don't normally do anything more than juice or fruit, but I can whip up something more substantial if you need it."

My stomach was still in knots, and it had nothing to do with the hangover, which was completely gone. "I should, but I can't. Maybe we can stop somewhere later?"

"Understood," she said with sympathy on her face.

She poured more coffee into a couple of travel mugs then motioned me to the front door. "Come on. Let's get this over with."

We were both quiet as she navigated Atlanta traffic back to the condo. After parking in a visitor's spot in the building's ramp, we took the elevator up to the twelfth floor. Walking down the hall, I saw a piece of paper taped to the front of the door and when I got close, found a note in Asshole's sloppy handwriting.

My place, too. See you tonight, babe!

I started shaking, my breath came in huge gulps, and my fingertips started tingling again. I felt Abby's hand on my shoulder, and shortly, my breathing became less ragged and my fingers stopped prickling.

"Don't want to set the building on fire," she murmured. "But he just upped the ante. This is *war*, and he has no idea who he's dealing with.

"Take a picture of that note and text it to Burke. Then you're moving in with us until all this is settled."

I took another deep breath, raised my phone, took the picture and texted it, then tore the note off the door before unlocking it so we could enter.

The perfume was still noticeable, and Abby wrinkled her nose. "What does she do? Bathe in that shit? It's awful."

"That was one of my clues when I walked in yesterday. Most women try to just have a hint of fragrance when someone gets close, but she must use a whole bottle at a time."

The condo was a mess. He hadn't made the bed, and dirty dishes were in the sink instead of the dishwasher. Two empty wine glasses sat on the coffee table, one with a noticeable smudge of lipstick.

Abby blew out a breath. "Not even bothering to hide it. I agree with the name you've given him."

Then she saw all the plants on the balcony and kitchen windowsill. "We can't move all this in one day. Time to call in reinforcements." She pulled her phone out of her pocket and dialed a number from memory.

I wandered around my home in a daze. I remembered moving in twenty years prior…we were so proud we'd saved enough for a down payment on a place to *own* rather than rent, and it only took two friends and one truck to help us move. We didn't have a lot. It took me nearly a year to furnish the place, saving up until we could afford to pay cash for each individual piece of furniture.

Now, I was about to abandon it. The tears started flowing again.

"Hey." Abby came to my side and pulled me into her arms. "It's okay to cry. But I need you to pull yourself together for a couple of hours. We need to know what you want to take."

"We?" I'd been paying little attention to what she'd been saying.

"Yes, we. A good friend is on his way to help move. He's a fucking awesome air witch, and rather than carry all your stuff down to the car in multiple trips, he's going to transport it all for us."

"What?" I was still staring at all my *stuff* and bemoaning its imminent loss.

Abby pulled away and glared at me with her chocolate brown eyes. "Get it together, girl. You can cry later. Right now, unless you want a man seeing your unmentionables, even if he is gay, you need to at least pack those into a suitcase or box. Timmy can move the plants and all your hanging clothes through the ether. But he has to be to work in three hours, so we need to get a move on."

I sniffed. "Okay. Wait. This 'Timmy' can move objects through the ether? What do you mean?"

She snickered. "Witch, remember? He can move your plants to my garden, and even your hanging clothes into the closet in our spare bedroom with magic. But I think you'd prefer he moved a suitcase rather than every bra and pair of underwear. So, where do you keep your suitcases and what do you want to take?"

I sniffed again and choked back more tears. She was right. There would be time for crying later. I pulled two suitcases out of the back of the hall closet and opened them on the bed. In minutes, we had my dresser drawers emptied, and I went into the bathroom to pull out all my toiletries and makeup. Just for spite, I let the anger flow back until my fingers sparkled then, squinting my eyes to ensure I focused, grabbed his monogrammed bath towel and watched as a few pieces of red glitter burned his initials out of it. I wondered at the glitter but thought I'd imagined it. Then I grabbed mine and burned the center 'S' out of that one, leaving the 'J' and 'F' in place. It left satisfying holes.

"Nice," Abby chuckled, reaching around me to grab an armful of bottles. "And great control, too! I'll do one better when we leave."

Just then, the doorbell chimed. "That's probably Timmy," she said, putting all the bottles back on the counter. "I'll get it. You keep packing."

I heard her talking with someone at the door as I threw bottles and jars into a carryon bag. I turned as I heard Abby's voice behind me. "Jo, this is Timmy. Timmy, Jo. I know you want all your plants, so we'll get started on those. Keep packing. And don't forget at least that picture of your mother on the side table!"

Timmy was probably in his late thirties with blond hair, blue eyes, and a body that told me the gym was one of his favorite places. He stood a great deal over six feet tall, and I craned my neck to look at him when we shook hands.

"Abby's explained the situation," he said. "I'm all on board not only moving your things but with whatever she and D are cooking up. I *hate* cheaters."

"Thanks for your help," I said. "I'm sort of in a tizzy about everything."

"Understandable. Like Abby said, we'll get started on the plants. You keep getting all your stuff together."

As I was putting the rest of the toiletries into the bag, my phone started playing Queen's "Another One Bites the Dust." It was my ringtone for Burke. "I know you can stay with Denise and Abby, and that's probably best for now," he said when I answered. "I've filed the preliminary paperwork. He's already hired an attorney, and it looks like it's going to be a fight. You know Georgia is an equitable division state, but I think we can sway an arbitrator or even a judge with those photos."

"I know," I sighed. And I did. Divorce in Georgia was more no-fault than severely penalizing a spouse for adultery. "But damn! He shouldn't be able to get away with cheating…and in my bed!"

"Oh, he'll pay," Burke chuckled. "One way or another. He hired Anthony Markham. You know he's a milquetoast. Don't worry. Just get all your crap over to Denise and Abby's and try to enjoy your weekend. We'll take it all back up on Monday.

"By the way, I know you two only have one car, and Rob probably has it. Do you want me to pick you up?"

One of the reasons Asshole and I had bought that particular condo was it was within walking distance of both our offices at the time. Our car only left its parking space in the garage when we visited friends in the suburbs or his parents in Florida. Five years ago, he'd been transferred to a suburban branch and started driving every day. I'd have to think about getting my own vehicle.

"Thanks, but no. I can get myself to the office," I told him. "If I can't borrow one of their cars, it's probably only a five- or six-dollar Uber ride. Besides, you don't usually come in until an hour or more after I get there. I don't want to upset your morning routine."

He chuckled again. "Independent, as always. Okay, then. I'll see you Monday." We disconnected, and I continued packing. Trying to remember what was precious to me – apart from *everything* – and what I could easily leave behind taxed my brain.

I went into the kitchen and noticed all the plants from that windowsill were gone. I opened cupboards and drawers, picking out a couple of items that had sentimental value. I put my grandmother's

Red Wing Pottery mixing bowl and great-grandfather's carving set on the counter, along with the aforementioned picture of Mom. I remembered to grab my e-reader off the side table and chuck that over, too. Books were my escape, and I'd need them more than ever right now.

Needing a box to put all that in, I went back into the hall closet and grabbed one. I dumped the contents – Asshole's high school golf trophies – onto the sofa and put what I'd placed on the counter into it.

Abby and Timmy came in from the balcony. I looked up to see that it, too, was empty of plants. "Wow," I said. "That was fast!"

"But not easy," Timmy said, rolling his shoulders to ease tension. "You have a *lot* of plants!" I smiled sheepishly. There had been ten small pots on the kitchen windowsill and nearly thirty of varying sizes on the balcony, including a five-foot bay laurel tree in a twenty-gallon pot that I babied. I *was* wondering how we'd move that one because it took two people just to slide it into the house for the winter. I was a plantaholic, what could I say?

"Closet, next." Abby shoved him toward the bedroom. "Then her suitcases and we'll release you from bondage."

Timmy sniggered then leered down at her. "You know, I could easily take that in a different way."

"Oh, go on with you." She shoved harder.

Out of curiosity, I wandered into my bedroom to watch. Abby opened the closet door and pointed to what was obviously my side. "We'll get the shoes. From here…" She held her hand between my clothes and Asshole's, pushing his a little to the side to make a defined split, "…to here…" Pointing at the left wall. "…into the closet in the spare bedroom. It's empty so you don't have to worry about mixing things up."

As I watched – stared, actually – one section of clothes at a time shimmered then disappeared from where they were hanging. It took less than five minutes before the closet was half empty.

"I can get the shoes, too," Timmy said. And he did. Two minutes later, my completely-full shoe rack was gone.

Rolling his shoulders again, he looked at me. "Suitcases?"

"Oh, sorry," I said as I scrambled to shut them. "I got caught up watching you. That is *so cool!*"

"I know. Handy, too!" he said as he stared at the two suitcases in turn, each of which just shimmered a little then…weren't there anymore.

Abby hugged his waist. "Thanks so much for doing this. As soon as we get home, I'll put an energy drink on the counter for you, then call so you can get it."

I added my profuse thanks to hers, walking him to the door. "Like I said." He reached down to hug me. "I *hate* cheaters. You need something moved, or maybe even someone's air cut off, you call me. Abs has my number."

"How does he do that?" I asked after he'd left and I went back to perusing the living room, trying to decide if I had missed anything important.

"Near-perfect control of the air element," she replied. "I'm not sure *exactly* how it works because I really suck at air magic, but it has something to do with displacement. He has to see what he's moving or know *exactly* where it is, and know where it's going, but he described it like he creates a pocket of air at the destination and squeezes the air around whatever he's moving to push it to where it needs to go.

"And he wasn't lying about cutting someone's air off. He owns a bar, and that's one of the ways he keeps trouble out of his place. Someone starts mouthing off or getting violent, and all of a sudden, they can't breathe. Stops 'em in their tracks."

"How'd you meet him? He's younger than we are, isn't he? Cute, by the way."

She laughed. "Yes, he's younger – late thirties or early forties, I think. And yes, he's cute but not in the least straight and married to boot. You'll see him, and his husband Chaz, again this weekend. They own the Cozy Cauldron. We'll probably go there tonight or tomorrow."

"I've never heard of that place. Where is it?"

"You wouldn't have. It's a bar on Virginia Avenue for paranormals only. Well, paranormals except for vampires and predator species weres on the full moon. Chaz has put up some awesome wards around the place.

"If you're not a magical creature of some kind, your eyes will either slide right by it, or it'll look like the building is empty, depending on your mindset at the time. Now that your magic has finally woken up, you'll see it just fine.

"What else do you want to take?"

I looked around the home I'd had for twenty years…maybe for the last time. I knew I wouldn't come back as long as Asshole thought he could live there, too, and perhaps never again. It would all depend on the divorce proceedings. Not that I was sure I wanted to live in a place where he'd screwed his secretary.

"I can't think of anything else. Apart from what's in that box and my jewelry box, there weren't any family heirlooms."

"Cool. Then let's haul this down to the car and go find some breakfast – or brunch. I'm starving."

I grabbed my purse and the box, motioning Abby out the door with my chin. As soon as I'd set the box down in the hall to lock up, Abby laid her hand on my arm.

"Lock it then step aside," she said.

I did as she asked and watched as she put her hand on the knob and muttered some words. There was a brief flash of red light then it looked normal again.

"What did you just do?"

She grinned. "He's going to see an image of you every time he opens this door – from either side. Enough to remind him every damned time just what he did. Maybe even think he's just a little crazy. But that's not all that'll be happening to him."

"I remember you two said something last night about revenge, but then I got too wrapped up in my own misery."

This time, she let out a belly laugh as she picked up the box and started walking toward the elevator. "How about a little reverse Viagra for the cheater? Think that sounds good?"

I stopped in the middle of the hall and stared. "Are you saying what I think you're saying?"

"Oh, yes." Her eyes glittered as she gave me an evil smile. "When we're done, he won't be able to get it up, even taking the little blue pill. And a urologist won't be able to find a thing wrong with him."

"You can do that sort of stuff?"

She reached out and punched the elevator directional button. "That and more. D and I don't usually go in for the nasty stuff, preferring healing to hexing, but we're both damned good at either – they're just flip sides of the same coin, after all. You will be, too, with a little training."

I whistled which, for me, was closer to just blowing my breath out. "Fantasy is my favorite book genre, but I never thought it was *real*, much less that it applied to me!"

"Welcome to the world of Harry Potter…in real time."

We stopped at a small restaurant on the way for a quick breakfast (I still wasn't very hungry), then once back at the house, I officially moved into their spare bedroom.

CHAPTER THREE

"Next up," Abby announced, "is to settle your plants in with mine. I would have had Timmy move your laurel into the greenhouse, but I wasn't sure if I had a clear space for it. We'll need to make that happen, somehow, since it won't be long before winter's here. So, change into grubbies."

I didn't really have "grubbies." My extent of getting dirty was just my hands when I repotted a plant. Jeans and a T-shirt would have to suffice, as well as a pair of old loafers. I didn't even own a pair of running shoes.

When I emerged from the bedroom, Abby eyed me. "If you're going to work in my garden, you're going to need worse clothing. And a cheap pair of running shoes. You'll slip on wet grass in those."

Before I could protest, my phone pinged with a text from Burke. ROB JUST FROZE YOUR BANK ACCOUNTS. IT'S NORMAL AND I EXPECTED IT, BUT DO YOU HAVE ENOUGH CASH TO GET BY FOR A WEEK OR SO?

I grabbed my purse to look in my wallet. As long as I could borrow a car, I was fairly certain I had enough for lunches for a week and told Burke.

Abby had been standing quietly until I finished my text. I simply turned the phone so she could read the exchange.

"Whatever you need, we'll supply it. You can pay us back when it's possible to do so. And yes, you can certainly borrow one of our cars to get to work. D usually takes hers in case she needs to make a house call, but I walk unless the weather's bad. If it's raining, you can drop me off."

I hugged her hard, my cheek brushing against the tight curls on her head. "I don't know what I'd do without you two. You're the best."

"Come on. We have plants to work with. And some magic to learn!"

It took us a couple of hours to ensure my plants were properly positioned to get enough sun without squashing any of hers. She pulled a hand cart from the storage shed and together, we managed to get my tree into her tiny greenhouse. Three sides were already taken up with tables where she'd overwinter her delicate plants, so my tree sat dead center. Working in there would be a tight fit.

After we got all the plants settled and had eaten a light snack, she sat on a bench and motioned me to join her. "Time for a lesson or two," she told me.

"Okay. I know, after watching you with the towels, that you've figured out focus is the main thing. No matter what you want to accomplish with magic, ensuring you're thinking about *nothing* other than the task at hand is paramount."

"How do I zap someone rather than set them on fire?" I asked.

"Intent. Do you *want* fire, or do you simply want electricity? And if electricity, do you want a small zap like static or a big one like a Taser? Decide what you want then *focus*. Try zapping me with just the static you'd get scuffing your shoes on carpeting."

My jaw dropped. "What? No. I'm not going to hurt *you*!"

She laughed. "I trust you. Think about how absorbed you get in a book, not paying any attention to what's happening around you. Think about your laser focus when you just burned initials out of the towels instead of causing a conflagration. Apply that to the type and intensity of the fire."

I stared. "Are you sure about this? I mean, I could set you on fire!"

"I have faith," she said.

"Okay. Here goes nothing!" I closed my eyes and followed her instructions, thinking about just the snap felt when static electricity was discharged, then held that thought firmly while touching her bare arm. I waited for her scream and the smell of burning flesh, or at least hair. It didn't come.

I opened my eyes to her grin. "You did it! I only felt the pinch of static. Nothing else! We'll practice that frequently. You need to be able to do this with your eyes open and in a heartbeat instead of a few seconds.

"Now, onto the plants. How is it, without using magic, yours are thriving? I mean, look at your basil. It's not leggy like most indoor basil gets. Are you just a natural gardener, or is there something else?"

"I don't know," I said. "It's just a feeling I get…they need more or less water, it's time to repot or divide, or they need pruning. I do whatever my gut is telling me to do and this is the result."

"You *are* an earth witch, whether you realize it or not. It's not your gut talking to you; it's the plants! You've been using magic all along!

"Based on the bottles and jars I saw in your bathroom, you're making your own creams and such, too, am I right?"

I nodded. "I found recipes on the internet and adapted them to what I had." Then I had a horrible thought. "Oh, shit. I left all my ingredients in the pantry. All the oils, dried herbs, and even a big block of beeswax. That shit ain't cheap, and he'll probably throw it all out."

"No worries. I have all the supplies you need and probably more. You can use whatever you need if you have to make something else up while you're staying with us."

"I think I'm good for now, but thanks. I have a question."

She cocked her head. "Ask. That's what this time is for."

"You obviously use herbs in magic because Denny said you didn't have everything in stock for what you wanted to do to Asshole. Yet when you did whatever to the doorknob, you didn't use herbs. Nor did I when I zapped you. What's the difference?"

She smiled. "Only your intent and personal magic is necessary for small stuff like zapping. What I did to the doorknob is also small, in the greater scheme of things. For larger acts of magic, like healing or hexing, herbs are our allies. They add their own energies to the spell, along with the witch's. Healing is usually generic, like my hangover remedy or the energy potion, and the energy of herbs and the witch are enough. For specific targeting, like what we're going to do to your soon-to-be ex, we need a bit of their DNA. Which is why I grabbed hair from his razor. He really ought to clean that more often."

She pulled a small ziplock bag out of her pocket and waved it in front of me, grinning. I could just see tiny pieces of dark hair clinging to a toothpick.

"So, next time you make up a headache tisane, just focus on the cup and push a little intent to get rid of the headache into it."

"It's that easy?" I asked.

"Most of the time, yes. If you're a witch, that is. Mundanes can actually do it, too, but it's a *lot* harder for them, and they probably don't even know to do it in the first place. Everyone can use magical energy. It surrounds and is in us. It's a question of knowing you can, then how easy or hard it is for the individual in question."

"Wow." It was all I could think of to say.

"Cool, huh?" She stood and motioned me toward the house. "Come on. Enough school for the day. We need to start dinner. D is going to be exhausted when she gets home. She always is on surgery days."

Denise was, as predicted, exhausted when she got home. She explained her fatigue by telling me when she's taking care of animals, especially when in surgery, she uses a lot of healing energy.

"Most of the time, I can help them recover faster than without," she told me. "Sometimes, though, the damage or illness is too much even for magic. Those are my worst days. I hate losing a patient."

Saturday evening I was introduced to the Cozy Cauldron. It was an eye-opening experience. With so many paranormal people in one place, the magic in the air was palpable, even to me. It made the hair on my arms stand at attention, and I started feeling itchy until Abby taught me to shield against it – basically, telling my brain to ignore it.

Denise and Abby pointed out witches (both female and male) they knew, along with their primary ability, werewolves, were-raccoons, and even a were-mouse, all of whom resembled their non-human animal in some way, whether it was facial features or hirsuteness. I even met a dwarf who lived in one of the tunnels in downtown Atlanta. He could hold his beer better than anyone I'd ever met, if the number of empty mugs in front of him and his apparent sobriety were any indication.

Timmy gave me my first gin and tonic on the house as a welcome gift. His husband, Chaz, was shorter than Timmy, obviously shared his love of the gym, and dark where he was blond, but just as eager to help incapacitate Asshole.

"Let us know when you do the spell," he told Denise. "We want to add our intent, too."

Denise laughed. "It'll probably be tomorrow, but I'll call to let you know. Mona just dropped off the poppy leaves today."

"Poppy leaves?" I asked.

"You know about the opium poppy, right?" I nodded. "Opium comes from the latex in the seed pod, but the rest of the plant has *some* of its qualities, just not anywhere near as strong. We don't want the full effect of opium; we just want him to lose his sex drive. So, yeah, we'll use the leaves in the spell."

"But wait," I interjected. "Erections are caused by blood flow. How does relaxing him, or whatever, counteract that?"

Chaz laughed. "Okay, male brain lesson. We can find something arousing, but if we're *too* relaxed, like drunk? Whatever brain signals are necessary to get it up don't work, no matter how much we wish it would. The spell Abby's writing will be specific enough to point to that physiological response."

"Writing a spell? I thought you just used intent," I said.

"It helps with focus, especially if there's more than one witch involved in the working," Timmy told me. "Even if you're doing a spell solo, verbalizing what you want is sometimes more powerful than just thinking it."

I filed that knowledge away, then went back to the original point of the conversation. "Wow! I'm looking forward to seeing this *working*," I told them. I knew I'd never see Asshole's embarrassment, or even hear about it, but the thought of him not being able to pleasure his nubile mistress was gratifying.

Timmy and Chaz left us to pay attention to their other customers. We stayed for a couple of drinks then went back to the house. I didn't like crowds and was glad to get away from so many people.

Sunday I got to glimpse my first real magical spell. All four witches forbade me from participating. My anger, they said, could add unwanted consequences.

"You need a cool head for a spell like this," Denise said. "I don't think you qualify at the moment."

She was right, and I knew she was. As mad as I was, his penis would probably shrivel and fall off. Although…No, I wouldn't be *that* vindictive.

The four friends formed a circle around a small pot sitting on a tripod above a fire in the back yard. They didn't hold hands like I'd read in my fantasy books, but at a signal from Abby, they all read the words she'd written on four pieces of paper as she crumbled dried leaves (poppy, I presumed) into the pot then dropped the toothpick with tiny pieces of hair from Asshole's razor into a puddle of stale beer Timmy had poured into the pot upon his arrival.

"Limp as a wet noodle, no more fucking like a horny poodle. No more sex says this hex." They said it nine times then tossed their paper into the mixture in the pot, too. All four pointed their index fingers toward the pot, and I saw red sparkles come from each until a poof of smoke rose.

Chaz dusted off his hands. "He's done for," he said with a laugh. "But damn, Abs. The wording?"

She laughed. "Best I could come up with, without incapacitating him further. It rhymed, though, didn't it?"

"Wish I could be a fly on the wall when he tries to bang his secretary again," Denise said. "I wonder if she'll stay with him after that?"

"What's with the different colored sparkles I saw?" I asked as Abby poured the remains of the pot's contents onto the fire, dousing it. "When Timmy moved my stuff, the sparkles were…silver, for lack of a better color. What I've seen since, including when I burned the monograms off the towels, was red."

Timmy laughed and draped his arm over my shoulder, guiding me back into the house. "Depends on the spell. Red is 'danger' for lack of a better word. Or 'meanness' if you want to go there. Silver or white is benign. If you watch Abs make a healing potion or D working on one of her animals, you'll see green. Each kind of intent generates a different color, and it's not all primary colors because every intent is different. You'd need one of those color match chart thingies if you wanted to see them all."

I spent a pleasant but overwhelming afternoon with four magical teachers and a couple bottles of wine. I knew about Abby and Denise's healing and Timmy's "near-perfect control" of air magic. Chaz's abilities also were with air, but I was told his focus was warding magic, like what was around the Cozy Cauldron, or around their house to deter thieves.

Once Abby told them about my affinity for plants and being able to make up skin care or medicinal products more-or-less on the fly, everyone decided I'd probably be pretty good at potions.

"I can teach you more, if you're interested," Abby said.

"Maybe," I replied. "Although I like playing with my stuff, I think I'd like to get comfortable being a witch before I delve into it any further. Not to mention I have a job and a divorce to pay attention to."

Speaking of the job, I went back to work Monday morning. Burke had gotten a colleague's secretary to do most of my typing, but there were still piles on my desk of tasks only I could do. Burke actually came in about a half hour earlier than normal, and as he passed my desk, said, "Get the retainer form filled out and back date it to Thursday. I've already paid myself the fee so the firm won't bitch."

"That was the first thing I did this morning. But thank you for your retainer. Right now I have only the money in my wallet and one credit card that's in my name only with no way to pay it. I'm screwed."

"Working on it. We should be able to divide at least the bank accounts by the end of the week. Decide where you want your account to be and have it ready to receive funds by Friday. Oh, and don't forget to change your automatic payroll deposit with Human Resources."

It was about this time I started having the strangest dream. It repeated nearly every night. I was standing in front of a small cabin surrounded by trees. It was so peaceful compared to the constant background noise of the city. All I could hear was the squawk of a crow standing on the railing of the front porch. It looked right at me as it cawed. I woke up every time, feeling a strange sense of loss. Finally, after almost two weeks, wondering why I had this recurring dream, I recounted it to the girls over breakfast one Sunday morning.

Denise's eyes widened. "Dreams can be messengers, and I think this one is loud and clear. You're supposed to buy that cabin, and I think the crow is your familiar, calling to you."

"W…What?"

Abby took another bite of pancake, swallowed, then looked at me intently, "What D said. Dreams can be messengers. Especially when they recur so frequently, you're being hit over the head until you get the message.

"A lot of witches have familiars. They're always pets, yes, but they also can strengthen your magic by adding their own energy. The bond between a witch and familiar is tighter than any friendship or marriage bond – sort of like two halves of a whole."

I was feeling apprehensive at this information. "So what? Yes, I do want my own place but I doubt that cabin is in the heart of Atlanta. I can't move much farther away from work than I already am. Not to mention I couldn't afford it until the divorce is final. And I'm supposed to search the world for this particular cabin and crow? How am I supposed to do that?"

"The Universe will make it happen, one way or another," Denise said. "And you can control the dream, if you want. Tell the crow you're working on it but there are some things, like your divorce, that need to happen first. The dreams should calm down if you do that."

I just nodded. Shit was getting weirder and weirder. But I did as she instructed, and it seemed to work – I only dreamt that about once a week instead of every night.

***

Weeks turned into months, and although I loved Denny and Abby, I *really* wanted a place of my own. They had been nothing but kind, although I was certain they wanted their privacy back.

About a month after the big spell, I'd taken Abby up on learning to make potions. It wasn't that much different than what I'd already been doing, but I had to learn the magical applications of herbs then how to add magic without my emotions getting in the way.

My first attempt at a magical potion was a *disaster*. I tried to make a version of Abby's hangover remedy. No one is sure what, exactly, I did wrong, but when I tried to infuse magic into the gloopy-looking mixture, the whole thing erupted in my face…and all over the workroom. After I took my second shower of the day, it took me three hours to clean virtually every surface, including the ceiling.

"I think you should table that one for now," Denise said, laughing so hard tears were streaming down her cheeks.

Given how much we imbibed on a normal basis and how low my tolerance had gotten as I aged, I was determined to come up with a recipe, if not to get rid of a hangover the next morning, then to sober me up the night of – at least enough to drive home and pass a sobriety test if pulled over.

After a couple months' trial and error, I got good enough that Chaz bought that potion to combat drunkenness from me. It had stimulant herbs like sage, peppermint, and rosemary in it as well as what I called a "sobering thought" intent. The effects only lasted about a half hour and didn't get rid of the morning hangover, but I was proud of my first *real* potion.

"Making someone too drunk to drive sober up is awesome," he exclaimed after trying it on a particularly problematic customer. "It saved us nearly thirty dollars in cab fare, not to mention the hassle of pouring him into said cab. Keep 'em coming!"

Surprising myself, I found potion-making a de-stressor after a long day at the office – or in the arbitrator's conference room. Abby let me have free rein in her workroom, and they often found me there long after it should have been time to go to bed.

I still had a lot of learning to do, though. After one particularly stressful day at the office, I'd retired to the workroom, determined to come up with a potion that diffused tension out of the air. I wanted it to work similar to a room freshener but without the scent. My determination was my downfall that particular evening, though. I had just started to pour my magic into the mixture, watching the light blue sparkles flow like a river into the pot, when I became lightheaded – and passed out. I must have made a loud noise as I fell to the floor because the next I knew, Abby was leaning over me, a worried expression on her face.

"What did you do?" she asked.

"Huh?" I looked up at her, feeling rather fuzzy.

Denise joined Abby, staring at me as I raised myself to a sitting position.

She reached down to probe the back of my head then pulled a penlight out of the pocket of her scrubs and shined it first in one eye, then the other.

"No damage," was her pronouncement. "Now, what did you do? Walk us through it."

I slowly climbed to my feet, still feeling woozy but able to stand on my own. I recounted my steps in the potion-making.

"Ah," they exclaimed, giving each other a knowing look.

"What?" I didn't like that look.

Denny sighed. "You used *too* much energy and depleted your normal supply."

I stared at her. She sighed again. "Think of it as being a marathon runner. You can't sprint the whole twenty-six miles. You have to pace yourself to be able to cross the finish line without collapsing before you're even halfway through. Magic is the same. If you pour *all* your energy into a potion or spell or whatever, it doesn't leave enough for you to function, and your body shuts down for a time.

"You have to learn to use just a *little* of your energy in a spell. Don't empty the reservoir because it'll take quite a while to replenish it. You want to sleep for a year right now, don't you?"

I nodded sheepishly.

Abby chortled as she looked at the potion in the pot. "I think we'll toss this and you can start fresh tomorrow. The energy you infused is so strong, it'll put whoever you want to calm down to sleep."

She yawned as she said that last sentence. "Good thing it's almost bedtime anyway. I'll toss this on the compost pile while you put tomorrow's coffee together, D. Jo, go to bed before you fall over."

I learned my lesson, and with their help, was able to regulate my use of energy. It all came down to how many sparkles I saw. A river? Too much energy. Water flowing from a halfway-open tap? Just enough.

It took two more weeks, but I finally had a potion that, without Burke's knowledge, I tested at the office using a reed diffuser I'd placed on his credenza. He only remarked that it didn't smell like much, but I could tell a couple of his clients weren't as agitated as they'd once been. Score!

CHAPTER FOUR

My arbitration meetings, mostly attended by just the attorneys but sometimes by the parties involved, were rather funny at times. Asshole seemed to be a shadow of his former self. Gone was the self-confidence and arrogance I'd become used to. Instead, he sat quietly at the table, only speaking when spoken to, and nearly as much of a doormat as his attorney. Burke had heard through the grapevine that his secretary/lover, Camilla, had left him nearly as soon as I had, taking a job in a different branch. I did not hold back my laughter.

Thirteen months and an appearance before a judge later, I was finally divorced and kicking myself for not paying closer attention to our finances, letting the business major handle everything. I'd gone to the bank to get statements of our checking and savings accounts for Burke and noticed the deposits weren't as large as they should have been. Asshole made twice what I did, yet the direct deposits of his paycheck were considerably less than mine.

Burke got a court order to search for any financial accounts in Asshole's name and came up with two more besides the ones I knew about – one savings, one investment account. For almost ten years, he'd been splitting his paycheck, depositing only a quarter into our joint account, meaning my salary had been paying the majority of our bills. Between that and the damning photos I'd taken, the arbitrator had awarded me two-thirds of our *complete* assets. Asshole had fought to keep the condo and car, which I didn't really mind. The more I thought about it, the more I no longer wanted to live in a place he'd defiled. I'd already purchased a six-year-old SUV that got decent mileage, so didn't need the car. On top of the condo and car, he got the mortgage and auto loan payments while I got most of the liquid assets. I wasn't wealthy by any stretch of the imagination, but comfortable. He couldn't say the same.

Now that the divorce was final and I knew what I had to work with, I could finally start looking for a place to live. But where? I was still having the dream about the cabin yet couldn't see a way to live there and maintain my job in the city.

Denise's earlier prediction came true. Immediately after his arrival one morning about a week after the divorce was final, Burke called me into his office, telling me to shut the door behind me. I got nervous, wondering what I'd done to deserve the dressing-down I was about to receive.

"I hate to say this," he said as I sat, "but I am retiring at the end of the year. I wanted you to be the first to know, after Cindy, of course."

Cindy was his wife, and she had been a homemaker for their entire marriage, which was going on fifty years. Burke was nearing seventy-five, and although he'd cut his hours back about eight years previous, I could tell he was tired of coming into the office every day. I wondered how Cindy would take having him home *all* the time.

"I understand completely," I told him, relieved that I wasn't in any trouble. "Actually, it's about damned time you got out of the rat race altogether. Got any plans? More golf? More fishing?"

He laughed. "I hadn't quite gotten that far. But probably more travel. You know the kids and grands all live out of state, and we'd like to see more of them. Then there are all the beaches in the world to explore. As you know, Cin loves the ocean. I'm pretty sure we can fill up the time and then some.

"But my question is, what do you want to do? I can poll my colleagues to see if anyone needs a top-notch secretary. I know there are no openings here, but I'm sure there will be one at another firm somewhere in the city.

"Or do you want to do something else? You've mentioned helping Abby with her herbalist stuff. Do you want to go back to school and be like her? You've got a lot of options."

I grimaced. "Not as many as you'd think, Burke. I'm nearly fifty. That's old in today's workforce. With your announcement, I have a lot of thinking to do. Like, my job, wherever it might be, will determine where I move. Now that the divorce is final and I know how much I can afford to spend, I'd like my own place." I left out the dream of the cabin and the crow. Burke was a magical nonbeliever if I ever saw one.

"Take your time. You have almost five months, and if I recall the settlement correctly, quite a bit in savings. And let me know how I can help. You know I will."

"I know, and I appreciate it. Give me a couple of weeks to cogitate."

That night, I sat on the back deck with a glass of wine, thinking about what I wanted to do for the rest of my life, and where I wanted to do it. I looked over their garden, and for the first time, really wanted someplace with a yard instead of shared walls.

Denise joined me. "What'cha thinkin' 'bout?"

"Life," I murmured. "Burke told me he's retiring at the end of the year. I need to figure out whether I want to continue being a legal secretary before I decide where I'm going to move."

"Have you thought about making potions full time?" Abby said from the doorway behind me. "You've gotten really good at it."

I sighed. "I don't want to go through all your schooling. Not to mention dealing with people every day. I don't think I could handle it."

She laughed as she sat on my other side and topped up my wine glass. "I wasn't talking about medicinal potions. Chaz and Timmy are over the moon at your sobriety potion. And I, for one, am in love with your face cream."

I'd developed a face cream that – for real – inhibited wrinkles. I had noticed crow's feet at the corners of my eyes when putting on my makeup one morning about ten years previous and was horrified. I started experimenting that night. I'd been unsuccessful until I'd learned about my magic. Now, I added a smoothing intention to my regular moisturizer. Not to brag, but it worked better than any commercial cream I'd bought – and I'd tried pretty much every product on the market.

"Yeah, but…the FDA and all their regulations. I don't want to go through that either," I whined.

"If they're sold as magical potions, the FDA won't get involved," Abby told me.

"Hold on," Denise interjected. "Sure, she's good at potions, but how's she going to get paid? Remember Anna telling us most of the credit card companies don't work with magical people anymore?"

"Who's Anna?" I asked.

"She used to sell charm bags. Damned good ones, too. Then all the ways of processing credit cards dried up. She couldn't make enough cash sales, even at metaphysical fairs, to keep the business viable. Now, she does them on a commission basis and works at Target to make her bills."

"Oh, that sucks."

Abby sat up straight. "Wait. What if you did it all wholesale? Okay, not the face cream. That probably *would* get the FDA's attention. But the sobriety potion – wait. Not that one either. But maybe develop some others that were strictly magical in nature? There are *hundreds* of metaphysical shops in the country that would probably buy them. Most people nowadays either don't have all the ingredients or don't want to make their own shit from scratch – which is stupid because it's better if you do it yourself. Anyways, selling wholesale, you could insist on a check as payment." She dusted her hands. "Problem solved!"

"As if I didn't have enough to think about already," I chided her. "But your idea might have merit. Thankfully, I have time to work this all out."

In my spare time over the next several weeks, I did a *lot* of market research. What types of potions were out there, what people were charging for them on a retail basis, and I had a pages-long list of brick-and-mortar and online metaphysical stores in the United States. I also had spreadsheets galore, trying to figure out if I could make enough money to live on.

The more I thought about it, the more I really liked the idea of living in that cabin in the woods and making potions and shipping them to customers without having any personal interaction. After over twenty years of dealing with irate spouses – even if it was just transferring a call to Burke or showing someone into his office – I could do with some solitude.

In exchange for a year's worth of sobriety potions, Chaz paid a friend who specialized in graphic design to come up with a logo, a website, and labels. I knew enough from hanging around lawyers to do my own incorporation. By the middle of September, *Perfect Potions* was an official business.

My research also found that *some* credit card processors would deal with magical businesses, so I wouldn't necessarily have to rely on a check from customers. That would probably ease the payment process since so many places relied on plastic nowadays. Abby crowed at this information and texted their friend almost immediately with my findings.

With the help of Abby, Denise, Timmy, and Chaz, I came up with formulae for potions for protection (personal and property), general health, assistance in legal matters, and prosperity. We spent an entire Sunday afternoon addressing postcards to every shop on my list (four hundred and twenty-six), offering a sample of two – their choice – to test the efficacy.

The return cards poured in, and again, my friends helped me package and ship.

By mid-October, I had proved to myself this was a viable option. Abby and I had to schedule time in her workroom so we wouldn't be bumping into each other, and I knew it was really time to move to my own place. I started the online search to find that cabin in the woods.

November rolled around, and Burke started transferring cases he knew wouldn't be closed by year-end to other attorneys in the firm. He asked me what I was going to do. "The end of the year is coming up quickly," he said. "I'd feel better if I knew you had a plan in place."

"I'm still formulating an *exact* plan," I told him. "But I can tell you I'm not staying in the city. The more I think about it, the more a cabin in the country sounds like heaven. I'm investigating working remotely from home."

That wasn't a lie. I was. He'd just read it as doing secretarial or transcription work. "Good. I know you have some savings, so don't take anything until it feels *right*."

I knew from my feelings in the dream that the cabin was still in Georgia – just up in the mountains somewhere. After slogging through the hundreds of listings online, I set an alert with a couple of websites to be informed when a two-bedroom cabin in one of eight counties in Georgia came on the market. My phone pinged occasionally, but none of the listings was *the* house.

Thanksgiving was a fun affair. Timmy and Chaz hosted a feast at their bar for all paranormal folks without family nearby. Although they'd hired a catering firm, Denise, Abby, and I helped ensure everything ran smoothly so the guys and their staff could concentrate on selling booze to wash down the food. The responsibility of overseeing the buffet table didn't stop me from joining the customers in imbibing, though. I was having fun!

The following morning, I'd taken another one of Abby's hangover potions (which I hadn't quite perfected on my own) and while we were drinking coffee at the kitchen table, my phone pinged with a text. It was an alert from one of the real estate companies. I gasped as I clicked on the link. The photo was the cabin in my dreams. I turned it so Denise and Abby could see.

"This is *it*," I exclaimed. "This is the house from my dreams. The only thing it's missing is the crow."

Denise grabbed her laptop and typed in the URL so we could see the entire listing on a bigger screen.

"Jo," she crowed, "it's being sold fully furnished! Can you swing this?" She pointed to the price.

I knew without a steady paycheck I'd have to pay cash for whatever I bought because no mortgage company would lend to me. After looking at the price, I did some mental calculations. "Eighty percent of the asking price, yeah. Not sure about the other twenty. But if they come down…"

The girls looked at each other and nodded in unison. "We'll lend you whatever you need to cover the balance," Denise said. Abby nodded and smiled at me.

"What? No."

Abby put her hand on my arm. "This is the house you were meant to live in. Your dreams prove that. And I have faith that you'll be able to pay us back in no time. Hell. You're taking up more time in the workroom than I am at this point, and I'll bet you'll just get busier. It's a no-brainer for us."

My jaw dropped. I had no words. "Um. Okay. I think. Click on the link to schedule a viewing. This weekend if they can."

The real estate agent could and did schedule an almost-immediate viewing. We made an appointment for two o'clock, which would give us time to leisurely start the day before hitting the road. Denise had to go into the clinic because of a really sick ferret, so Abby and I made the drive up to the mountains.

I was so nervous, Abby insisted on driving. I was glad she did because that gave me a chance to just *look* rather than concentrate on the road and traffic. It was a gorgeous day. Even before we left the interstate, the view of mountains gently pushing their way into a cerulean sky dotted with cotton puff clouds made my heart soar. *This* was where I was supposed to be – I was certain of it.

Although the interstate ended, we were still on a four-lane highway until nearly at our destination. Following the GPS on my phone, Abby pulled into a gently sloping driveway off a two-lane country road. Kay, the real estate agent, was already there, waiting for us.

She had her back to the house as she stood next to her car, watching as we parked then disembarked from our vehicle. Behind her, a crow flew out of the woods and perched on the front porch railing, just as they had in my dream. Cocking their head, I swear they winked at me before flying off again.

"Did you see that?" I murmured to Abby.

"Yeah. Cool."

Kay strode toward us with an uncertain look on her face as she saw the color of Abby's skin. With a slightly-forced smile, she shook both our hands then asked which was the potential buyer.

"Me," I said. "Jo Schm…Foster." I'd taken my maiden name back at the divorce but still wasn't quite used to using it.

"And I'm one of her best friends, Abby Morton," Abby said. "This is such a cool place! Can we see inside?"

"Of course!" After finding out the white lady was the potential buyer, Kay relaxed and her smile became genuine. She led us up the porch stairs, punched a few numbers into the lockbox to retrieve the key, then let us in.

The house had obviously not been long empty. It didn't have that musty smell that comes with being shut up for a long period. As I wandered around, I felt a sense of coming home. The décor was exactly what I would have put in a cabin – somewhat rustic but comfortable in brown, forest green, and burgundy. A small grouping of sofa and chairs encircled the rock-faced fireplace. There were a couple of bookcases to either side, empty now of contents. A flat-screen television was mounted on the wall above. The kitchen was a little small for my needs if I was to use it for my potion-making, but otherwise, perfect for one or two people.

The two bedrooms continued the rustic theme, with quilts on the beds and chintz curtains covering the windows. Someone had made both, because the curtain fabric could be found as blocks in the quilts. The bathroom looked like it had been remodeled sometime in the not-too-distant past because it had a jetted tub and walk-in shower.

"So, what do you think?" Abby asked as she trailed behind me.

"It's nearly perfect for me," I said. "If the business continues to grow, I'll probably have to add a workshop out back somewhere, but for now, I think I can get by in the kitchen."

"That's what I thought, too," she grinned. "Let's go look outside."

We walked out the back door onto a small deck. It was only half the width of the house, with steps down to the ground. Four Adirondack chairs faced the woods. What passed for a back yard wasn't any larger than the city lot Denise and Abby had, but I didn't need much, anyway. I had no plans to have a garden.

Off to the left, a path led into the woods that surrounded the house. I pulled the listing up on my phone and heaved a sigh of relief after looking at the accompanying map. Most of the woods was owned either by the Forestry Service, this homeowner, or the neighbor to the east. There would be no encroaching development for at least a few years.

"I'm almost jealous," Abby said with a laugh. "I wonder if we can transport this place back to the city. I could live here if it was closer to civilization!"

"Isn't that the whole point of living in the woods? *Farther* away from civilization?" I teased her. "Besides, this is only ten minutes from town and less than two hours from city life. I'm going to make an offer. What do you think? Should I offer eighty percent of asking or go up a bit?"

"Start there. They can counteroffer. And don't worry – we have your back!"

I found Kay sitting in a rocking chair on the front porch, looking at her phone. It took us about ten minutes to complete the paperwork, and she promised she'd be in touch as soon as she heard from the seller.

"She's anxious to sell," Kay told me. "Her husband died tragically about seven months ago, and this place was their dream home. She can't handle living here anymore and has moved in with her daughter in Savannah. Your all-cash offer and not having to wait for a mortgage company may work in your favor."

"Savannah? Wow. That's a drastic change of scenery. I hope it works well for her." I crossed my fingers that it worked well for me, too.

CHAPTER FIVE

Abby drove us back home, and Denny was waiting for us, still in her scrubs. "Well?"

I laughed. "Of *course* I put in an offer. I mean, it's literally the house of my dreams! We have to wait to see what the seller says."

"Her crow showed up, too," Abby said, pulling the cork from a bottle of wine. "That's an awesome sign."

"It did? What did the real estate agent say to that?"

I laughed. "Smart crow. They landed on the porch railing when the agent had her back to it. They winked at me then flew off again. I wonder if they're male or female."

"Far as I know, you can't tell by looking. Voice, maybe." Abby was carefully pouring the wine so it didn't splash.

"Voice? Don't all the caws sound the same?"

Denise grabbed one glass, handing it to me. "No, silly. The voice they'll speak to you with."

I was even more confused and said so.

She took another glass and sipped before answering. "From what I've been told, familiars speak mind-to-mind with their humans. You hear it in your native language, English, in your case. No idea how it works, but it apparently does."

I choked on my wine. Denise thumped my back, and I had to grab a napkin so I wouldn't spew red wine all over my shirt as I coughed to get it out of my windpipe.

Once I could speak again, I asked, "So, if they're telepathic or whatever, does that mean they hear every single thought I have? That could get uncomfortable if not downright embarrassing!"

"No idea. Guess you'll find out! What are we having for dinner?" Abby was now looking in the fridge.

"Oh, hell," Denise said. "Order a pizza. I've been working hard to save a life for the last six hours, and you've been driving. No cooking tonight."

I spent Saturday on pins and needles, waiting for word from the real estate agent. I had a couple of orders to finish but was too keyed up to concentrate as I needed to for the magical part of the potion. I couldn't even focus enough to read and instead paced around the house.

"I'd say go for a walk, but it's raining. On second thought, take an umbrella and go for a walk. You're driving me nuts!" Denny had watched me make a circuit from the living room, through the kitchen, to my bedroom and back again, only to repeat the pattern again and again.

"Sorry," I said. "I just hate waiting. Especially when it's this important."

"Got it. But go for a walk or *something*. Wearing a path in our floors isn't going to help."

I knew she was right. I changed into tennis shoes (I *had* made some new clothing purchases in the last few months) and took an umbrella from the stand by the door before meandering around their neighborhood for a half hour.

The walk didn't help, though. I blindly went through the rest of the day, staring at the television set but not watching. Denise put a plate in front of me for dinner but if asked, I couldn't have told you what I ate. I took a bath, hoping it would relax me, but still tossed and turned all night. Sunday was no better (except it wasn't raining when Denise shooed me out of the house) and I was bleary-eyed when I went into the office Monday morning.

Uncharacteristically, my phone sat on my desk where I could grab it the moment it pinged or rang, rather than in its normal spot in my pocket. Burke noticed when he came in.

"What's with your phone?"

"Waiting on a real estate agent. I made an offer on a house on Friday."

"Really? Where?"

I pulled up the listing on my computer and turned the monitor so he could see.

He whistled. "You weren't kidding about a house in the country, were you? Any luck on the home working front?"

I hated lying to him but just couldn't bring myself to tell him I was making magical potions. "Think so. I've started part-time with one place. I'll see how it goes."

Patting my shoulder, he said, "I have faith it'll all work out. Can I have the Porter file, please?"

Finally, my phone pinged just after lunch. It was a text from Kay. SHE ACCEPTED YOUR OFFER. FINAL PAPERWORK TO FOLLOW VIA EMAIL.

I whooped with joy, which brought Burke out of his office. "You got it? On the first offer?"

I stood and hugged him. "Yep. My dream home, and it's fully-furnished!"

He hugged me back. "Call Adam. He can do the closing for you."

Three weeks later, I closed on my house on our last day at work with the firm. They gave us a celebration party in the afternoon because Burke had transferred all his cases and was just going through the motions for the next two weeks. As I packed a few personal items from my desk, Burke handed me a gift-wrapped box.

"What's this?" I asked.

"Something from me. Twenty-three and a half years is a long time to put up with me, and I wanted you to have a reminder of how much I value that."

I gasped as I pulled the paper off to see the Tiffany logo on the box. Opening it, tears filled my eyes. Nestled in the velvet was a necklace of the scales of justice, with a peridot (my birthstone) in one pan and a diamond (Burke's) in the other.

"I was going to get you a really nice watch," he said, choking a little himself, "but Cin convinced me that would be impractical for someone living in the country. I hope every time you wear it, you remember not only our hard work but some of the fun we've had over the years."

I hugged him. "I'll treasure it. You know that. And once I'm settled, you two need to come visit. It really is gorgeous up there. Cin and I can drink margaritas on the deck while you're off dropping a line into a stream somewhere, bringing dinner back with you."

He laughed. "Nah. I'll join you for margaritas. In the house. I want to visit sooner rather than later, and it's too cold right now to stand for hours waiting for a bite or even sitting out on a deck."

Leaving the office with my box of belongings, knowing I wouldn't return, was bittersweet. I caught myself tearing up on the elevator down, but by the time I got to the parking deck, I felt a sense of adventure…I was off on a new phase of my life.

The next morning, my car and Abby's were stuffed to the gills with suitcases of clothes, boxes of potion supplies, and bags of groceries and other necessities. Timmy rode shotgun with me to see the house so the next day, he could move all my plants and hanging clothes. Chaz was in the car with Abby and Denise. I didn't even have to ask him to put up wards around my property – he volunteered.

As we pulled into *my* driveway, Timmy let out a long, low whistle. "This is so cool!" he exclaimed. "We get to visit, right?"

I laughed. "Of course you do. There's a spare bedroom."

The moment I parked in front of the house, a crow flew out from the woods and, typically, landed on the front porch railing.

"It took you long enough," I heard in my head as soon as I got out of the car. The voice was female and somewhat scratchy, like an old woman who'd smoked too much. I was *so* grateful for what Denise and Abby had told me. Otherwise, I'd have thought I'd lost my mind.

"Sorry!" I told her. "This was honestly as soon as I could manage it."

Timmy laughed. "Familiar being a little impatient with you?"

She cocked her head and glared at him. *"Impertinent boy. I have been waiting years for this one to come into her magic."*

His eyes widened. "Wow. I heard that. I didn't think anyone but their bonded human could hear familiars."

"We can make ourselves heard by others if we want. At least those with magic in their blood, which you have."

I watched the exchange with interest. I knew I probably had a steep learning curve ahead of me. I just hoped she didn't peck me when she got *too* impatient.

"Can we table this discussion until we get her stuff moved in?" Abby asked, looking at the sky. "It looks like rain, and I'd like to keep everything dry if we can. Not to mention Timmy and Chaz need to open the bar in a few hours."

I unlocked the front door and before any human could enter with their armload, the crow flew inside, landing on the fireplace mantel. As we carried my belongings to their designated rooms, she groomed her feathers. Although at first glance, she looked like every other crow I'd ever seen, on closer inspection she had *one* white feather on her left wing, right up at the shoulder. At a distance, I probably wouldn't see it, but if she was near, I'd be able to tell her apart from others.

Thirty minutes later, Chaz had walked the perimeter of my property to do his thing, my bedroom floor had suitcases on it, boxes formed a maze from the living room to the kitchen, and the shopping bags were piled on a counter. Timmy screwed up his face in concentration, and a moment later, a bottle of champagne with the cork already popped and five flutes appeared in a bare spot on the table. He poured, handing each of us a glass.

He raised his glass. "A toast to the new homeowner!"

"*Where's mine, you imbecile?*" the crow croaked.

"Crows shouldn't drink alcohol." Denise *was* a veterinarian, after all.

"*In cases of celebration, we certainly should.*"

Timmy shrugged his shoulders, opened several cupboard doors until he found the crockery, then poured a small amount into a bowl before carrying that over to the mantel and placing it in front of the crow.

"*Now we can toast. But to hell with the new homeowner crap. Here's to the fully-fledged witch, even if she is a little long in the tooth.*" She dipped her beak in the champagne then tipped her head back to swallow. I swear I heard her burp a moment later.

All four of my friends laughed, raised their glasses to the toast, then drank. I drank, too, but eyed the crow over the rim of the flute. *This* was going to be one hell of a relationship.

After the toast, my friends departed. Timmy told me he'd put all the plants in front of the sliding door to the deck, so I should probably make room for them.

I finished my champagne, eyeing the chore of unpacking in front of me. The crow, however, had different ideas.

"I need a way to come in and go out on my own. Open a window."

"I'm not leaving a window open year-round," I told her. "I can't afford the heating or air conditioning bills with that. I'll figure out something, though. Do you need to go out now? And by the way, what should I call you?"

"Humans and their money concerns. Fine. Put one of those little doors in a window like other humans have for their four-legged friends. I can push that with my beak. No, I don't need to leave right now.

"And you may call me Esme. As to your education on having a familiar, we..."

"Can we postpone that? I'd really like to get unpacked a little. At least to the point I'm not tripping over boxes."

She sighed. *"In that case, yes, I'll leave. Situate yourself so you can pay attention to me as soon as possible. Would it be all right with you if I tapped on a window to come back in?"* I heard sarcasm in her voice. She wasn't asking permission.

"Of course. It'll probably be a couple of days before I can get something set up in a window for you. The kitchen window, perhaps? I'll be spending a lot of time there." I walked to the window in question and opened it. Then had to push out the screen. She lightly pecked my hand as she flew by. She may have to give me some pointers on having a familiar, but *I* was going to give her some pointers on not pissing me off, which pecking certainly did.

Grousing to myself about the crow's attitude, I closed the window then headed for the bedroom to get that in order. I first moved the furniture a little to suit me. Then I got all the suitcases unpacked and put them in the closet in the spare bedroom. After that, I had to go dig in the bags in the kitchen for the linens I'd purchased. While the place did come fully stocked, I wanted my own and planned on donating the sheets and towels that had been left.

CHAPTER SIX

I was about to download the Domino's app on my phone to have pizza delivered for dinner when there was a knock at the front door. I hadn't heard a car pull up and, looking out the window, only saw mine, parked in the drive. I hadn't taken the time to pull it into the carport. Not knowing anyone in these parts, I opened it cautiously.

"Welcome, neighbor!" said a woman about my age, holding a covered dish in her hands. She was a couple of inches shorter than I and almost skinny in comparison. Brown hair sprinkled with gray was pulled into a ponytail, and her green eyes twinkled. Sitting at attention next to her was one of the largest dogs I'd ever seen. His head came nearly to her waist, and he must have weighed as much as she did.

"My name is Ellen, but most people call me El, and I live next door. Well, as next door as it gets in these parts. I know what a pain it is to move and brought a pan of lasagna for you. I hope you're not vegetarian because it does have meat."

"It's nice to meet you," I said, still a little cautious. "I'm Jo. Please excuse the mess but come in. Your dog is welcome, too."

"*Thank you*," I heard in a man's baritone as the dog rose and walked into the house.

"You're welcome," I said automatically, before realizing I'd replied to…a dog?

My eyes widened at the same time as Ellen's.

She cleared her throat as I closed the door behind them. "This is going to sound really strange, but did you understand my dog?"

"*She has magic. She did*," I heard in that deep voice.

I choked. "Yes? At least, I heard a deep voice thanking me. That was your dog?"

She followed me to the kitchen and put her pan on the counter. "Not something I'd normally ask someone I just met, but are you a witch? That might explain why you heard Coop."

I might have blushed. "Um. Yes again? Are you, too?"

From the bag slung over her shoulder, she produced a bottle of wine. "The rest of your welcome gift.

"And the answer to your question is no. According to my mother, hearing animals is an inherited gift in our family. But Coop tells me people with 'magic in their blood'…" She used air quotes. "…can hear animals, too."

"Would you like to stay and share a glass with me? I'm rather curious about my new neighbor." I opened drawers but found no corkscrew, then cupboards until I found glasses. They weren't goblets but tumblers. I put two of them next to the bottle with a frown. "Looks like the former owner wasn't a wine drinker. I'll have to add a corkscrew and goblets to the shopping list."

She dug in her bag again and came up with a corkscrew. Grinning, she said, "I didn't know Harvey and Myrtle except to say hello, but on the off chance they didn't drink, I brought one – in the hopes I'd be able to get to know you a bit better on the first try."

She opened the bottle, put the corkscrew back in her bag, and poured two glasses. I motioned for her to sit in the living room. As I sat, I cleared my throat.

"Anyways, I know you're Ellen. How did you know I was moving in today? We can't see each other's houses."

She sipped and pointed to her dog with her other hand. "Coop said a crow told him yesterday that a single woman around my age would be moving in today. How they knew or why they told Coop, I have no idea, but I just went with it.

"By the way, if you want the lasagna for dinner, you need to put it in the oven now. It's fully-cooked but will take about an hour to heat back up."

I got up and put the pan in the fridge. "I'm rather hungry now after moving then starting to unpack. Want to share a pizza with me?"

In just a few minutes, I'd come to like Ellen quite a bit. She seemed a no-nonsense sort of person, and one who believed in magic on top of it.

"Dominos to the rescue!" she laughed. "Do you have the app on your phone, or should we use mine?"

"I was just about to download it when you knocked. Give me a minute. I like pepperoni, black olives, and onions on mine. What about you?"

"That'll work for me, too," she replied as I busied myself on my phone. Five minutes later, the pizza had been ordered.

"If you don't mind me asking, what's in all the boxes? I know Myrtle sold this place completely furnished. Can I help unpack some more?"

Although she was obviously okay with it all, I still was hesitant. But, plunging into the deep end, I said, "Mostly supplies. I make magical potions. For now, I'll need to use the kitchen, and I haven't looked at the cupboards to know what needs rearranging so I have room. Some of it will go into the spare bedroom, which I'll have to use as an office in addition to a guest room. So, thanks, but no. I'm going to leave that for tomorrow."

"Potions, huh? Cool. Changing the subject, what brought you to the mountains?"

Uncharacteristically, I opened up, giving her the whole sob story of Asshole's betrayal, my discovery I was a witch, the dreams, and Burke's retirement. It had been over a year, yet I still felt my fingertips tingling as I related my tale. I saw El's eyes widen and looked down to see the beginnings of sparkles. I had to pause the telling for several deep breaths to calm myself.

"Does that happen all the time?" she asked…after taking a huge gulp of wine.

I groaned. "Only when I get really angry. I mean *really* angry. I thought I'd gotten that out of my system but apparently not completely."

"Remind me never to piss you off. That looks dangerous."

I heard Esme caw in amusement. Ignoring that, I said, "It can be. I learned – mostly – to control it. But yeah, fire can happen." Then I told her about burning the initials out of the towels.

She guffawed. "Fitting!

"So the crow who spoke to Cooper, assuming it's the same one, is your familiar? What does that entail?"

I gave her a wry smile. "I have no idea. Although I've dreamed about her, and she was here briefly when Abby and I looked at the house, I just met her in person today. She says her name is Esme."

As if I had called her, there was a loud tap on the kitchen window. "Excuse me. I think I'm being summoned." I rose, went into the kitchen, and opened the window. Esme flew past me, and I closed the window before returning to my seat. I mentally made a note to find one of those pet doors ASAP. Opening and closing that window would get old in a hurry.

Esme perched on the mantel, looking down at Coop, who had been snoozing at Ellen's feet.

"Wake up, you behemoth. We need to talk with our humans."

"I can understand why you'd need to speak with Jo, but why me?" El asked.

There was a knock at the door, so I got up again to answer it before Esme had a chance to explain herself. Dinner had arrived. As soon as I'd closed the door and the aroma permeated the house, Cooper sat up. *"Food?"*

I laughed. "I've never had a dog, but I imagined they liked pizza so I ordered an extra-large. There's a couple of slices for you, too."

"They're all spoiled too much," El said as we went into the kitchen to portion out the pizza.

"*Hey*," Esme yelled. "*I get a piece, too.*"

Although I wasn't sure she'd be around, I had assumed she'd at least eat the toppings, so factored in a piece for her, too. There would be no leftovers this night.

In between bites, Ellen told me her story. I initially was so sad at the death of her husband but then perked up considerably when she told me about the sheriff's deputy she was now dating. I commiserated with her at developing odd abilities late in life and congratulated her when she told me about her job as a paranormal consultant for the law enforcement community in the mountains.

"Is there a lot of paranormal activity up here?" I asked.

Her jaw almost dropped. "You didn't hear about the killings earlier this year?"

"When? If it was spring or summer, I didn't watch much in the way of news then. I was already depressed about Asshole and losing my home. I didn't need any help in that department."

"Girl, you really missed it. Yeah. There was a rogue vampire in the area last spring. He killed a *bunch* of people. It not only hit the Atlanta news, but CNN picked it up, too."

Esme had been delicately picking the toppings off a piece of pizza I'd put on a plate for her on the mantel. Now she piped up, "*Your girl took care of that, though, didn't she, Gargantua?*"

"We *took care of him, yes,*" Cooper replied with a hint of pride in his voice. He'd already inhaled his two slices and was eyeing Ellen's plate.

"What?" I paused taking a bite. "What are they talking about?"

Ellen finished eating and used her napkin before replying. "He broke into my house one afternoon, and I shot him. Coop finished him by biting his face off."

I put my slice back down, appetite gone. "Ew. Gross. But you're okay, right?"

She laughed. "Right as rain. Fairies even finished cleaning and repairing the damage. I got lucky."

"Wow," was all I could think of to say. My appetite had not returned, so I put the remaining half-slice on Cooper's plate. He ate it in one bite and gave me a pleading look.

"Sorry, Coop. That's the last of the pizza, unless Esme wants to share hers."

"*He eats enough for an elephant. He doesn't need mine.*" I took that as a 'no.'

Laughing to myself and still trying to figure out Esme's caustic personality, I cleared the table, put the plates in the dishwasher, and the empty box in the trash.

Ellen finished her wine and rose. "We should go and let you relax a little before bed. Thanks for dinner, by the way. But before I forget, what's 'Jo' short for?"

I made a face. "Josephine. My mother was a fan of *Little Women* growing up, and Jo in particular. The full name is so damned old-fashioned, I hate it. So, don't use it unless you want to get zapped."

She laughed. "No worries. Ellen is rather old-fashioned, too, and I prefer 'El.' Let's swap phone numbers. I'm less than a five-minute walk away through the woods and am happy to help with unpacking. Shit, in all honesty, I'm bored. It's too cold to play in the garden. Give me a project that isn't reading."

"Is there a path to your house?" I asked. "Is it the one that goes to the left off my back yard?"

She grimaced. "No. That path curves around south then west and will join up with the Forestry Service hiking trail in about a mile. Hate to tell you this, but Harvey was one of the vampire's meals and he was killed on that path. I'm pretty sure that's why Myrtle sold the place.

"To get to my house, go in the opposite direction of that path. It's almost a straight shot from your back yard to mine. Come to think of it, we should probably clear the way. I'll have to ask the trees about that."

"You talk to trees, too, not just animals?" I was slightly aghast.

"One tree. A big oak at the edge of my back yard. He speaks to the others then relays stuff to me. You *do* know trees talk through their root systems, right?"

I remembered reading something about that in some scientific-type article several years prior and nodded.

"Anyways. Holler if I can help. Come on, Coop. Let's go home."

Surprising me, I got a big hug before she let herself out the door. "Friends are good!" she called as she walked around the side of my house toward the woods. It was dark by this time, and she activated the flashlight on her phone. She and Coop walked side-by-side into the trees and disappeared.

I plopped down on a chair, amazed at the swift formation of a friendship. Then wondered if I could be as self-assured as she seemed to be.

"*Pshaw,*" Esme croaked. "*You're fine. Just need to get your feet under you in your new life.*"

I looked at her, still perched on the mantel. "You told Cooper earlier you two needed to speak to your humans. Was it important?"

She cawed, bobbing her head up and down. I was fairly certain she was laughing. "*No. I just wanted to mess with him.*"

I stared at her. "I take it you already know each other. And was it you who told him I was moving in today? If so, why?"

She flew off the mantel and landed on my knee. I winced as her talons dug into flesh. She saw that and hopped onto the table next to me.

"*You need friends in these parts. Many do not believe in magic and will not befriend a witch. She will be good for you. The beast will also be good for you because he will make you laugh. He's okay as far as dogs go.*

"*Yes, I knew you were coming today. I have monitored you for many years, waiting for your magic to burst forth instead of trickle out.*"

I wondered at all the epithets for Cooper. But he was a *big* dog. Then I took in the rest of her words. "I…what? You've *monitored* me?"

"*I'm a bloody familiar! Of course I've monitored you. I knew where you were, what you were doing, even what you were thinking every hour of every day for the last however many human years. We're bonded, girl, and have been since you started bleeding.*"

I looked longingly at the now-empty wine bottle. I should have bought at least one with the other groceries and supplies I'd purchased in Atlanta. Or maybe even my own bottle of gin (I'd been drinking Denise and Abby's supply). Instead, I turned my attention back to the crow, who was preening again.

"Why now?"

I heard a sigh before she looked up at me. "*Because if you weren't strong enough in your magic to do anything but make plants grow, I wouldn't be needed. I had a hunch, though, so stuck around. Turns out I was right, huh?*"

"Why have I never seen you before?"

She snorted. I wasn't aware crows could make that sound, but take it from me, they can. "*What? Hang around in a dirty city just in case? I prefer the country, thank you. More to do, better eating, and a lot more trees. You wouldn't have understood me unless your magic was strong enough so I'd have just been another bird to you. I don't need to be close, so why inconvenience myself?*"

I yawned. It had been a long day, and looking at the still-huge pile of boxes, the next day would be just as long.

"I really need to go to bed," I told Esme. "I suppose you want out before I go?"

She flew to the kitchen and perched on the edge of the sink. "*Of course I want out! I'm not sleeping in some human house.*"

"Fine," I said as I opened the window. "I suppose you'll know when I'm awake. I'll meet you here in the morning," I called after her as she flew out, blending with the dark in seconds.

I turned my attention to getting the coffee ready for the morning. At least the former owners were coffee drinkers and had left a machine. I made the rounds, ensuring all windows and doors were locked, then went to bed.

It took a long time to fall asleep, though. It was too damned quiet! I was used to the background sounds of the city – cars on the street, people talking or the neighbors' television heard through the condo's walls, and the occasional airplane overhead. Without those noises to distract me, my brain continued to work. My head was swirling with thoughts of Esme, El, Cooper, and what I needed to accomplish the next day.

All of a sudden, I felt Esme sigh as she settled into a nest I just knew was high in a tree, tucking her head under her wing. I thought my imagination had taken off until I remembered the *bond* and that Esme had known everything about me since I started menstruating. *This* would definitely take some getting used to. But I, too, sighed and finally drifted off.

CHAPTER SEVEN

The following morning, I took my cup of coffee and stepped out onto the deck, presumably to admire the view. At the same time as I startled several deer munching on whatever they could find for food at this time of year in the yard, my bathrobe-clothed body and bare feet informed me it was too damned cold to spend any time out there. I retreated to the living room.

After copious amounts of coffee and a shower, I was ready to spend at least the rest of the morning sorting out the kitchen. Esme hadn't yet appeared, for which I was grateful. I had things to do that didn't involve a snarky familiar.

First, I had to move boxes away from the deck door so Timmy had room for my plants. Several piles became precariously tall when I'd finished, and I turned my attention to what I'd originally planned. By the time I'd pulled everything from cupboards and rearranged to suit myself, it became plain there simply wasn't enough room to use the kitchen for more than cooking on a regular basis. I'd need an outbuilding sooner than I'd hoped. Knowing no one else, I called El.

"Hey!" She didn't bother with any pleasantries. "What's up?"

"I had hoped to be able to use the kitchen to make potions for at least a year, but even after rearranging all the cupboards, it's obvious that's not going to happen. There simply isn't enough storage room. Do you know anyone who can build me a workshop out back, complete with electricity, water, heat, and all that?"

She laughed. "I know how you feel. I didn't know anyone when I moved here either. Still don't know many, but I *do* know a good general contractor. My son found him when I needed to remodel this place. Hang on. Let me go get his number."

I heard her walking, a drawer opening, and paper shuffling. "Ah. Here he is. Appropriately named John Carpenter. Here's his number." She rattled it off and I wrote it down. "He's good so you may have to wait a few weeks, but I'd say it'll be worth it.

"My kitchen is bigger than yours. If you want to use it, come on over."

"Thanks, but that would mean hauling supplies and equipment over there. I'll just have to work around the clutter. It'll be tight, but I can manage."

As I was speaking, the first of my plants shimmered into existence next to the deck door. One by one, nearly forty pots appeared, stems and leaves rustling with the movement. He got a little careless with the last one because it landed with a thump, spilling some of its dirt. I was thankful I had wood floors, making the cleanup easy. I'd cleared *just* enough space, and it was apparent

I'd need to move more boxes because at the moment, I couldn't get to the plants to water them.

"What's the noise over there? I'm hearing loud rustling and thumps in the background."

"A witch friend of mine is moving the rest of my belongings." The sound of hangers hitting a pole came from my bedroom. "What you heard is my plants coming from a friend's greenhouse to my dining area in front of the deck door."

"I didn't hear a door opening, just rustling. No other voices, either."

"You wouldn't," I laughed. "Timmy's moving them…through the ether I think is the way he described it. He does it with magic."

"*Really*? Witches can do that kind of shit, too? Wish I'd known a few when I moved. Would've saved me a ton of money!

"Wait. You said plants. How many? What kind? Are you going to build a garden, too?"

I laughed again. She had mentioned gardening the previous day. "All herbs in pots, including a bay laurel tree. I've had them for years. And no, I'm not building a garden. They're used to being inside in the winter and wouldn't be happy outside year-round."

Esme tapped at the window. I sighed into the phone. "I have to go. Esme wants in, and I have to continue the unpacking. Thanks for the contractor's number!"

I disconnected, put my phone down, and opened the window. Esme flew in with a croak, once again taking up her perch on the mantel. *"It's good I can fly. This place is a labyrinth! When are you going to neaten it up?"*

"Hey, I haven't even been here twenty-four hours. Give me a break!"

However, she was right. I had to do *something* with all the boxes. I went into the spare bedroom and pushed all the furniture against two of the walls. Then I hauled seventeen boxes in, piling them against a third wall, covering up the closet. That wouldn't do (it was also my coat closet), so I made taller piles, ensuring the boxes with glass bottles and vials were on the bottom, just in case I got careless.

After all that, I was more than ready for lunch. A sandwich and soup were fastest, so I set to work making a grilled cheese sandwich and heating a can of tomato soup. Esme sat on the counter to watch.

"Can we talk about my role as your familiar now?"

It was probably as good a time as any, so I nodded as I stood at the counter and bit into the gooey cheese goodness.

"About time. Anyone tell you about familiars? Any of those witch friends of yours?"

I swallowed before speaking. "Denise and Abby told me not all witches have familiars; the bond is tighter than family, friendship, or marriage; and that you're here to strengthen my magic. Or something like that. I think that's all."

"Basics," she spat out. *"It's better than that. Yes, I can add my magic to yours, but I can also help you figure out new spells. And if you're in trouble, I'll know it and can get help. By the way, you don't need to* speak *to me. I can hear your thoughts as easily as my own. Just direct your thoughts at* me so I *know to listen."*

Having a conversation in my head was too much like schizophrenia for my comfort level so I still spoke aloud. "How old are you? Crows don't normally live more than about ten years."

"You're asking a woman her age?"

"No, I'm asking a crow hers."

"I'm not entirely certain, to be honest. I think a couple hundred of your years? I had two humans before you, and you live to be about eighty or so, right? Math isn't my strong suit."

"Have you always lived around here?" I wasn't looking for a rote recitation of her life, but more information might come in handy someday.

"Yes. These mountains are my home, just as they are now yours. I was hatched not too far from here, as a matter of fact."

"Are you immortal?"

"Think so, unless someone kills me. Pretty sure I can die from injury, but I'd rather not find out. No one's told me anything and I don't know anyone to ask. And before you ask, I was hatched with the knowledge I have. As soon as I was fledged, I knew to seek out my human and did."

I finished my lunch and looked around, trying to decide what to do next. The dining table would have to be my office for the time being, so I moved the cabinet with all my paperwork into a corner there and put the printer on top of it. The box with all the labels went on the floor next to it. My Virgo's sense of organization protested the lack of it.

It was time for a break, so as I sat with a glass of water, I called the contractor. Not surprisingly, I got his voicemail. I left him a message, telling him I was El's neighbor, that I needed a workshop built out back, and my cell number. (I had opted not to get a landline. The cell tower was just a half mile away, and I had a strong signal.) Once I'd done that, I figured I ought to have an idea of how big it had to be and what I needed in it. I had to rummage in yet another box to find a pad of paper.

"Make it bigger than you think you'll need," Esme advised. *"You never know when you'll need another countertop or more cupboards."*

"You've had experience with workshops before?"

"My first human was a blacksmith." She smoothed a feather on a wing with her beak. *"He had to add onto his shop twice as his business expanded and then when he added two helpers. So, yes."*

I thought of Abby's workshop and how it was arranged. As a spare room off their kitchen, there was no need for a separate water supply. She also kept most of her stock at the office, so she didn't need storage for completed items. Nor did she have need of an office at home since she had a separate one. I was going to have to come up with a design from scratch.

I looked up sizes of prefab buildings on the internet, deciding starting with one of those might be easier. Eyeing the back yard, I thought a ten-by-twelve building would be large enough for my needs and easily fit behind the carport, although it would occlude my view of the woods in that direction. If it could be raised to the deck level, I could go to work in my slippers or bare feet. I liked that idea.

I sketched out what I thought would be a nice "kitchen" with plenty of countertops and shelving, leaving room for a lot of windows – underneath one of them I put a desk with more shelves and a tall filing cabinet to either side. Esme sat on the back of the chair, peering over my shoulder.

"If you take out one counter on the end, you could have all glass and a place for your plants."

"Some of them will stay in the house," I told her. "Once I get you a door thingie and put it in a different window – like in the living room, I plan on putting a shelf above the kitchen sink for them, just as I had in the condo. The others can move between the deck and where they are now, depending on the season. I like having my plants in the house, but yes, I'll probably put a few in the workshop, too. I don't need a whole wall of windows, though. I've made shelves for them here and here." I pointed to a couple of windows I'd drawn in.

I looked at what I'd drawn out. It was feasible but…how much was it going to cost? *That* was a major concern. However much, I'd have to take it out of savings, and I still wasn't quite making a full-time income. I sighed.

Just then, my phone pinged with a text. SOS, it said. I KNOW YOU'RE SUPPOSED TO BE ON VACAY CUZ OF MOVING BUT NEED 24 PROSPERITY POTIONS – 12 BIG, 12 SMALL. WILL PAY FOR OVERNIGHT SHIPPING. PO TO FOLLOW SOON. It was from a shop in Arizona that, in the last couple 0of months, had become my best customer.

Esme cackled. *"The Universe provides. Time to go to work!"*

I went into the spare room, first pulling out the box with my master potion bottles. I only had enough of this one for three retail bottles. So I made another mess as I unpacked one-ounce bottles, two-dram vials, bags of dried herbs, and my "cauldron." It was actually just a cast iron Dutch oven, but I had been taught magical potions should only be made in cast iron. I bought this one in-person instead of online because I needed to ensure the lid fit tightly for steeping.

I eyed my familiar. She could make herself useful. "I've always used bottled spring water because of the treatment they use on city water. Will the well water here be okay?"

She cackled again. *"It will. It's natural."*

I blew out a breath. I didn't need to go to the store just yet. *And*, I thought, that lowered my cost of production by a few cents per bottle. I was quite happy about that!

It took two trips to haul all the supplies into the kitchen, dumping the armload of herb bags on the counter and gently placing the boxes of empty bottles beside it. Then I had to figure out cooking. I had always worked on an electric range, and this house had a gas stove.

I immersed myself in potion-making. I was in my happy place! I measured water and brought it to the point of boiling before lowering the heat until the gas nearly went out. I didn't want it to boil again, but it needed to stay hot for three hours before I allowed it to cool. Then I measured the herbs before crumbling them into the hot water. I stirred until the herbs swirled in the pot like a whirlpool, muttered my spell, and watched the gold sparkles spin into the water, then stirred again. Finally, I clapped the lid on.

"That's a good potion there," Esme said from the counter. *"No wonder you have happy customers. But if you eliminate the dill and add alfalfa, it'll be more generic."*

"We considered that," I answered. "When thinking about "prosperity," most humans equate that with money, not just success in a given venture. This works better for the way people think nowadays."

"Humans and their preoccupation with money. Okay. We'll do it your way."

I set the timer and carried all the herbs back to the bedroom for storage, then unpacked the apparatus I'd concocted to easily strain a gallon at a time. It consisted of a commercial double-boiler Abby had taken to a metalsmith witch she knew to have holes, similar to but smaller than a colander, punched in the top section. Into this, I placed an old, worn T-shirt for the first strain. The second strain would take longer. That was done through a coffeepot setup with a coffee filter. Only then would I pour the potion into either my master bottles or those smaller ones for retail purposes.

While I waited for the potion to cook, I pulled up my email to get her purchase order and prepared not just the invoice but the shipping label. Then dug labels out of their box near the filing cabinet and put those on the bottles, filling three small bottles with the remaining contents of my master bottle. That went into the dishwasher.

Esme watched me from the counter the entire time. *"Quite a process,"* she commented. *"Different than making up one at a time for sure. While you're on that contraption of yours, find a door for me."*

I assumed she meant the computer and laughed…a little. She *had* been paying attention all these years because she obviously knew about online shopping.

"Good idea," I told her. "I have other things I need, too. Did you see where I put my list?"

She unerringly flew to the kitchen counter and returned with the paper in her beak. I pulled up my Amazon account and started shopping for what I needed. When I got to pet doors, she hopped onto my shoulder. I winced again as her talons dug in. "That hurts."

"Sorry. We'll have to devise a pad. Sitting on your shoulder gives me a good vantage point."

"You can sit on the table in front of the computer," I said, moving the laptop to give her room. "I'm not going to put a pad on every single shirt I own." She hopped from my shoulder to the table and peered intently at the screen. I had to reach around her to access the keyboard, but it was considerably less painful.

As I scrolled through the pages, she hmmed. Finally, on the third page of images, she said, *"That one. Third one down."*

Naturally, she'd chosen one of the more expensive ones. But this one had a small shelf on one side on which she could perch as she pushed the door open from the outside. She'd be able to sit on the windowsill on the inside. It was also made so you could slide part of it to fit the window's width tightly. I clicked "add to cart."

"If I put a shelf for plants in the kitchen window, that will obstruct this door. So where do you want me to put it?"

She took off and flew around the house, inspecting every window. Returning, she landed on the table next to my laptop.

"The kitchen window is the easiest for me. Next best would be the bathroom window, but I imagine you wouldn't like that, nor would your guests. So, your bedroom. The window that looks out over the back."

I silently grumbled. I had the bed under that window. I'd have to rearrange the bedroom – again.

I placed my order and closed the laptop. I still had another hour before the potion would be ready to cool, and another several hours after that before I'd be able to strain it. My phone rang.

"Good afternoon, Ms. Foster," a deep voice rumbled on the other end. "This is John Carpenter. You called me about a potential workshop?"

"I did," I replied. "I just moved into this house. The kitchen is too small for my business so I was thinking about a separate building out back."

"When would be convenient for me to come by? I'm working the next three days then will be off until the first of the year."

Well, shit. I'd completely forgotten about the holidays. Then smacked myself. I was supposed to be back down in Atlanta the next day to celebrate Yule.

"Either yet today or Friday. I have to be back in Atlanta tomorrow. If that's not convenient, I can wait until you're back at work."

I didn't *want* to wait but…

"I can come by in about two hours, if that's okay," he said after a moment. "Since Ms. Mackay referred you to me, I assume you're in the old Jackson place?"

Wow. With just my neighbor's name, he knew where I lived. Rather creepy! "Two hours would be fine, and yes, I bought the house from Myrtle."

He sighed. "That was so sad. I grew up with Harvey and his brother Mike. I'll see you in a couple of hours."

After we'd hung up, I eyed the place, hoping it was clean enough for company.

"You told him you just moved in. He'll expect some disorder." Esme was, if nothing, practical. However, I went into the kitchen and made a fresh pot of coffee. I'd drink it if no one else did.

The timer dinged, and I took the pot off the burner, putting it on a trivet on the counter to cool. As I drank yet another cup of coffee, I eyed the bookshelves to either side of the fireplace. They looked so empty, yet I had no books to put on them. I'd even forgotten my herb books in the rush to grab my stuff that first day, and Asshole had disposed of them all. There hadn't been room in the condo for any bookshelves, and I had embraced e-reader technology in addition to regular trips to the library. I knew I couldn't afford new books, but I loved flea market shopping and was certain there were still used book stores around. I vowed to buy one physical book a month until they were filled to overflowing.

A knock at the door announced the arrival of Mr. Carpenter. With that knock, Esme instructed me to open the window for her so she could leave. "*He won't understand a crow in the house,*" she told me as I let her out. "*I'll be back when he leaves.*"

When I opened the door, he looked around. I asked him if he'd like coffee, warning him I had no milk or sugar to doctor it with.

"Thanks, but I've had my caffeine allotment for the day. Is this all the Jacksons' furniture? I haven't been in here since they remodeled nearly ten years ago."

"It is," I told him, refilling my cup before sitting. "Myrtle sold the place fully furnished. I like how it looks and have no plans to change much."

He, too, sat and opened the notebook he'd been carrying. "So, how can I help?"

Sort of lying but not really, I explained I made lotions and soaps and that sort of thing, and there wasn't enough storage room in the kitchen for all my supplies. Then I got my sketches off the table to show to him.

"I thought about putting a workshop off the deck and behind the carport," I explained. "That way, I could go to work in slippers. This is sort of what I was thinking."

He looked at my sketch then at the kitchen. "I assume you'd want water, electricity, heat, and air?"

I nodded.

"With a ten-by-twelve building, solidly built rather than a pre-fab, and extending the necessary utilities out there, that's going to run you somewhere around fifteen grand."

I choked. But before I could protest, he held up his hand. "But what if we enlarge your kitchen?" He got up and walked over to the deck door then faced the counter (I caught him glancing at the pot on the trivet and inhaling the aroma that permeated not only the kitchen but the house), pointing to the sink.

"We could move that wall out to be even with the end of your deck, either lengthening your counter or adding another sliding door, and adding a floor-to-ceiling storage cupboard over there." He pointed to the counter on the opposite side of the sink. "If that would give you enough storage and workspace, the only utility-type work would be moving some of your plumbing around and probably adding an electrical outlet or two. I'd have to run the numbers, but I think that would only be about six or seven grand."

I walked over to him and looked out the deck door. Enlarging the kitchen would mean it would stick out from the back like a sore thumb and take out almost half of the deck. It offended my sensibilities. The more I thought about it, the more I wanted that separate workshop.

I mentally went over my finances. If I was able to make enough money to pay all my bills in three months, I could swing the separate building. If not, I'd probably have to do what I'd been telling Burke and actually get a job of some kind, at least part-time.

"Do what you want," I heard Esme say. *"Have faith in yourself."*

She was listening to my thoughts again. It was disconcerting to know she heard whatever I thought even when she wasn't anywhere nearby.

I heaved a sigh. "While I like the lesser expense of enlarging the kitchen, I don't think I'd like the way it would look. So I really want the separate building."

He smiled. "I kinda thought you'd go with that. Give me until after the first of the year to come up with plans and a firm price before we sign a contract. Can I take your sketch with me?"

I nodded. "Of course. And if you have any ideas on rearranging anything to make it easier to build, I'm all ears."

He chuckled. "It looks like you arranged it rather logically. But as I'm plotting it out, I might see a thing or two." He shook my hand. "I hope you have a wonderful holiday season. I'll call you when I have the design and quote ready."

As soon as his truck had left the drive, Esme said, *"Let me in."* I heard an accompanying peck on the kitchen window. When I opened it, she flew in and perched on the counter next to the cooling pot.

CHAPTER EIGHT

"If you're low on stock, you need to make more potions. I have a feeling with all those resolutions *humans make at the start of the year, you're going to need them. I think you ought to develop a love potion, too. Humans like that sort of stuff."*

"I refuse to make anything like that," I huffed. "Love should be naturally occurring, not forced by magic."

"Oh. You're one of those humans who won't put profit before morals. Good on you! But there are other potions you can make to…um…cash in on the hype."

"Such as?" I side-eyed her.

"Well…let's see. What do humans make those resolution things about?"

"Losing weight, getting in shape, finding a new job…I don't know all of them. The first two are a matter of willpower and sort of covered by my 'general health' potion. The third I could probably come up with a variant on the 'prosperity' potion. What else?"

"Look on that contraption of yours — the computer. You search for all sorts of information. Why not potion ideas?"

"We did that already when coming up with the potions I have. Besides, the holiday season is *not* the time to develop and market new products. That needs to be done months in advance. And I only have stock for what I currently make. There's no time before the first of the year!"

She harrumphed. *"Fine. We'll have to do that later. But I'm telling you, make more stock. I have a feeling you'll need it."*

"I will. On Friday. There won't be enough time to start a new batch after finishing this one today, and I have to go to Atlanta tomorrow. Satisfied?"

She harrumphed again but said nothing.

Thursday was lovely. I drove back to Denise and Abby's house, and the three of us celebrated Yule. We'd purchased and decorated a ball-and-burlap tree two weeks previous. Just as most people exchange gifts on Christmas, we did ours on Yule. They gave me a new cauldron, telling me I would need a second. I had paid for the tree — over their objections, and my wrapped gift was a friendship ornament.

After a scrumptious dinner of ham and homemade scalloped potatoes, we took all the decorations off the tree and planted it in their backyard, along with ten previous Yule trees already there. There was no magic, *per se*, but once we'd gotten it into the ground, I felt a magical stirring, like the trees greeting each other as old friends.

Nice as the day was, I was eager to get back to my own home – and cranky crow. Esme wasn't pleased I was returning to the city, even just for the day, and refused to accompany or meet me there.

"Fine," she'd said with a huff. *"I'll spend the day by myself. Have done for years so no different. Enjoy yourself."*

I wasn't surprised by this pouting. I knew she didn't like the city and hadn't thought she'd come with me, but she would have to learn I had a life outside of making and selling potions. I wasn't giving up my friends – my *human* friends – to spend all my time with her.

I made good on my promise the next morning, and as soon as I'd inhaled a cup of coffee, started another batch of the prosperity potion under Esme's watchful eye. I had *just* enough dill to complete this batch, and that prompted me to inventory the rest of my herb stock to see what else I'd need. I added only rosemary and myrrh to the list. I had a problem, though. I'd been buying my herbs from a health food store in Atlanta to avoid shipping charges. Living up here meant I'd need to either drive back into the city or pay for shipping. That would add to my production costs, and it grated.

I grabbed my laptop and did a quick search. There was indeed a health food store on the outskirts of town, and they mentioned selling organic herbs, but there was no list. It was time to make their acquaintance because if they stocked or could get what I used, I'd be a good customer.

Looking at the potion's timer, I would have to delay leaving the house for another two hours. So I took my time with breakfast and my shower, glancing at social media perhaps a little more often than I should.

The timer finally dinged. I took the pot off the stove and placed it on the trivet then grabbed my purse and headed out.

"If they have sunflower seeds, get those, too." Esme was sitting on the porch railing, watching me do a three-point turn to head out of the driveway. I waved at her over my shoulder, mentally acknowledging her request.

Twenty minutes later, I pulled into a graveled front yard that passed for a parking lot and walked into a cramped storefront. It was, in reality, the front parlor of an old house and nearly as small as my future workshop. Except for the fireplace, the walls were lined floor-to-ceiling with shelves of various products, from powdered alfalfa to the latest organic cream for varicose veins. On one wall was a pegboard system with silvery bags of dried herbs hanging from hooks.

"Hi!" said a woman sitting at the cash register. She looked to be in her early forties, with dark blonde hair pulled into a ponytail. I could see a silver highlight or two shimmering under the fluorescent light. "Can I help you find something?"

I pointed to the wall of bags. "That's what I'm looking for." I perused their selection, which had been hung alphabetically by common name. Taking a bag of dill off a hook, I wanted to sniff it to see if it was still fairly potent, only to find the bag sealed. Between that and the opaque bags, she at least knew storage requirements.

Assuming they were purchased wholesale in bulk, I turned back to the lady at the counter. "May I ask if you know how fresh these herbs are?"

She shook her head. "Sorry. My supplier guarantees freshness but doesn't tell me *how* fresh. They all smell right when I package them up, though."

I grabbed two bags each of dill, myrrh, and rosemary. "I'll take these to start. Do you have an inventory list so I know what you carry? I go through quite a bit over the course of a year, and if your stock is good, I'll be buying a lot." I held out my hand. "I'm Josephine – Jo."

Shaking my hand, she said, "I'm Marie. What do you do that you use a lot of herbs? Do you make something I might want to carry?"

I thought for a moment. Living in the Bible Belt, I knew to keep my mouth shut about magic. There was *no* way I would tell her about my potions. However, I was thinking about making and selling soap. I enjoyed doing that for myself using a melt-and-pour stock and thought I could incorporate that into the business. My research told me as long as it was labeled properly, I could sell it commercially without the FDA climbing in my shit.

"Handmade soap. I haven't gotten my formulations exactly right, but I think it'll be with goat's milk, and maybe a glycerin one, too."

Her eyes lit up. "I *love* goat's milk soap. There's a couple up here who make it, but I don't like that they use synthetic fragrances. I'd like to talk with you about selling your soap here when you're ready.

"Also, if you need more than two ounces at a time, let me know. I can package any amount you need, up to a pound."

While we'd been speaking, she'd been moving her mouse around on its pad, clicking here and there. I heard a printer fire up in a small room behind her.

"Hang on," she said, rising from her perch and grabbing a cane I'd not noticed before. She hobbled a couple of feet to the printer. Walking was obviously painful for her, and I now understood why she'd stayed seated and not risen to greet or help me. Returning to her chair, she sat with a grunt, put the cane back where it had leaned against the back of the counter, and handed me a sheaf of paper. "Two lists. One is what I carry, the other is what I can get. It's all organic.

"Since I have a feeling you're going to be a really good customer, I'm going to put you in the database for a ten percent discount on whatever you buy. I'm not set up to do wholesale to someone else, but this is as close as I can get. Will that work for you?"

I grinned. "Better than! I've been paying retail since I started on this journey. Any discount helps a great deal."

"*Sunflower seeds?*"

Damn. I nearly forgot. "Do you carry sunflower seeds? My pet bird loves them."

"*Pet?*" I heard the indignation in Esme's voice.

"*Shut up,*" I remembered to *think* back to her. "*That's the easiest way to describe you to a stranger.*"

Marie, oblivious to my silent conversation, nodded and pointed. "They're on the next-to-bottom shelf over there. But they're salted. Your bird probably wouldn't like those. However, if you're willing to drive down to Canton, there's a pet store that carries an organic mixture just for birds. It has sunflower seeds in it."

I was fairly certain I could find Esme's snack on the internet but thanked her for the information. I gave her my last name so she could put me in the database, and she finally rang up my purchases. She looked at the business credit card I handed her.

"Perfect Potions? Is that the name of your company?"

I nodded and said, "It is," without giving further explanation. Then gulped. An internet search would tell her I was a witch. Oh, well. She'd either accept it or not.

She said nothing more as she bagged up my purchases. We shook hands once again, and she told me she hoped she'd be seeing a lot of me. I told her she probably would before leaving.

I mused about outing myself on the drive home. I knew there were some up here in the mountains who quietly accepted witches, others who vehemently and vocally disparaged them, and some who didn't believe in magic and laughed it all off. I wondered which Marie was. I liked having a supplier so close, but if she was in the middle bunch, I'd probably end up driving back to Atlanta. I sighed.

"She's a businessperson first and foremost. Your personal predilections shouldn't bother her."

"I know," I replied, still rather amazed at how easily I'd accepted a bird speaking in my head. "But I'd prefer to do business with someone who didn't scowl at me throughout the transaction."

As I pulled into the drive, my cell phone rang. My car wasn't new enough to have Bluetooth built in, so I let it go to voicemail. I put the herbs in their proper box and got myself a glass of water then checked. It was El.

"Hey," she said. "Wanted to know what you were doing for Christmas. If you're not busy, come over here about one. My kids and mother arrived last night, and we're cooking a big spread. Dinner's at two. Dave is on duty but will join us when he gets off shift. No reason for you to spend it alone if you don't have any other plans. Call me!"

To be honest, I hadn't really thought about Christmas. Sure, we sort of celebrated when I was a kid, and again when I was married to Asshole, but we weren't church-goers so it was more of a secular holiday. Mom was gone, so it was just me, Asshole, and his family, which wasn't much fun. (I never got along with my in-laws. I wasn't good enough for their darling son.) I'd gotten into celebrating Yule after Denise and Abby got married, leaving the husband, who didn't like my friends, at home. But I *didn't* have any plans, and since I wanted to meet this supposedly hunky man of El's, it was something to do that day. I called her back.

"Thanks for the invite," I told her. "I'd be glad to come over. What can I bring?"

She laughed. "Just yourself. Trust me when I say my family is *all* prepared for a holiday meal. Mom even packed ingredients for sweet potato soufflé in her suitcase!"

I choked. "She *what?*"

I heard a door open and close, then the sounds of nature rather than a television in the background.

"I may be fifty years old, but she still thinks I'm twenty and this is my first go-round with a family dinner," El grumped. "She said she wasn't sure I'd remember the recipe correctly and running into town to the store wasn't on her agenda."

I started snickering. "Did you just go outside so your mom wouldn't hear you complain?"

"Okay, I sometimes feel like I'm still a kid when she's around. Yes, I'm out on the deck."

My snickering grew into full-blown laughter. Calming myself, I said, "But I should at least be able to bring a bottle of wine or something!"

"My son, Jason, took care of that," she laughed. "I have a…fondness, shall we say…for the wines from a local vineyard. He and his sister – Samantha, by the way – stopped on their way from the airport and picked up a whole case as my Christmas present. Not that it'll go bad before I get around to all twelve bottles, but I don't mind sharing. 'Sides, consider this a 'welcome to the neighborhood' party. Since we're the only two in the neighborhood…"

"Okay, okay, I get it," I laughed. "See you Monday about one-thirty."

We hung up, and I went back to business, entering the herb purchase into my financial software before checking on the potion. It still wasn't cool enough to strain and I was about to go rearrange the boxes in the spare room to make them more accessible when Esme tapped on the window.

I went into the kitchen to see her fluttering outside. She dropped down, disappearing from sight, rose to tap on the window with her beak, then dropped out of sight once more. When I opened the window she flew in, landing on the mantel. Before I could even get the window closed again, she complained.

"When does that door thing arrive? I'm not a damned hummingbird who can hover in front of the window. It's a pain to hop up and down like that."

I cleared my throat. "You could have just said you wanted to come in. Since I can't seem to tune you out, I would have heard that."

She ignored me. "*I heard you think about soaps. You could make 'em magical, you know. We should talk about that.*"

"We can talk about it after I get the potions re-stocked. Like, next week. In the meantime, I want to get the spare room organized. There *has* to be a better system until I get the shop built!"

I spent the better part of an hour moving the boxes and furniture, trying to at least get the room situated so the bed could be used. I had a feeling at least two of my Atlanta friends would be up for a visit sooner rather than later. Once I had everything arranged as best I could, it was time to strain and bottle that potion, and start on another.

"*You have a second cauldron now, idiot. Start two.*"

I had indeed forgotten about my Yule gift. I'd even left it in the car. I got that out and added it to the burgeoning pile of supplies in the kitchen.

CHAPTER NINE

Christmas morning dawned bright. It was like the day I'd first looked at this house – clear, blue skies, and puffy white clouds. Forgetting my previous experience, I stepped out on the deck with my coffee, intending to enjoy the view, then retreated quickly back inside. Instead, I stood in front of the glass door, admiring the woods surrounding my home. It was so peaceful!

I was ready to go long before noon but politely waited until just before one-thirty to ask Esme to guide me to El's house. She croaked a laugh.

I left the house with only my keys and cell phone. After locking the front door (I had no key to the deck door), I walked around back to see why Esme had laughed.

"*Observe*," she said.

Off to the right of my back yard, I could see the beginnings of a path through the woods, almost identical to the path on the opposite side. As I watched, one pine tree *slowly* moved itself a few inches to the north while another close by it, some deciduous tree because I could see no leaves, moved a bit to the south. My jaw dropped in astonishment. I knew El had said she was going to speak to the trees about clearing a path between our houses, but they could move like that?

Esme, of course, heard my thoughts. *"It will take several months, but yes, they are moving out of the way. The underbrush, which generally goes dormant in winter, won't reappear next spring. You* do *realize the sacrifice they're making?"*

"I do!" I exclaimed. "How do I tell them?"

"Your friend has already done so. A libation of wine from you, though, wouldn't go amiss. The fairies are helping with the project. In return for this clearing, the trees and shrubs will take over the other path, and by summer, it will no longer exist. That is the path the man was killed on and it will help heal the pain over there."

"Wow." It was all I could think of to say. I was about to follow what path there was, hoping I wouldn't get lost in the trees, when Cooper came bounding out of the woods. He came to a stop about three feet in front of me and sat, looking up.

"She said to come get you because I would be easier to follow than an airborne creature."

"I could have hopped on the ground, you monster. But as long as you're here, I'll fly ahead." Esme launched herself into the air as Coop turned back toward the trees.

"Thanks, Coop," I said as I followed.

We slowly wound our way through the woods. As I walked, I saw more trees noticeably shifting themselves in one direction or another. Cooper was very deliberate in his steps, avoiding anything looking remotely like a plant. I followed as closely as I could in his footsteps.

Then, suddenly, there were no more trees in the way, and we emerged into El's back yard. The back of her house looked very similar to mine with its wood siding and deck, but she had a full-blown raised-bed garden with gorgeous stone walls. A three-tiered fountain stood in the center, and as I watched, a few birds perched on the top tier to get a drink. Most of the plants in the beds were dormant, but I could see a green stem or leaf here and there, peeking above the straw mulch.

Her deck door slid open, and El emerged, wearing one of the gaudiest Christmas sweaters I'd ever seen. She waved and said, "You're here! Come on in!"

Before I could say a word back, Esme flew from somewhere in the branches, past us, and into the house. El instinctively ducked then chuckled. I heard exclamations coming from the interior.

"It's okay," she called over her shoulder. "That's Esme, Jo's familiar. She's just as much a part of the family as Cooper so give her some love."

"I don't need love *from your hatchlings. Stop!"*

I followed Coop onto the deck and hugged El before entering behind him. "Thanks for having me," I told her then said to the two youngsters standing by the fireplace and reaching for Esme, who was perched on the mantel, "I wouldn't try to pet her if I were you. She pecks."

The young woman, a blonde rather than El's brunette but with the same delicate facial features, drew her hand back. The young man was tall, over six feet, and he must have taken after his father because there wasn't much of a resemblance to his mother. His hand continued on. And was rewarded with a jab. Thankfully, it didn't look like Esme drew blood. That wouldn't have been a good way to start off the holiday.

"She did warn you," I heard a woman's voice coming from a chair. "I know you can't understand the crow, but that caw wasn't a friendly one."

El said, "Let me introduce you. Jo, this is my mother, Marty Bixler, and my kids, Samantha and Jason. All, this is my new neighbor, Josephine."

Ellen's mother rose, and I saw where she and her daughter got their looks. "You're the witch? Glad to meet you. And you, too, Esme. Forgive my grandchildren. They're still not used to the paranormal. Well, Sam's not. I'll let Jay tell you his story, if he wants."

The aroma of a traditional Christmas dinner assaulted me. I could smell turkey, stuffing, and yes, sweet potato casserole. An apple pie sat on a trivet on the counter. The table was set for five with Christmassy plates. "It's nice to meet you all. Is there anything I can do to help?"

"Nope. Sit. Mom and I have this." Ellen moved from where she'd been standing by the door to grab a goblet from the counter, fill it from an open bottle of wine, and hand it to me.

Marty motioned to the chair she'd vacated. "You're a guest so yes, sit. Besides, this is really only a one-butt kitchen. Three would be overcrowding."

So I sat. As did El's kids. "So, you're a witch," Samantha said, eyeing me with interest. "Don't think I've ever met one before. What do you do?"

Jason, who sat next to his sister on the sofa, elbowed her. His eyes, the same emerald green as El's, narrowed. "Not polite!"

She poked him back. "Hey, I'm still learning about all this stuff. I want to know."

I smiled at both of them. "It's okay, Jason. When I'm in company such as this, I don't mind talking about it."

Turning to face Sam directly, I said, "I think you've probably met a witch or two in your life. We just don't advertise it. Today's society may be more accepting, but still, it's not fun to be looked down upon or even persecuted for who you are.

"To sort of answer your question, I just found out a couple of years ago that I'm a witch. Even though I don't remember, I apparently got scared when my abilities manifested at puberty and suppressed it. So I'm still learning about it."

Sam's eyes widened. "Was it when you hit menopause, like Mom and Gran?"

"Sam!" El hollered. "That *really* isn't polite, and it's none of your damned business!"

I laughed. "It's all good, El. If I don't answer, how will she know?"

I looked back at the young lady. "No, it wasn't menopause. It was anger. I caught my husband cheating on me. From what my friends – and Esme – have said, it took that strong emotion to burst the dam I'd built.

"Now, as to what I do? I've always been good at growing plants and have a huge collection of them. For the last, oh, ten or twelve years, I've made my own lotions, soaps, and herbal remedies. My friends tell me my abilities there were my magic trickling out. Now, I make magical potions."

Sam's mouth opened in astonishment. "Wow. There's a market for that stuff?"

"Before she gets any further," El interjected from the kitchen, "I should warn you my daughter is a marketing guru. She'll probably want you to hire her."

I took a sip of my wine then raised an eyebrow at the young blonde sitting across from me.

"Ummm," Sam stuttered. "I wouldn't have a clue where to even start. But sure, if you want some help in that area, I'm happy to do some research."

I let out a laugh. "It's okay. Right now I think I'm doing quite well in that regard. But if I need some advice, I know where to go!"

Before we could delve any further into the subject, Marty said, "Dinner!"

We all grabbed a plate off the table and loaded them from the buffet she and El had created on the island counter. Ellen filled a spare plate, covered it with foil, and stuck it in the oven.

"Dave's dinner," she replied to my questioning look. "I'll keep it warm in the oven for him. The microwave would dry it out too much."

I had forgotten about the law enforcement boyfriend. "What time will he get off shift?"

She shrugged as she sat. "Unless something happens, he should be here shortly after four. But he warned me that on holidays, there's usually at least one family fight they need to break up, so it could be later."

As we all started eating, I had the feeling of being watched. Cooper was sitting, somewhat patiently, at El's feet and eyeing her fork every time she took a bite. It wasn't him. Across the table from me, Jason snorted then pointed at me with his fork. "Your crow is sitting on the back of your chair, staring at your plate."

I twisted my head. Sure enough, Esme was there. "What?" I asked.

"You're not sharing."

Marty laughed, nearly choking on a piece of turkey. "I doubt she has to this point. We'll give you a plate when we're done. Just like Cooper and Patches get their treat when we're finished eating."

I didn't want to contradict Marty, but I *had* been sharing my meals when Esme had been around for them – and it was food she was interested in. Breakfast foods I got to eat by myself. Most everything else, she wanted at least a small bite – even fruit.

I nodded at Marty then looked back at Esme. "What she said. We're guests, remember?"

"Fine!" Esme harrumphed and flew back to the mantel.

The food was delicious, the conversation even more so. I got the feeling this was the first time the family had been reunited since Samantha found out about her mother's and grandmother's ability to speak with animals. And her brother's unusual talent. Apparently Jason was empathic, meaning he could feel others' emotions. That was a new one on me. Sam grilled everyone, trying to understand, I thought, something that was completely foreign to her. I learned right along with her.

The animals got their own plates after we'd eaten dessert. Cooper, naturally, inhaled his. Patches, the cat, also ate her turkey quickly. Esme was a little more delicate in her pickings but nonetheless, finished in what I thought was record time. Coop moseyed over to his bed by the fireplace and was shortly asleep. Patches disappeared, probably also to nap. Esme went back to the mantel and, tucking her head under her wing, followed suit.

After I'd shooed Ellen and Marty out of the kitchen and loaded the dishwasher, we sat with another glass of wine, continuing Sam's education on the paranormal. I even made my fingertips light up for her, which elicited a "whoa" from everyone.

"Remind me never to piss you off," Marty said. "That there looks dangerous!"

Ellen chuckled. "That's almost exactly what I said!"

The door opened just as the sparklers dissipated. In walked a man dressed in full cop kit, down to the heavy belt with filled gun holster. He took the gun out and put it on the table next to the door before making his way over to El and giving her a good, long kiss.

"Hi, sweetheart," he said after they came up for air. "And hi, Jason. I presume the others are Samantha, your mother, and your neighbor? Merry Christmas, everyone."

Dave was, as advertised, a law enforcement professional. It wasn't just the uniform. He had the bearing of, oh, I don't know, a drill sergeant. Anyway, someone in authority. He was also, as advertised, handsome, with salt-and-pepper hair and Sinatra-blue eyes.

"Hi hon," El replied, her cheeks bright. "Since you already know Jay and have met Sam electronically once or twice, yes, this is my mother, Marty, and my neighbor, Jo. On the mantel is Jo's familiar, Esme. If you're hungry, there's a plate in the oven. You know where the goblets are.

"Did you have any problems today?"

He shook Marty's and my hands on his way to the kitchen, murmuring more polite words in greeting. "Surprisingly, it was a quiet day. Only one minor fender-bender. I didn't even get to leave the station." He retrieved a goblet from a cupboard and poured himself a glass of wine from the bottle on the counter before pulling the plate out of the oven.

"However, it's early, yet. The booze has only been flowing for four or five hours. I give it until about seven, and the middle shift will start getting calls." He took both plate and glass over to the table and sat to eat.

At that point, I started yawning. The tryptophan in the turkey had finally kicked in.

"Sorry," I said to the room, "but I think I need to go home and take a nap." I stood and turned to El. After stifling another yawn, I told her, "Thank you for an excellent dinner, which I wouldn't have cooked just for myself." Looking at each in turn, I told Marty, Samantha, and Jason it was a pleasure to meet them, and again to Dave on my way out the door.

Then I noticed Esme was still asleep. "*Hey, familiar!*" I called in my head. "*Coming?*"

She pulled her head out from under her wing and, ruffling her feathers a bit, grumbled her acquiescence.

"Do you want me to guide you back to your house?" Cooper asked.

"I can do it, you mammoth," Esme shot back.

Marty guffawed, and El snickered. The kids looked at them questioningly while Dave continued to eat, apparently used to seemingly random outbursts of hilarity.

I heard El tell her children what the animals had said as I closed the deck door behind me, Esme flying on ahead. She did indeed guide me back, landing on a branch where I could see her before flitting from tree to tree, always keeping me in sight. Honestly, it took longer than following Coop, but I wasn't going to gainsay her.

As I walked, the trees were still moving, and I almost tripped over an exposed root that had shifted right in front of me. "Sorry!" I called out, unsure of the correct etiquette for dealing with trees…and maybe fairies.

Once finally back at the house, Esme returned to her nap on my mantel. I snoozed on the sofa for a couple of hours, and it was full dark when I woke. I turned on a few lights and after I'd poured myself a glass of wine, Esme said without taking her head out from under her wing, *"You had a visitor while you were asleep. Your friend left extra food on the deck for you."*

Curious, I went out to the deck. On the railing was a huge plastic container with a note taped to the top that read, "A 25-pound turkey goes a <u>long</u> way. Too long. Have some leftovers."

In the container was enough turkey for four or five sandwiches, a pile of stuffing, another pile of casserole, and several rolls. I wouldn't have to worry about what to eat for a few days!

I spent the following week restocking. My enforced "vacation" due to moving would be coming to an end at the first of the year, and I wanted to be ready for what I hoped would be a huge influx of orders.

While the potions cooked, Esme and I started brainstorming new potions and magical soaps. Although I'd never tell her and thus inflate her ego even further, she really did know her magic – and herbs. Experimentation would be necessary, but I was comfortable with our potion formulations for Stop Procrastinating, Concentration, Confidence, and Reduce Stress. The soaps, all goat's milk at that point, would be, Wake Up!, Calming, Sleep Time, and Aura Cleansing.

When I told Denny what I was up to, she instructed me to send a sample of each down to Atlanta. "We can use every single one of those!" she told me. "Especially the procrastinating one. You know I'm bad at that. On second thought, send two of each. I'll pass them along to Timmy and Chaz. The more opinions you get, the better."

CHAPTER TEN

True to his word, John Carpenter called on January fourth. "I have the plans for your workshop. Would it be convenient for me to come over this afternoon to finalize the project?"

My workshop would be a dream when he was done, but my place would be a mess during construction. He'd have to dig up nearly the entire back yard to put in a solid foundation and extend the utilities from the house. The deck would need to be rebuilt, too, as he had plans to attach it to the shop rather than just butt the shop up against it. "It'll make it stronger," he told me.

In the intervening two weeks, the business had nearly taken over the kitchen, leaving me little room to cook. I had started eating frozen meals heated up in the microwave, rather than continually rearrange my work area. Mr. Carpenter saw the piles of bags of herbs, blocks of soap base, finished soap, and packaging. (I'd put all the potions out of sight for his visit.)

"Thankfully, our ground never freezes, so we can work year-round. As long as the weather holds, we can start two weeks from today and it'll take us about a month. Would that work for you?"

I said it would, swallowed my gulp at the cost, and wrote him a check for five thousand to get him going. If Esme was correct in her assumptions and my projections held, I should recoup my costs in five years. I crossed my fingers.

Two weeks later on the dot, I woke to the sound of a bulldozer right outside the bedroom window. I had, naturally, forgotten about the construction and not set an alarm to get up before they arrived. Esme was sitting on my bedside table, glaring at me.

"I won't be able to come and go while they're working," she grumbled. *"They'll see me and wonder why you're letting a crow in your house."*

"It's only for a month," I mumbled, putting on my robe and padding into the kitchen for the necessary infusion of caffeine. "It has to be done sometime, and sooner rather than later is preferable. You can either stay inside or outside all day. Your choice."

"Well, since you'll be working — you will *be working, won't you? I'll stay inside during the day. You have a lot of seeds, right?"*

I'd found Esme not only enjoyed sunflower seeds, but unsalted peanuts, as well, and I'd found a type of bird seed at Walmart that contained both. I bought it in twenty-pound bags and used a scoop to refill her dish on the kitchen counter at least once a day. "I do, but don't you dare poop in here."

She glared again. *"Now that's just insulting. I do not randomly poop inside. Leave the toilet lid up. I can manage that."*

I sipped my coffee and watched out the back window as the back yard was dug up and dirt piled around the perimeter. At the same time, two men with sledgehammers broke apart the deck, throwing pieces to the side as they worked. I hoped it wouldn't be so messy once everything was done.

I had to throw a towel over the bathroom window so I had privacy for my shower then left it there so if anyone looked in the window while Esme was on the toilet (didn't that sound weird?), they wouldn't wonder about the crow.

It was time to go to work, whether I had an audience out the window or not.

For five weeks, I was up before dawn so I could be showered and dressed by the time the workers arrived. It only took two weeks before the walls were up, the deck was rebuilt, and the plumbing had been extended from the house. The weather continued to hold, and three more days saw it "dried in" – the siding and roofing had gone up on the shop. I thought that was quick and they'd be done sooner, but then there was a delay – the electrician had come down with the flu.

Both Timmy and Chaz had called several times, begging to come up for a "weekend getaway." I had put them off, citing the chaos of construction and the mess in the house, but finally, I acquiesced, and they arrived about noon on a Sunday – one of the two days the bar was closed (the other being Monday). I had made a path to the bed in the guest room and they both told me they didn't mind the maze that was my house at the moment.

"We just needed to get out of the city for a bit," Chaz told me. "Despite things supposedly calming down after the holidays, it seems all the crazies have come out of the woodwork."

Timmy nodded in agreement. "A quick trip up here to the quiet of the country will be enough for us to relax a little. Thanks for having us."

Due to the mess in the kitchen, we went into town for dinner that night. Both of them eyed the bar setup with professional eyes, and both nodded their approval before we sat. After our food arrived, I could tell they were mentally critiquing that, too. I wondered if they ever stopped working.

Thankfully, the weather was nice the following morning, and it was during the lull in construction so once they woke, we had coffee out on the deck. Although I was now used to it, Chaz exclaimed when he opened the deck door and startled a half dozen deer that had been grazing at the back of my yard.

"Do you always get to see deer?" he asked, settling himself into one of the Adirondack chairs.

"Almost daily," I said as I sat, pulling an afghan around my shoulders. The weather may have been unusually spring-like, but it was still February and chilly in the morning. "Sometimes only one or two but I've counted as many as eight."

"That is so cool," Timmy murmured into his mug. We sat in companionable silence, listening to the birds sing. The men stared out into the woods, sighing occasionally.

They left late afternoon, thanking me for sharing my quiet and promising to be back soon.

It was blissfully quiet for three more days, and Esme was back to her normal in-and-out. (I still left the toilet lid up, though.) I spent that time perfecting all the new potion recipes. Esme was almost spot-on with her suggestions for formulations, and it only took a tweak here and a change there to make them *Perfect Potions.* I packaged up small samples and got them mailed out to my one-hundred-seventy-four customers with a note that magical soap samples would be on their way soon.

El and Cooper had visited shortly after construction started to see all the goings-on. While I stirred potions and packaged soap, they regaled me with their most recent paranormal investigation. It had been a band of pixies damaging the bottling equipment at one of her favorite vineyards. They didn't show up on the security video, but she and Coop had spent the night there only once and caught them. She never did get an answer as to why they were doing it but convincing the vintner to put a jar of peanut butter outside the bottling shed's door every week kept the pixies satisfied. For this, she had forgone her usual pay from the sheriff's office and accepted a case of wine a month for six months from the winery. She'd brought two bottles with her and placed them on the counter.

"Sharing the spoils," she said. "I love my wine but I can't drink *that* much in a month!"

I started to work on the Concentration potion and Cooper sneezed several times, finally asking to be let back outdoors. El chuckled. "He's not allergic, at least not according to the vet, but rosemary makes him sneeze. It at least keeps him from digging near those plants."

"Since you can talk to him, can't you just ask him not to dig?"

"I *did*," she whined. "He leaves the garden beds alone, but for some reason, the shrubbery around the front is fair game, no matter what I say. He always apologizes, but then a week or two later, I come out to find more holes and dirt scattered. My only consolation is he doesn't actually dig the plants up."

I could only laugh. I'd never had a dog – or a cat – but I'd heard friends' stories of their pets' peculiar habits.

"*At least I don't destroy plantings,*" Esme said with a huff from her perch on the mantel. "*You're lucky to have a crow as a familiar instead of a creature with four legs.*"

"Yeah, but I bet you don't cuddle close on cold nights like Coop or Patches do. There are tradeoffs to everything," Ellen shot back.

Esme only glared before returning her attention to the construction outside. She had been watching it with the proverbial eagle eye. I wondered if she actually knew enough to supervise. Of course, I forgot she could hear my thoughts.

"*I have seen a lot of buildings go up in my time. I think I have learned enough to ensure they are doing their job properly.*"

"And if they weren't? How am I supposed to correct them? I don't know a damned thing about construction."

"*Not my problem. If I see an issue, I'll tell you. It's up to you how you phrase it.*"

"John knows his stuff," El interjected. "Jason wouldn't have hired him to remodel my house if his reputation wasn't sterling. I think you can relax, Esme."

The crow harrumphed, rearranged herself on the mantel, and continued to watch out the window.

"*Are you done with the stinky stuff? I'd like to come back in. The sawdust is making me sneeze worse.*" Cooper was at the front door.

"I think that's my cue to head home," El said with a laugh.

"Hang on. Take these, try them, and tell me what you think," I handed her a sample bar each of the Wake Up! and Sleep Time soaps. "I think I have the formulations right this time but want another opinion."

She sniffed them. "Ohmigod. This one smells *awesome*. I am a coffeeholic, and it's like a delicious cappuccino. And this one? I'm ready to go home, put my PJs on, and head into bed in the middle of the day. But yeah, I'll actually *use* them instead of just inhaling the aroma and let you know what I think."

The electrician recovered and finished his wiring in two days. It took a little over a week more before John knocked on the deck door with an invoice in his hand.

"Before we settle up, please come give the place a final look," he said.

In my slippers, I followed him across the deck and over to my new shop. Once through the door, I stood in awe. I know I had picked everything out and peeked in during construction, but this was the first time I'd actually seen it all put together. White marble counters topped oak cabinets, which sat atop a tan tile floor. The deep, stainless steel double sink gleamed, as did the white countertop electric stove. Between the light coloring and the windows, the small shop had an airy feel.

"Well?" he asked.

"I'm thrilled," I told him. "It's everything I'd imagined and more."

"Good. I always like a client who's satisfied on the first go-round. May I have a final check?"

We went back in the house, and once again, I swallowed a gulp as I wrote the check. He shook my hand and told me if I ever needed anything else done, to give him a call. I promised I would and waved as he climbed in his truck to leave.

Esme was on the mantel when I turned back into the house. "*It's a good shop,*" she murmured her approval. "*When will you move out there?*"

I looked at the time on my phone. It was already late afternoon. "If it doesn't rain," I began.

"*Not for a few days.*"

"Then I'll do it tomorrow. I already know how I want things arranged, and it shouldn't take but a day to get all the supplies moved. I must admit, it will be nice to have my kitchen back. Not to mention the spare bedroom."

The following morning dawned bright and clear, just as Esme had promised. It was still cool in the mornings, but knowing I'd be working up a sweat, I dressed in jeans and a T-shirt. Crowing to myself as I picked up one of the cauldrons, I walked it over to the shop in my slippers. I loved not having to dress in a suit and full makeup to go to work!

Three hours later, I had moved everything from the house and I took a break for lunch before starting to put it all away. My phone pinged with a text from Marie.

Your herbs are here.

In the intervening months, we'd struck up, if not a friendship, a good working relationship. She hadn't said a word about me being a witch, but we'd had a few nice conversations about herb usage…my study of their medicinal properties for my own use had come in handy. I'm sure part of it was the fact that I was now ordering my stock in pounds rather than ounces. Even with my discount, she was making some money off me.

My fingers flew in reply. MOVING INTO THE NEW SHOP. WILL COME BY MONDAY. ALSO HAVE SAMPLES OF THE SOAP FOR YOU TO TRY.

She answered with a thumbs-up emoji. As I put a reminder in my phone to go pick up the herbs, I finished my lunch, then started to put all my supplies away. A place for everything and everything in its place. Now that I had real cupboards for storage, I moved the herbs from their bags into large amber jars I'd purchased, putting a pre-printed label on each. Once I'd filled the cupboards, flattened the boxes I'd been using for storage, and put them near my garbage bin, I moved the office out there, too. I had to unload the filing cabinet to get it moved, and even then, it was a struggle because I didn't own a hand cart and a solid oak cabinet was rather heavy. But John's measurements were spot-on and once I'd gotten it up the step into the shop, it slid neatly under the desk.

I was catching my breath when I heard El knock on the still-open shop door.

"I bring wine to celebrate your new shop," she said with a grin, holding up a bottle.

"How'd you know? No wait, let me guess. Esme told Cooper, who told you," I replied.

"Got it in one. I wanted to come see the finished product anyway." She looked around. "This is great! Are you going to move some of your plants, too?"

"A few. The majority will stay in the house because that's where I use them most. Not to mention I have to leave one window for Esme to come through. Let's go in the house. I want to shut the door so I can turn the heat on. It's still too cool to work out here without it."

While I normally tried to work only Monday through Friday, I ended up spending a few hours in the shop on Sunday, finishing up the soap samples and getting them packaged for shipment. I put one of each into a small shopping bag for Marie and called it a day.

CHAPTER ELEVEN

Esme's prediction of rain "not for a few days" held until Monday. It was raining when I got up, and I cursed myself for not putting the soap shipments into my car the previous day. Eyeing the flattened boxes, I re-taped four of them and used them to haul the smaller shipping boxes.

Grateful that the post office had an overhang at the entrance, I piled the boxes there before parking the car and racing back to the building. A kind gentleman held the door, and another helped me carry them up to the counter. I thanked each, then stood in line until it was my turn at the window.

"These smell wonderful," the postal worker said. "What are you sending out now?" I'd seen the same lady every time I'd had to make a trip in, rather than just put a small box or two in my mailbox for our delivery person to pick up.

"Handmade soap samples," I told her.

Her eyes lit up. "Really? I love homemade soap. Are you going to sell it on the internet?"

I shook my head. "I only do wholesale. If she likes them, Marie at Blue Ridge Health Foods will be selling them locally."

"Ooh. I can't wait. I'll check with her in a couple of weeks, shall I?"

I paid my bill then raced through the rain back to my car. As I started it, I heard, *"The soap will sell well, if that's any indication."*

Damn the crow and her listening in on my every thought. But she was right.

It was *pouring* by the time I got to Marie's store, just ten minutes away. This time, though, I wasn't hauling huge boxes and could use my umbrella for the fifteen feet between car and door.

I held the door open with my hip as I shook the water off my umbrella and put it on the floor where it wouldn't get anything else wet. Surprised not to hear Marie greeting me, I turned to face the counter and froze.

She was slouched in her chair at the counter, head thrown back and right hand clutching the shirt at her chest. Her left arm hung at her side. She wasn't moving. At all.

"Marie?" I called. She didn't answer. Scared out of my wits, I walked on stiff legs to the counter. I said her name a second time and again, she didn't respond. The closer I got, the more I could see she wasn't breathing. Swearing under my breath, I walked behind the counter and reached for her neck. It was warm, but I couldn't find a pulse. At least her eyes were closed but her face was frozen in a grimace. With shaking hands, I pulled out my phone and called 9-1-1.

"9-1-1. What's your emergency?" A female voice was calm and soothing.

"Um," I stuttered. "I'm at Blue Ridge Health Foods, and the owner is dead, I think."

"Would that be 2165 Lakewood Highway?" she said after a brief pause.

"Yes," I gulped.

"Ambulance is on its way. Is she breathing? Have you checked for a pulse?"

"No, she's not breathing. I checked for a pulse on her neck and couldn't find one."

"Are you able to do CPR?"

"She's sitting in a chair. I don't think I could get her out of it and onto the floor by myself without hurting her further, if she is hurt."

"Okay. Do you need me to stay on the line with you?"

"No, thank you. I think I'll manage."

I hung up and stared out the front window, waiting for the siren and lights that would indicate help had arrived. My whole body tingled, and I rubbed my arms in an attempt to warm up.

"*Hey,*" Esme said. "*Are you cold, or are you feeling magic?*"

Now that she mentioned it, I *wasn't* cold. Damp, yes, but it was warm in the store, and I wasn't even feeling a chill. The tingling was my response to magic in the air. I never felt my own magic, but this was like when I was at Timmy and Chaz' bar. Just not nearly as overwhelming. More like when Denny or Abby did a spell when I was in the room.

I looked around. I couldn't see an obvious source for what I was feeling, but there was magic there, I just knew it. With trepidation, I looked more closely at Marie. There. Around her mouth were faint dark red sparkles that were slowly fading. She had ingested a magical substance, and not a good one, in the last fifteen minutes or so. Whatever was in her stomach would still be twinkling at least as deep a red as cabernet sauvignon or maybe even darker. I swore some more.

The siren and lights arrived. Although the siren had cut off when they got to the end of the driveway, blinking red lights illuminated the store. Two paramedics rushed in, towing a gurney with a bag on top, and I simply pointed to Marie. They ran over to her, checked her vitals, moved her from the chair onto the gurney, and one started CPR after applying an oxygen mask to her face.

"Unit Four. Patient is in cardiac arrest," I heard the other say into a radio as he strapped her down while the other continued his ministrations. "Initiating CPR and transporting."

"Ten-four," the radio crackled. "Transport to FRH ASAP."

Another siren sounded then cut off outside. A few moments later, a sheriff's deputy, who looked like Hulk Hogan in a uniform, walked in. Water dripped off his Smokey the Bear hat and rain slicker. It didn't seem to bother him that he was getting the shop floor all wet.

"What do we have?" he asked the paramedic who was still working on Marie.

"Probably cardiac arrest," came the reply as he stopped his ministrations and pulled a defib unit out from the huge case. I turned away. I didn't want to see Marie's body jerking as the electrical impulses hit her.

The officer turned to me. "Do you know this woman?" I heard "clear" in the middle of his sentence, followed by the distinctive "thump."

"Only slightly," I told him. "I get herbs from her and she was thinking about stocking my soap. I had brought samples." I pointed to the small bag in my hand. "Her name is Marie, but that's about all I know."

"And when did you arrive? Did she have the heart attack while you were here?"

I shook my head. "I got here *maybe* a minute before I called 9-1-1. She was sitting in the chair, looking dead."

He took my name, address, and phone number, and asked me to leave the premises. "We'll be in touch if we have any more questions for you."

I grabbed my umbrella and went out to my car.

"You need to call El," Esme said. *"That's probably magical murder. Local cops won't know that."*

I nodded then remembered to reply in my head. *"When I get home."*

I watched as the paramedics slowly came out of the store with Marie on a gurney and put her in the ambulance. There was no oxygen mask on her face, so I knew she was really dead. The police officer stayed inside. Once the ambulance had left without siren and lights, I pulled out of the parking lot, my foot shaking on the gas pedal. I took a deep breath to calm myself and managed to get home without any mishaps, although my speed may have been somewhat erratic.

It was only eleven in the morning, but I poured a shot of gin and downed it before sitting. Esme flew in from outside and landed on the side table. While she shook herself, rain droplets flying, she said, *"Get a grip, girl."*

"Hey," I growled. "I've never seen a dead person before. Give me a break!" I really hadn't. The closest I had come to death was my mother. She'd been in the hospital, recovering from a severe asthma attack. I hadn't been there when she unexpectedly died from an aneurysm. Denny's mother took care of everything, arranging for cremation as Mom had wanted, and because my father was nowhere in the picture, remained my guardian for the next two years until I graduated high school and went out on my own. I never saw my mother's body.

"You need to call El who needs to call her boyfriend who needs to call someone else. Unless her family wants an autopsy, they won't do one to find out what killed her but just say she had a heart attack and leave it."

I sighed. "I know. Just…give me a minute, will you?"

The shot of gin warmed its way down, and I felt a little calmer. I pulled my phone from my pocket and called El.

"What's up?" she asked.

Taking a deep breath, I said, "I just got back from the health food store where I was *supposed* to pick up an herb order and drop off some soap samples.

"When I got there, the owner was dead. The paramedics said it was probably a heart attack, but I know it wasn't natural. There was magic residue around her mouth. She'd eaten or drunk something magical, and it wasn't good."

"*What?*" El yelled into the phone. "What do you mean, *she'd eaten or drunk something magical, and it wasn't good?*"

I took a deep breath. "Magic has different colors. At least to a witch. Harmful magic, whether a potion or something else, I see as red sparkles. Healing stuff, like what my friends do, gives off green sparkles. Like that.

"Marie had deep red sparkles around her mouth. That means she ingested a harmful magical substance. Based on how they were fading, probably only about fifteen minutes or so before I got there.

"Esme says we need to tell someone or they'll just write it off as a heart attack and bury or cremate her or whatever she wanted."

"Holy shit. Esme's right. Let me call Dave. I'll call you back."

She hung up without another word. I sat there staring at the phone, hands still trembling.

"*You should go work in the shop. You like that, and it'll calm you down.*"

"I suppose you're right, but I want to wait for El's call, first."

I stared at the phone, willing it to ring. Finally, after what seemed a lifetime but was probably only five minutes, she called back.

"Dave says because the cause of death is unknown, they *will* do an autopsy unless the family forbids it. But the magic stuff? He'll mention it to the sheriff, but unless the coroner comes back with 'suspicious death,' it won't get investigated. If she does, chances are the investigator will want to talk with you since none of us have a clue about magic. You willing?"

"Not sure how I can help, but sure. She didn't deserve to be murdered."

After El promised to keep me in the loop, we hung up. I ran out to the shop, my hair and shoulders only getting slightly damp in the short distance. I pulled out a cauldron then remembered I needed the herbs I'd ordered from Marie to start the next batch of potions.

"Shit, shit, and fuck," I said, kicking the cupboard door. "I could kill whoever killed Marie. Now I have to drive into Atlanta – in the fucking rain."

Esme flew in her window, landing on the counter in front of me. Once again, she scattered rain droplets as she shook herself then leaned forward and butted her head into my stomach. Thankfully, she tilted far enough that it was the *top* of her head and not her beak.

"Short term problems," she said. *"Get a grip."*

I was getting tired of being told to "get a grip." But she was right. I headed back to the house, grabbed my purse and soap samples once again, and headed toward Atlanta.

After stopping at a drive-thru for lunch, I finally made it to my favorite health food store a little over two hours later. As I ran through the rain to the door, I heaved a sigh. I would be driving home at the beginning of rush hour traffic.

The store was a co-op, meaning it didn't have just one or two owners. I dropped the bag of soap samples I'd originally intended to give Marie with the cashier to pass on to the head of purchasing before going to the back of the store to get my herbs.

Thirty minutes later, I was headed home. True to form, I hit the brakes after only fifteen miles. My phone rang, but I let it go to voice mail. Even though Georgia had outlawed holding a cell phone while driving, Atlanta traffic was *not* the place to divert your concentration! Two minutes later, the phone rang again. Someone really wanted to talk with me, so I maneuvered my way over to the side of the road.

Both missed calls were from Fannin County. Which department, I had no idea, because that was all that showed up on Caller ID, but it seemed prudent to return the call sooner rather than later. I hit the button to return the call.

"Sergeant Anderson." The voice was familiar. It was El's boyfriend.

I heaved a sigh of relief. This one I knew. "Dave, it's Jo Foster. You called?"

"I did. Thanks for getting back to me so quickly." A semi's horn blared right next to me as hydraulic brakes squealed. "Where are you?"

"On the side of I-75 in Marietta, on my way home from Atlanta. What's up?"

"The health food store owner? Marie Rice? Her daughter's raising a stink. Says she's certain her mother was murdered, and you had to be the one because you were the only person in the store this morning."

I was extremely glad I had put the car in park because I started trembling.

"*What?*" I yelled into the phone. Then, taking a deep breath to calm myself, I continued, "Why in the world would I have killed Marie? I barely knew the woman!"

"That's what Deputy Sorenson told her, but she's insistent. Can you come into the station tomorrow morning? We need you to make a formal statement."

I took another breath. "I have to know – did she identify me specifically, or just because I was the one to report her mother's death? And if she named me, how did she know? I've never met her."

"Can't tell you that. Not right now. Can you come in about nine?"

I started shaking. Being accused of murder had not been on my bingo card for this year. My voice shook, too, as I said, "Um. Sure. Nine. I'll be there."

"Calm down, Jo," Dave soothed. "This is just a formality. I volunteered to call so it would be someone you already knew and wouldn't sound like law enforcement is accusing you of anything. I'll see you in the morning."

"*I'm telling El,*" Esme said after I'd disconnected. "*She should go with you tomorrow since I can't.*"

"No, it's okay," I replied, trying to calm myself before getting back on the road. "I didn't do anything wrong. And Dave said it's just a statement. I'm a little shocked, that's all."

"*If you say so.*" Her voice was full of doubt.

I'd finally gotten enough control of myself I felt I could drive again. I eased my way back into traffic and fretted all the way home.

El and Cooper were waiting on my front porch when I pulled up. She didn't even wait for me to unlock the door but hugged me hard, ignoring my laden arms.

"Dave told me what that young lady has accused you of," she said as they followed me into the house. "He's honestly flabbergasted on your behalf, but they have to follow procedure.

"Do you have receipts from the times you've been in the shop? Might be handy to know exact dates. And by the way, I'm coming with you tomorrow."

"You don't have to," I said as I put my shopping bags on the kitchen counter. "Dave said it's just a statement. Since I haven't done anything wrong and barely knew the dead woman, it shouldn't be more than a three-minute interview."

Esme flew in from the hall and landed on the counter in front of me. "*Take El with you. The monster, too. You'll need moral support.*"

Coop nudged my hip with his head, and I almost lost my balance. He really was a *big* dog. "*The small bird is right.*" Esme snorted but he continued, "*We are your friends.*"

"Okay. Fine." I blew out a breath. "Seems I'm going to have company tomorrow. In the meantime, I need to put my supplies away and eat dinner. Meet me here at eight-thirty?"

"You got it. We'll be here!" She and Cooper left. I ran the herbs out to the shop but didn't feel like actually putting them away so left the bags on the counter. Taking El's advice, I looked up my visits to Marie's shop. Today had been the fourth time in nearly three months, the previous three for only two or three two-ounce bags at a time. I noted the dates in my phone.

I didn't really sleep that night. I tossed and turned, visions of being led to the cells in handcuffs dominating my thoughts. I felt Esme wake and grumble, but she did nothing to help me sleep. Therefore, I was up before my alarm in the morning.

CHAPTER TWELVE

Copious amounts of coffee and a shower later, I eyed my closet, trying to decide how I should dress for a formal interview with the cops. *Professional* and *no nonsense,* I thought. I pulled out one of my office pantsuits and put that on.

El knocked on the door promptly at eight-thirty. She eyed my outfit as I let her in. "Hon, you are *so* overdressed. Quick. Jeans and a collared shirt."

"What? I want to appear professional and…and confident. This works."

"Not up here. You look like a city slicker. Go change. Now."

I hurried to the bedroom and changed, not even taking time to hang the suit back up but tossed it on my bed. I was back in the living room in less than five minutes.

"Much better. Let's go." She dragged me out to *her* car, where I saw Cooper taking up most of the back seat. He probably would have covered the whole thing, but he was buckled into a harness that kept him in place. Underneath that peeked a vest I hadn't seen before.

"What's with the vest?" I asked as I climbed in the passenger door of her SUV. "Isn't his collar enough?"

"*I am official,*" he intoned at the same time as El said, "That's his working vest. We're actually part of the Sheriff's Office, you know, and he's certified in track-and-trail. It'll let him come into the building with us if there's someone I don't know at the desk."

She drove quickly into town, parking across the street from the courthouse, where the Sheriff's Office was located.

"Five minutes to spare. Good," she said as she clipped a badge to her belt after leading me through metal detectors into the tiny reception area. She greeted the deputy at the desk by name, and without asking, he paged Dave, who appeared from the back of the station so quickly, he must have been waiting for the call.

He gave El a quick peck on the cheek, ruffled Cooper's fur, then shook my hand. "Once again, Jo, this is just a formality. Inspector Woods is going to ask you to go through yesterday in more detail than Deputy Sorenson got. Come on. Let me introduce you."

We followed him back to a small room off a narrow hallway. It was so small, I was afraid I'd become claustrophobic, with only about three feet of spare space surrounding a table with two chairs situated across from each other. Waiting for us was a man in his forties, I thought, in a business suit rather than a uniform. He was a little shorter than Dave, with blond hair and hazel eyes behind wire-rimmed glasses. Dave made the introductions then motioned El and Cooper out of the room. I immediately felt *alone.*

"Please sit, Ms. Foster," the inspector said. "As I'm sure Sergeant Anderson has told you, this is simply a formality. I'd like to take you through the events of yesterday morning."

I sat, took a big breath, then said, "As I told the deputy yesterday, I'd only been in the store maybe a minute before I called 9-1-1. She wasn't breathing when I got there. I'm not sure what else I can tell you."

He took out a recorder. "Do you mind if I record this?" I shook my head. "Please respond verbally."

"No, you may record this," I said. He stated his name, the date and time, and the case number, which he read off a folder in front of him.

"Now, Ms. Foster, when did you arrive at Blue Ridge Health Foods yesterday morning?"

"I'm not sure of the exact time. Maybe around ten?"

"Did you go there directly from home?"

"No. I stopped at the post office first. Then I went to Marie's store."

Even though he was recording the whole conversation, he scribbled on a notepad. He looked up. "And exactly what did you do and see when you entered the store?"

I thought back. "It was raining, and I shook out my umbrella outside, then put it on the floor so I wouldn't drip water all over. I was surprised Marie didn't say anything when I walked in – she usually does. When I turned to face the counter, she was slumped in the chair with her head back. One hand was grabbing her shirt.

"I said her name. Twice. She didn't respond. I didn't see any evidence of breathing so I walked over and checked the pulse on her neck. I couldn't find one. Then I called 9-1-1 and stepped away to watch out the window for the ambulance."

"You didn't try to do CPR?"

I shook my head then remembered I had to verbalize my responses. "No. She was sitting in a chair. I wouldn't have been able to do CPR in that position and I was afraid if I tried to get her on the floor, I might hurt her. We're about the same size and I'm not all that strong. The 9-1-1 operator said 'okay.'"

"How well did you know Ms. Rice?"

"Not well at all. I looked at my receipts – that was the fourth time I'd been in the store in the three months I've lived up here. I didn't even know her last name until Sergeant Anderson mentioned it yesterday."

"No other interactions?"

"A few text messages? The order I was supposed to pick up yesterday was larger than what I normally got from her. When I'd decided to increase the amount, I texted her so she could get more from her supplier if she had to." I pulled out my phone and showed him the thread on my phone. "Here. You can see the whole exchange."

He read the messages – all seven of them. Then scribbled something more in his notebook. "Thank you, Ms. Foster. Give me about fifteen minutes to type this up, and I'll have you sign it. El knows where the coffee is." He ended the recording verbally before punching the 'off' button, then escorted me back to the reception area.

El and Cooper were waiting for me, Coop stretched out on the floor at her feet. They both stood when I arrived and El said, "Well?"

I shrugged. "I told him what I knew. He said to give him about fifteen minutes to type it up for me to sign then said you know where the coffee is."

She smiled. "I do. Come on."

They led me back through the door and down the same hall but turning right instead of left into a small kitchen. A coffeepot and mugs sat on the counter.

"It's standard police-issue coffee, I'm afraid," she told me as she poured two mugs' worth. "Tasteless but caffeine-laden."

As I sat at the single table, she took a bowl out of a cupboard and filled it with water from the tap. She set it on the floor before joining me at the table. Cooper lapped up about half of it before groaning and laying back down again.

"You seem to know your way around this place." I tried to start a conversation that didn't involve me being accused of murder.

She smiled. "We've been in and out of here for the last, oh, six months or so. Mostly just to meet Dave for lunch or bring him dinner when he's working late, but sometimes it's been an official visit, bringing a report in for an incident they had me look into.

"The department is small, only about thirty people, so I've gotten to know most of them, as well as some folks in other counties."

"You do a lot of – what did you call it? – paranormal consulting for them? Are there a lot of non-humans up here?"

She chuckled. "More than you'd think! The mountains and woods are ideal homes for a lot of creatures, especially were people, gnomes, and fairies. One vampire I met said Blue Ridge can support about a half dozen vamps, even though it's a small town. Something about the tourist population.

"According to Sheriff Danforth, paranormal activity has increased over the last couple of years. Mostly mischief-type stuff, but there *was* that rogue vampire last year. Since they can't see any of the non-humans, they need someone like me, who can. So yeah, I've been doing some work for them. It's interesting, and no two cases are alike."

I mulled over her words. "Why would the activity be increasing?"

She shrugged. "No one knows. There must be something riling them up when it's been quiet for at least the last decade, but none of the creatures I've spoken with seem…different than normal, I guess would be the phrase. Who knows? Climate change?"

Inspector Woods poked his head in the door. "Ms. Foster? I'm ready for you."

El grabbed our mugs and Cooper's dish, emptying them into the sink before putting them in the dishwasher. "We'll meet you out front," she told me before I followed the inspector back to the itty-bitty room.

We sat again, and he placed a couple of papers on the table, turning them toward me. "Please read this and if it agrees with what was said, sign at the bottom of the third page."

I read, and it was a verbatim transcript of our conversation, including a summary of the text messages. I signed where indicated and passed the papers back to him. He took them, stood, and held out his hand. "Thank you for coming in, Ms. Foster. I don't think I'll have any further questions, but if I do, I'll call you."

I shook the proffered hand, and he once more escorted me to the reception area. El and Cooper were waiting, ready to leave.

They dropped me off and headed home. Since I was already in jeans, I headed out to the shop. Esme was waiting for me on the counter, poking her beak at the bags of herbs I'd left there the night before.

"Now that's over, it's time to go to work."

She was right. I spent about twenty minutes putting my purchases away then started in on the Concentration potion we'd come up with. It was getting to be exam time in schools, and I wanted to be prepared for orders.

***

Three weeks later…

"Need your expert witch advice," El said after I'd answered her call.

"What?"

"Why would someone ingest snakeskin?"

"What?"

She sighed. "This is a semi-official call. I've been asked to call you as their paranormal investigator, but you'll be getting an official call from Inspector Woods in about fifteen minutes.

"First, what I'm about to tell you is confidential. Not that I'm worried you'll speak with anyone but me or the sheriff's department but I have to say it anyway.

"They've determined Marie Rice *might* have been murdered, but the autopsy and tox report aren't adding up. They found powdered snakeskin, copperhead to be exact, in her stomach contents."

"Holy shit," I said, taking a breath. "I can't think of any reason whatsoever someone would eat snakeskin. At least, not intentionally. Don't they skin snakes before eating them?"

I could hear the grimace in her voice. "As far as I know, and this is just from reading because there's no way I'd eat snake, yeah."

"In that case, snakeskin is used to increase the potency of some spells."

"Thought it might be something like that," she said. "Looks like you were right, that magic was involved. I'm going to hang up now and call Will back. He'll probably call you after we speak. Okay?"

I blew out a breath. "Okay."

I looked at the soap I'd been working on while a potion simmered on the stove. Thankfully, I was done with infusing the potion, and all I had to do to the soap was cut it into bars. My concentration for the day was now shot to hell. I picked up the pastry scraper I used for cutting, and my hand shook. So much for making straight cuts. I put the scraper down, grabbed my coffee cup, and sat to wait for the phone to ring.

Ten minutes later, the phone rang. Caller ID said "Fannin County," and it was indeed Inspector Woods on the other end of the line.

"Ms. Foster," he began, "El tells me you're a witch and know about herbs and magic and stuff. I am out of my element when it comes to that, and I'd like to pick your brain. Instead of doing this on the phone, may I come over?"

"If I can help, of course," I said. "Now or later?"

"Now, if it's convenient."

"Come on over. I'm in the shop around back of the house."

"*You need to get that off the heat before he gets here.*" Esme was in her usual spot on the counter, watching the potion simmer.

"It still has twenty minutes to go. If I need to interrupt our conversation, I will."

I prepared a couple of invoices while I waited. I still didn't feel steady enough to cut soap, so that was on the counter, too. He'd get an eyeful of witchcraft at work.

Fifteen minutes later, I heard a car pull into the drive and shortly, a knock at the door. I let him in, and he took in the scene, with the cast iron pot bubbling on the stove, and the blocks of soap on the marble counter.

Then he took a deep breath. "It smells marvelous in here!"

I laughed. "I can't smell anything different because I'm in it nearly every day, but it's all the herbs. Even though they're stored in airtight containers, the scents still escape when I'm working with them.

"I'm not set up to have guests back here. Do you want to go into the house where we'll be more comfortable?"

He shook his head. "No, if it's all the same to you, I'd rather stay out here. I'm interested in what you do as well as what you might be able to tell me."

"Coffee?" I asked as I poured myself another cup from the thermal carafe I'd brought from the house.

"Yes, thank you!"

I grabbed a spare mug, poured him a cup, then said, a little sheepishly, "Sorry. Creamer and sugar are back in the house since I don't use them."

He smiled as he took the mug from me. "I take it black."

I motioned for him to sit in the desk chair. "I still have…" I looked at my phone's timer "…three minutes before I can sit. So, you sit and ask your questions. I'll answer if I can, or even call a friend or two if I can't since I haven't been at this as long as some others. Marie didn't deserve to be murdered, if that's what it was."

He sat and pulled out a notebook and pen, just like every investigator on every cop show I'd ever watched.

"We think it was," he started. "Of course, this conversation is confidential."

I nodded. "The one I had with El was, and I assumed this one was, too."

"Wait," he looked up. "You said you haven't been at this very long. I thought witches were born as such."

I smiled at him. "They are. We are. But I got scared when my magic manifested at puberty and blocked it. I just unblocked it a couple of years ago. A traumatic experience."

"I think I understand." He wrote something down. "Okay…

"Ms. Rice's heart appeared to be healthy, according to autopsy, but there was evidence of a heart attack. However, the coroner smelled something…" He consulted his notes. "…bitter almond, she said, and decided further tests were needed.

"After conducting her tests and sending samples to the toxicology lab, she determined Ms. Rice had ingested a highly sugared sweet tea that contained hydrogen cyanide…" My eyes widened. "… and the snakeskin El asked you about and…" He looked at his notes again. "…mugwort?

"The amount of cyanide in her system shouldn't have been enough to kill her, the tox report said. Maybe give her a headache or make her nauseated. Yet, she died. And there were the other things in there that made no sense.

"El said you suspected magic. Would you explain?"

I blew out a breath at the same time as my phone timer went off. "First, you need to know that witches can *see* magic," I said as I turned off the stove and moved the pot to the trivet on the counter for cooling. Then I leaned against the counter to look at him.

"While we all see it a little differently, to me, it looks like colored sparkles. Sort of like glitter. I *felt* magic in the shop – it makes my skin tingle or itch. I looked around and didn't see anything out of the ordinary, but when I took a closer look at Marie, I could see red sparkles around her mouth. They were fading quickly, which told me she'd eaten or drunk something magical maybe fifteen minutes or so before I got there.

"The sparkles were red. That means 'harmful,' more or less. Anything from a minor hex to a curse, but the way I see it, the darker the color, the more harmful the magic. These sparkles were really dark."

I took a sip of my coffee. "As to the snakeskin, that's used to strengthen spells. You can use any type of snakeskin, to be honest, in any spell, but my guess is whoever prepared the potion that went into Marie's tea probably used copperhead because of the snake's venomous nature. The mugwort is also used for strength. It's generally meant to strengthen one's courage, or confidence maybe, but given that magic is all about intent, your witch probably meant it to strengthen their spell, doubling down, as it were, with the snakeskin."

"What does this mugwort taste like?" he asked after furiously scribbling notes.

"It's bitter, but not as bad as the cherry water, or whatever produced the hydrogen cyanide, would have been."

Esme took that moment to make herself known. When the inspector had knocked on the door, she'd flown to the top of one of the cabinets and not said a word until now.

"*That there is some nasty work,*" she opined. I'm sure all the cop heard was a caw, and he started as she flew from the cabinet to the countertop.

"A...crow?" he asked.

I laughed. "This is Esme, and she's my familiar. Somewhat cliché, I know."

He eyed the bird. She eyed him back. *"He's not bad looking."*

"Hush," I looked up at her with a frown.

"She talks?" His eyes were about as wide as they could be.

"She does. To me, other witches, and those like El who can hear animals. I think all you hear is a typical caw, right?"

He nodded and swallowed. "Okay. Back to the poisoning. So, you're saying someone gave her a potion?"

"Inspector," I began.

"Will," he corrected me. "We don't really stand on formality."

"Will. A potion is nothing more than a liquid of some kind infused with magical intent. I could brew you a cup of Lipton's and infuse it with my intent that you break out in hives. You would."

He gulped. I continued. "The potions I make, while not all for ingestion, are simply herbs simmered in water and infused with my objective, if you will, for the potion. They work because I use herbs meant for the purpose *and* my intent for that potion.

"Even if your culprit isn't a witch, there *had* to be one involved somehow. Magic is infused into the potion during the making. I don't know how it would be done otherwise."

"Would you make a potion like that?"

I was horrified and hoped my facial expression showed it. "*No.* Absolutely not. I have no objection to hexing someone who deserves it, but I won't curse. And that definitely was a curse."

He frowned. "So I'm looking for someone who is either a witch or knows about witchcraft *and* knows about poisoning people with…" He looked at his notebook *again*. "…cherry pits? At least, that's the coroner's guess based on the tox report."

"That, and they must have had this idea for quite some time," I added. "Cherries haven't been in season for at least six months, and the dried or canned ones you can buy year-round are already pitted."

I mused for a moment, recalling all the studying I'd done for the last couple of years, trying to not only catch up on magical applications but general herbal knowledge. Then I walked over to the laptop sitting on my desk and pulled up a spreadsheet I'd compiled during all that work. My brain just didn't retain a lot anymore, and I'd discovered it was easier to use a computer to store information. I clicked on a cell in the "Genus" column, which took me to a "Notes" document, and read further. Will turned in the chair to watch me. "You know," I started, "it might not be cherries."

"What do you mean?"

"The *Prunus* genus, which includes cherry trees, is *huge*…over four hundred species. It includes apples, which are available year-round. Although it would probably take several hundred seeds, I think it could be managed. Also, the leaves and branches of several species contain the poison. You could just prune a tree or bush and soak those."

"One last question," he said as he pocketed his notebook. "Did you see anything near her, like maybe a glass, that might have contained the tea she drank?"

I thought back to that day and shuddered a little when I told him I hadn't. "Then again, I wasn't looking for it."

He stood, drained his mug, and handed it to me. "You've given me a lot to think about. And more research to do. Thank you." With a glance at Esme, he shook my hand and left.

"*He's all bewildered,*" she said after he'd left. "*I could see the confusion in his eyes.*"

"Well, it's a lot to take in. I mean, the poison aspect of it is bad enough, but then add magic into the mix. That's not something he's used to dealing with. Hell, two years ago, I'd have been just as confused."

"*You* did *take to all this like a duck to water. Or a crow to food. Speaking of, my dish in the kitchen is empty.*"

Rather than argue with her, I walked back into the house, carrying the empty coffee mugs and carafe, and refilled her bowl of seeds after putting the dirty dishes in the dishwasher. She ate several while I stood there. "Keep on eating like that, and you'll be too fat to fly."

She eyed me, then picked up another peanut. "*Hey. Flying — and magic for that matter — takes a lot of energy. I have to refuel constantly. So no nasty comments.*"

I snorted but held my tongue. She could read my thoughts, anyway, and they weren't complimentary. She ate nearly a quarter her weight in seeds every day, and that didn't count what she probably ate away from the house.

Now that the excitement was over, I went back to cutting soap into bars. I had taken the blocks out of the molds prior to Inspector Woods' arrival and now put one block into a box with slots to ensure equal-sized bars. Then I positioned the pastry scraper to cut directly down. I had to be steady during the cutting process…there was a little play in the slots, and if my hands shook, the cut wouldn't be exactly straight.

"There must be a faster way to do that," Esme said as she flew to her normal spot on the counter.

"There is," I replied. "But the contraption that would cut an entire block at one time is expensive. I want to make sure the soap is selling well before I invest in it."

A half hour and sore arms and hands later, I had five dozen bars of soap piled on the counter. It took another hour to wrap and label them all and another half hour to package up those I'd already sold and put the rest in airtight containers for storage.

After lunch, I made a quick trip into town to post the packages. By the time I'd returned, the potion had cooled and I set to straining and bottling. It was dark by the time I'd cleaned up the shop, and I was glad I only had a five-step commute. Quite a change from working in an office!

CHAPTER THIRTEEN

My phone rang bright and early the following morning. I was only on my second cup of coffee. It was Will again. "I have to ask. Do you have a receipt from when you were at the post office? I need to be able to pin down your movements."

My heart started thudding as I took in the implication of his words. I was still a suspect. "I do. Do you want me to scan and email it to you?"

"Please. And how long were you there before you completed your transaction?"

I thought back to that day. "Um. I had to get my load into the building, then stand in line for a bit before I got to the window. Then there was the number of boxes I shipped, which took her some time to process. So maybe fifteen or twenty minutes?"

While I'd been speaking, I went out to the shop and pulled the receipt from the filing cabinet. It was almost three feet long because

I'd shipped so many boxes. "I'm going to have to scan this in pieces," I told him. "It's too long for my scanner to do in one go."

"Do what you have to. I need the whole thing." He was curt as he recited his email address before ringing off.

I immediately dialed El. "What the hell is happening?" I asked when she answered. "Inspector Woods was all nice and polite when I was trying to help him yesterday, and now it seems I'm back in the suspect category."

"What happened?" She sounded as confused as I felt.

I recounted the morning's conversation while I dutifully scanned the first section of the receipt.

"I'm not a part of this investigation..." She tried to sound soothing. "...but I think Will's just trying to keep all his ducks in a row. I don't see how you could be suspected of murdering her. You barely knew her and had no reason."

"I *know*," I complained as I laid out the second section on the scanner bed. "But..."

"What did you tell him yesterday?"

"Mostly how I can sense and see magic and that I saw evidence of it around Marie's mouth. Then that it might not be cherries, as they suspected, but could be one of many other possibilities. That genus is huge. I mean, don't people who specialize in ferreting out poisoning know this stuff?"

"I would suppose so, but not my area. Let me see if I can stick my nose in to see why Will is seemingly concentrating on you. I'll call you back."

She hung up, and I stared at the scanner as if it would give answers. I sighed and scanned the last two sections of the receipt before saving the file and emailing it to the inspector.

"You have a prodigious amount of herbal knowledge." Esme flapped her wings from the counter, startling me. I hadn't heard her come through the window. *"Perhaps he thinks you used it."*

"But why would I have given him all that information if I was the one who killed her? Wouldn't I have tried to direct him elsewhere?"

"I have no idea. The way most humans think baffles me."

I plopped in the chair. "I don't understand what's happening. After the divorce and moving here, I thought my life would be, if not easy, then comfortable."

Esme shook her head from side to side then left the shop. My phone rang just as the flap on her door banged. It was El.

"So?" I didn't bother with any greeting because she never did.

"He's being close-mouthed." I could hear the displeasure in her tone. "Says it's his case, not mine, and to keep out of it."

I fidgeted in the chair. "El, I'm scared. What if he truly thinks I did it?"

"I don't see how he can come up with enough – *any* evidence you did. If, for some reason, he does, I'll figure out a way to convince the sheriff to let me in on it. Since you suspect magic, there must be *something* Coop and I can do to help, although I'm not sure what at this point.

"In the meantime, don't fret about it. That's not healthy. Just go about your business as usual. You've got friends, Jo. Don't forget that."

I heard Cooper's baritone in the background voicing his agreement. We hung up and, despite El's admonishment, I stewed about the situation.

Before I could stew too long, though, my phone rang again. This time it was Denny. "I got this bad feeling about you and had to call. Are you okay up there?"

I burst into tears. "No, I'm not! I think I'm a suspect in a murder!"

"What in the hell? Calm down enough to tell me what's going on."

I took big gulps of air and finally was down to sniffling before I recounted the last three weeks. She already knew about Marie's death, but I repeated myself so she had the full picture.

"I don't know him, but that cop is off his rocker if he thinks you killed that lady," she stated after I'd finished my story. "So what if you have knowledge of herbs, including the poisonous ones? So do a lot of people. Especially up in the mountains where herbal remedies are ages-old."

"I know, right?" I sniffled some more. "Hell, Marie probably knew. I don't think anyone who uses, much less sells herbs, wouldn't."

Then I had a thought. In one of our conversations not too long after Christmas about weird abilities and getting older, El had mentioned another friend, Anne, I thought her name was, who could see ghosts. Maybe Marie was sticking around? "Hey, I need to go so I can call El. I had a thought about another one of her friends."

"Okay, but you keep me informed, right? Abs and I can hex someone on a moment's notice for you. Love you, girl!"

"Love you, too!" I hung up and immediately re-dialed El.

"So soon?" she answered. "What's up?"

"You said your friend, Anne, can see ghosts, right? What if Marie is still around? Would Anne be able to get any information from her?"

"Oooh. I never thought about that. I think she's back in town. Let me call her, and I'll call you back once I've spoken with her." She hung up without further comment.

I had no potions or soap to make that day, so went back into the house and tried to while away the time by playing solitaire on my phone. It was the only activity that didn't require thinking, because my brain was consumed with being thought of as a murder suspect.

Finally, my phone rang again with a call from El. Once again, there were no pleasantries before she said, "Anne's in town, pissed for you, and very willing to see if Marie is around to talk with. She's tied up until mid-afternoon but will come over here after that. The three of us…" I heard Cooper's "*four*" in the background… "can go over to the store, wander around, and see what we can see.

"Do you know where she lived?"

I shook my head then realized she couldn't see me. "No. Above the store, maybe? It's an old, two-story house, and as far as I know, the shop was only on the main floor. If not there, I have no idea where."

She grunted. "Okay. Let me ask Dave for a favor. He'll be able to find out where she lived. If Marie's ghost isn't at the store, and she didn't live there, maybe she's hanging around home.

"Anyways, come over about three. We'll take my car because it has room for Coop plus the three of us."

Just as I hit the disconnect button, Esme let out a loud, "Caw, caw."

I turned to find her in her usual spot on the fireplace mantel, although I hadn't heard her come back into the house. "What?" I asked.

"Careful. Ghosts can be tricky."

"But I'm not going to be the one to talk with her if, indeed, she's around. Anne is."

"What I mean is, they can have their own agenda. Just because they're dead doesn't mean they won't harbor the same prejudices they had in life. What if she didn't like that you're a witch? She could give this Anne false information."

"I'll have to cross that bridge if and when I come to it," I told her. "But right now, it's a chance for information Inspector Woods won't be able to get."

"If you say so. My seed bowl needs refilling."

I dutifully went into the kitchen to get the tin of her seed mixture out of the cupboard. When I looked at the bowl, I glared at her. "I swear, you're as bad as all those cat memes I see. It's not empty!"

She glared right back but said nothing. I sighed and topped the bowl off. Then decided it was time I showered then found *something* to do until it was time to head over to El's.

When I'm upset, I clean. Living in a one-bedroom condo, there wasn't that much to do, and as a result, the place sparkled most of the time. With a two-bedroom house, however, there was *always* cleaning…or yardwork to be done. Instead of showering, I dressed in outside clothes and went out to do the first mowing of a very long season. It took me a few minutes to remember all the instructions the salesman had given me on the care and maintenance of a lawnmower, but I finally got it gassed up and started. The exercise of pushing the mower up and down the hill my house was built on worked off a lot of my frustrations. It also confirmed I was getting older – my hips ached from all that walking.

After showering and choking down a sandwich for lunch, it was finally time to head over to El's. Thanks to more than three months of making the trip, I needed no guide to get me there – the trees had nearly completed their move, and the path was obvious. I paused before heading into the woods to look in the opposite direction, past my deck and shop. The path that had been so visible when I moved in was no longer there. Instead, it looked like a normal forest, with both old and young trees filling the space. I was in awe.

Cooper flew through his door as I exited the woods into El's yard. *"Hi! We get to go for a car ride today!"* He nearly bowled me over in his excitement, but to his credit, he did not jump on me, just bounced around in a circle.

"Hi, yourself. I take it you like car rides?"

"Oh, yes! I get to smell new things, especially when she leaves the window open for me. It is so much fun!"

Esme flew from a tree and landed on Coop's back. "*Only a dog would prefer to ride in a motorized contraption. Flying is much better.*"

I laughed. "I suppose it might be. But we can't fly so a *motorized contraption*, as you put it, is the best we can do."

Coop shook himself hard enough to dislodge Esme, who flew to the deck railing. El opened her door and greeted me.

"Anne's not here yet. Come inside. I have coffee going."

Even without our shared age, singlehood, and weird abilities, our caffeine addiction would have made us fast friends. We both loved the stuff and probably drank more than was healthy.

She handed me a mug of steaming elixir and leaned against the island. "I heard your lawnmower going this morning. Do you always do your own?"

I nodded. "I can't say *always* because this is the first time I've ever owned a house, and it was after growing season when I moved in. Today was my introduction to yardwork. But a lawnmower is cheaper than a lawn service, and given the slope, is a damned good workout. No gym fees!"

She moaned. "My knees won't let me do that much up-and-down, so I have a service. But…" She looked at her hips. "…I'm going to have to figure out something. I've been doing too damned much sitting this winter, and maintaining the garden isn't *that* much exercise."

Just then, we heard a car pull into the drive and shortly, a knock at the door. "It's open," El yelled.

"You have coffee. I love you," said a woman with gunmetal gray hair and sparkling blue eyes. She walked over to where we were standing and, after giving El a hug, held out her hand to me. "Hi. I'm Anne Johnson, ghost whisperer." She grinned. "You must be Josephine."

I shook her hand and nodded. "Josephine Foster, but please call me Jo. I do hope you can help."

El shoved a mug into Anne's hand. "If Marie's around, Anne will get whatever information she has out of her. She's a whiz with ghosts!"

I cocked my head at this statement. "A whiz?"

Anne laughed. "Although I came into my ability late in life – as I think we all did – I seem to have no difficulty establishing a rapport with ghosts. Hell, I even have one who I consider a friend!"

My jaw dropped. "A friend?"

"Come on," said El. "We're not on any timetable, so let's go sit and finish our coffee. Anne can tell you her story."

We adjourned to the living room, and after getting comfortable, Anne smiled over her cup. "I don't know if El's told you, but I live in an RV. I'm currently staying at a park on the other side of the lake. Honestly? This is the longest I've been in one spot. It's been almost a year. I normally move every two to four months.

"Anyways, I had a hysterectomy about two years ago, throwing me into early menopause. After that, I started seeing ghosts *everywhere*. Not only seeing them, but able to talk with them as well. It's still weird but is an *is,* so I go with it.

"There's a ghost who hangs out at the beach near where I'm parked. He and his dog, who is also still around, were drowned when they flooded for the lake, which is a reservoir."

"Boo is so much fun to play with!" Cooper interjected from where he was stretched out next to El's chair.

After El translated, Anne looked at him and smiled. "El's brought Coop over a few times, and yes, the dogs play with each other in the water, although Coop is the only one who makes a splash. Joshua is a kindly man and rather lonesome, I think, especially since no one can see him. So I go to the beach every few days and we chat. He's up on current events because he eavesdrops not only around the lake but goes into town on occasion."

"He knows he's dead?" I asked in astonishment. "Why does he not go to wherever he's supposed to go?"

She shrugged. "Says he doesn't have anyone he's anxious to see on the other side, and this is his *home*. Who am I to gainsay him?"

We were all quiet for a few minutes, sipping our coffee and musing on this poor man who just hung around, probably eagerly waiting for the one person who could see him to come to the beach.

"Well," El said, standing. "Let's go see if Anne can work her magic. Dave said Marie lived above the shop, so it's a single stop. We'll take my car since Coop's harness is already in there."

We trooped into the garage, Coop joyfully leading the way. He grumbled a bit when El clipped him into his harness, but with a promise of an open window, the complaining stopped. I sat in back with him after Anne called shotgun.

"Where am I going?" El asked after backing out of the garage and turning around.

"The shop is in an old house off Highway 60. I think you probably pass it on your way to one of the wineries."

"Okay. I can get us in that direction. Tell me when to turn into a driveway."

CHAPTER FOURTEEN

Twenty minutes later, I told El to turn right into the next driveway she saw. She pulled into the graveled parking lot just as I had, and we all got out – Coop starting his own investigation into the smells around the yard and, typical for dogs, I thought, anointing a couple of shrubs along the perimeter.

I walked up to the door with its "Closed" sign, and looked first through that then the front window. It looked as if no one had been there in the intervening weeks. The shop was dark, lit only by light coming through the few windows. The setting sun through the back window glinted off dust motes floating through the air and settling onto all the horizontal surfaces.

Anne walked slowly around the house then stood next to me, peering through the front window as I did. "I'm not seeing anyone around," she said, "but maybe she's hanging around upstairs where we can't see. What was her name again? Maybe if I call her, she'll come. Happens sometimes."

"Marie Rice," I replied.

"Got a middle name?"

"No. I didn't even know her last name until Dave told me. Is it necessary?"

She shrugged. "Helps. But if we don't have it, we don't have it. Let me try."

Anne called Marie's name several times, telling her we wanted to talk with her if she was so inclined. El had joined us at the window, one eye on Cooper and one on us. We waited silently, hoping Anne's efforts would yield results.

After ten minutes, Anne shrugged. "She's not here, or at least, not answering. I have an idea, though. Let's go talk with Joshua. He knows *everything* that happens in the county, and if Marie is still on this plane, he'll know."

El called Cooper, who had meandered to the back yard, still checking out all the smells. I watched as he raised his head from whatever he was investigating and slowly made his way back to us. The tall, screening shrubs behind him, though, caught my eye.

"Hang on a minute," I said. "I want to check something out."

As I walked toward the rear of the property, I pulled up a plant identification app on my phone. I'd found it invaluable when learning about my new property and thought it might be helpful now.

"What?" Anne and El asked at the same time.

I walked to a line of shrubs that towered over me, with glossy green leaves and a few remaining clusters of off-white flowers. Because I had my suspicions, it only took me a minute to get a firm identification of *Prunus caroliniana*, or Carolina cherry laurel.

I held my phone next to the shrub. "Look," I said. "This shrub – the leaves and wood – contains the same poison Marie ingested. It's right on her property. The cops wouldn't have to look far for it."

"What are you saying?" El asked. "She poisoned herself?"

"No, not at all." I shook my head. "Based on what I saw, she wouldn't have had time to get rid of the glass or cup she'd drunk from. Eating something is another matter. But Inspector Woods said she ingested highly sweetened tea. The water the tea was made from could have been poisoned with plants right off her property."

El eyed the wall of green. "It doesn't look like there's been any pruning going on recently. I'm not seeing any evidence of clippings or new growth that generally happens with pruning. But if it was done a couple of months ago, it would have grown out by now. Or someone could have clipped branches farther into the shrub, or on the other side where we can't see."

"How does that help?" Anne asked.

"Not sure," I said. "But we need to keep that in mind. Let's go talk with your ghost friend. Maybe he can find out something."

We climbed back in the car for the short ride over to Anne's RV. As soon as he was unclipped from his harness, Coop raced down a path that ran alongside her parking spot toward the lake. We followed at a more sedate pace.

"Damn," El said. "He's going to run right into the water, and I didn't bring a towel for him."

Anne let out a guffaw. "You can use one of mine. I'll expect it back fully laundered, though. Bear doesn't like the smell of wet dog."

"Bear?" I asked.

"My cat," she said, pointing to one of the windows in her RV where a *huge* long-haired gray and black cat lounged. "Hang on. Let me go get a towel for Coop." She disappeared into the RV and returned a moment later with a towel in her hand.

While we waited, El walked over to the window. "Hi, Bear!" she said. "We're only stopping because we have some business down at the lake. Anne will be home in an hour or so, okay?"

Bear turned his golden eyes toward her. "*She will be back in time to feed me?*"

It was my turn to guffaw. "Animals are the same everywhere, aren't they?"

Anne looked at El. "What did he say?"

When El repeated Bear's question, Anne laughed, too. "He gets fed before I go to bed. Please tell him I'll be home long before then."

El dutifully relayed Anne's statement before we followed Coop down the path. Halfway down, I heard the sounds of splashing, and soon, the sight of the big dog gamboling in the water came into view.

"Oh, good," Anne said. "Boo's here, which means Joshua is around somewhere. They're never far apart. Let's go over to the picnic table. That's where I normally meet him."

A minute later, she raised her hand and called, "Hello!" to the picnic table. I walked behind her, careful not to veer anywhere, in case I should bump into – walk through? – a ghost. El was right behind me.

"Mr. Reynolds," she began. "I've introduced my friend, Ellen, before. This…" She pointed to me. "…is a new friend, Josephine. She's in a pickle, and we were wondering if you could help."

She moved aside, and I felt something cold touch my hand. Startled, I pulled it away, then figuring I was being an idiot, stuck it out as if I was going to shake his hand. Cold enveloped my hand again then retreated. The cold stayed with me a moment before my hand warmed to normal temperature again.

"Hard to get used to, isn't it?" El murmured as she stood at my shoulder.

"Joshua apologizes, Jo," Anne said. "He forgets how cold his touch can be to the living. But he says he's pleased to meet you and wants to know what he can do to help."

All of a sudden, I felt a rush of wind then sharp talons digging into my shoulder. "*Hello, you,*" Esme croaked. I turned my head in confusion.

Anne's eyes widened as she relayed a greeting from the ghost to Esme.

"You know Mr. Reynolds?" I asked Esme.

"*Know most ghosts in these parts. There are a fair few. This one is more coherent than most.*"

"Wait." I was still confused. "Was he a magic person in life? Is that why you can communicate with him?"

She cawed a laugh then finally left my shoulder for the table top. I massaged my shoulder, thankfully not feeling any blood come through my shirt. "*Don't know about him in life – never met him then. All ghosts can see and communicate with other beings – if they want. Most aren't like this one though. They just drift around, stuck in some time, and pay no attention to anything around them in real time. This one is in the here and now."*

El had been following our conversation with interest and relayed what Esme had said to Anne.

"She's right," Anne said. "I see ghosts drifting around, but most don't acknowledge me. Joshua and a couple in town are the only ones I've actually been able to hold a conversation with.

"Now, back to the reason we came here. Sit."

We sat, Anne telling me and El *where* to sit. Then she told Joshua what had happened to Marie and my plight. She told him where Marie lived then asked me to describe her, which I did.

Anne listened a minute, eyes apparently looking off into the woods bordering the beach but probably right at the ghost. Esme was still standing on the table, obviously watching the conversation. Then Anne turned to us.

"He says he hasn't met anyone newly dead of that description, but he'll go searching and ask around the few ghosts he knows. I'm supposed to come back down tomorrow afternoon, and he'll tell me what he found.

"I don't know about you guys, but I'm hungry. We need to go back to El's to get my car. Should we stop in town for dinner first?"

Esme hopped to the edge of the table where Mr. Reynolds was probably sitting. *"If you find anything out, I can fly to investigate. It'll save the ladies some time. Meet you here around noon?"*

A moment later, she bobbed her head in agreement and turned to me. *"I'm off for home. See you there."* Then she flew off.

My stomach rumbled in agreement with food. Although it was an hour earlier than I normally ate dinner, the sandwich I'd choked down for lunch hadn't lasted long.

I looked in the direction Anne and Esme had. "I appreciate any help you can give, Mr. Reynolds. I didn't kill Marie and would like to find out who did."

Anne told me he was glad to help – it would give him something to do. Then she said, "See you tomorrow!" and turned back toward the path.

Coop stopped his frolicking in the water, and his face looked sad. "*Do we have to go?*"

"It's time," El told him. "But if you stand quietly while I dry you off, I'll get you a treat when we stop for dinner."

"*Treat? I will be good!*" he said as he exited the water, shaking himself off and scattering cold drops on all of us. It was still too early in the year for the lake to have warmed up much, and I was glad he was several feet away. Otherwise, I would have been doused and shivering with cold. El toweled him off a little more before we headed back up the path.

I'm sure she was used to it, but the stench of wet dog in El's car was nearly overwhelming. Both Anne and I rolled down our windows after making it obvious by pinching our noses. El laughed as we did so. "Yes, I think I'm used to it after over twenty years of having dogs. Even after using a towel, it'll take him a while to dry off, but the smell will dissipate quickly."

After a delicious burger at one of the restaurants in town with an outdoor patio (including a plain patty for Cooper, which he ate in three bites), we parted ways at El's. The trees had cleared enough of a path between our two houses that, with the help of the flashlight app on my phone, I was able to find my way, even in the dark.

Esme was waiting on the porch railing. "*Why are you waiting for mundane law enforcement to solve the murder? You should use a spell to find out what happened to that woman.*"

I may have choked just a bit. "What?"

"*You never thought about that? Are you a witch or not? Use a finding spell…or better, do some divination. You should be able to figure this out with magic.*"

I had one foot on the front step and froze, staring at her. "That's possible? I guess it is if you say it is but I have no idea how to go about it."

She gave the crow equivalent of a snort. "*Honestly. Did no one tell you anything?*" She looked up at the sky where a waxing moon glowed brightly through the tops of the trees to the east. "*The moon will be full in a few days. Prime time for divination. I'll guide you through it.*"

I sighed. I thought I'd left all my witchy lessons behind when I moved. She obviously heard what I was thinking because she snorted again. "*You never stop learning. Or shouldn't. There's always something new to discover.*"

With that sage pronouncement, she flew off into the trees, and I went into the house. It didn't take long before I fell into bed, exhausted from the stress of the day.

The next day was Saturday and as I had no job that kept me tied to a desk Monday through Friday, weekends were no different to me. I decided I needed to invest some time updating my website to include the new potions and soaps. I really hated this part of being a business owner, but it had to be done. Thankfully, unless I was online shopping, the computer held no interest for Esme and she left me alone after, once again, topping off her bowl of seeds on the kitchen counter.

I spent the morning taking photos of stock, uploading them, and writing product descriptions. My stomach grumbled to let me know it was past lunch time, and I was about to go back into the house when Esme poked through her door and flew to the desk beside me.

"The ghost came up empty. Your murder victim apparently has crossed over."

Crap. But, "While it would have been nice for her to tell us who killed her, I think I'm glad she crossed over. I always feel sorry when I read about ghosts stuck, for whatever reason, on this plane."

"Makes your job more difficult, though. Guess you'll have to do that divination after all."

I paused to text El who, I assumed, would text Anne, since I'd failed to get the other woman's number the night before. Then it was sandwich time.

Rather than go back to work, I decided to relax the rest of the afternoon with a good book. I hadn't quite gotten out of the habit of my e-reader, although I *had* started picking up hardcovers of favorite books at flea markets in the intervening months to stock the bookshelves in the living room. So many good books nowadays were only in electronic format, though, that I felt little remorse in grabbing that rather than a physical book.

The next couple of days were rather boring. I heard nothing from the other ladies or the Inspector about Marie's death. But Esme was relentless. *"Full moon. Good time for divination. You* need *to find out who killed that woman.*" When I asked why *I* needed to solve the mystery, she told me it was a feeling she had. Crows were odd creatures.

I was in the middle of packaging up an order Tuesday morning when Esme came into the shop and landed on the counter…right in the middle of all my packing materials. I heard several pops as her talons punctured bubble wrap.

"Prepare yourself. That Inspector fellow is coming up the drive."

Not having a clue as to why he'd visit again, I continued on with my work. A couple of minutes later, there was a knock at the shop door, and I heard him call my name.

I opened it and, after greeting him, gestured him in. "Coffee, Inspector Woods?"

He shook his head. "This isn't a social call. I need to know where you were last night."

I stared at him. "Why? But to answer your question, I was here last night. I haven't left the house since Friday."

"What's your relationship with Katherine Rice?"

"Who?" I thought for a minute. "You said 'Rice.' Is she a relation to Marie? Her daughter, maybe?"

He continued watching me, his face grim. "May I see your cell phone, please?"

"Careful." Esme was perched on top of the cabinets.

I narrowed my eyes. "I have no idea what's going on, but I don't like the way you're acting toward me. Unless you have a warrant, no, you may not see my cell phone. Would you care to explain your attitude, Inspector?"

"Katherine Rice, Marie's daughter, was killed in a one-car accident a couple of miles from her house last night. One of her front tires blew, and we suspect it caused her to lose control, careening into a tree. Further inspection showed the other three tires were drastically over-inflated. They were all balloons, ready to pop as soon as they got warm enough.

"There was a text message from your number on her phone, asking her to meet you. That you had information on her mother's death. Time was of the essence, it said, and she should come right away.

"So, I ask again. May I see your cell phone?"

I shook my head. This could *not* be happening to me! "For your information, I had no idea who Katherine Rice was until you told me. Due to that, I have no idea where she lived. Because I didn't know her, I couldn't have done a damned thing to her car.

"And no, Inspector, you may not see my cell phone unless you have a warrant. I will be calling an attorney shortly. As soon as I've hired one, he or she will be in touch. Please leave."

His eyes tightened even further. "In that case, Josephine Foster, I am arresting you for the murder of Katherine Rice. You have the right to remain silent. Anything you say can and will be used against you in a court of law. You have a right to an attorney. If you cannot afford an attorney, one will be appointed for you.

"Will you come quietly or do I need the handcuffs?"

Before I could say a word, Esme flew off the cabinets, grabbed my cell phone off the counter in her talons, and took off through her door. *"Taking this to your neighbor and telling her what's happened."*

"That damned crow!" Inspector Woods exclaimed. "What did you tell her?"

"I said nothing to her. And yes, I'll come quietly." Tears were streaming down my face, and I was shaking like a leaf. Even though I knew I was innocent, I had no alibi. And no idea how a text message was sent from my phone without my knowledge.

As he tucked me into the back seat of his car and got in the driver's side, Esme flew by. *"Ellen says to not worry. She is on her way to the police station now with the behemoth. They will wait to see what happens. I will be nearby, too."*

CHAPTER FIFTEEN

I went through the humiliation of being booked. Once that was done, I was allowed my one phone call. Thankfully, I had Burke's number memorized.

"You *what?*" Burke was shouting after I tearfully explained what had happened. "What the hell have your gotten yourself into, Jo? You know I'm not a criminal attorney, but I'm on my way. I'll make a few calls from the car to get you one. I'll put up your bail and represent you until someone better qualified can get up there.

"Hang on. Help is on the way." He hung up. With my one connection to the outside world gone, I cried even harder as I was led to a holding cell.

The door had clanged shut, and I was about to collapse on the cot to continue crying my eyes out when it opened again. Dave rushed over and enveloped me in a hug, which surprised me. I didn't know him *that* well.

"The hug is from El. She said Cooper said to give you a lick." He laughed. "I won't do that. They got here about a half hour ago and made a beeline to my office to tell me. She can't come back here, but I can.

"Will is so far off base with this one, he's not even in the ballpark. Do you have an attorney yet?"

I sniffled into his uniform shirt and nodded. "My old boss is on his way. He's not a criminal attorney but will find someone who is."

"Good. Ellen and I have already spoken with the sheriff. As a favor to me, he's trying to get you arraigned yet today. If not, it'll be tomorrow. We don't get *that* many criminal cases up here, and the judge may grant an expedited arraignment. It depends on her calendar. Can you raise bail? El and I will come up with it if you can't."

I sniffled again. "Burke said he'd post my bail. Given it's a murder charge, it's probably going to be astronomical. He can probably afford it better than you two. I certainly can't."

He smiled down at me. "Then dry your eyes. We'll have you out of here as soon as possible." His voice lowered to a whisper. "Tell your attorney El has your cell phone. I also know a top-notch forensic electronics expert in Atlanta he can take it to. Have him come see me after he's seen you, okay?"

I nodded.

In a normal voice, he continued, "El and Coop are hanging out in the reception area. I'm going to go tell her what we've spoken about. Since Coop is rather obvious, your attorney should have no problem spotting them. They'll wait until we know more. Hopefully, they'll be able to take you home yet today.

"I have to go back to work. Chin up, Jo. Everyone *but* Will is on your side, okay?"

He let me go, and with a small smile, left me alone. I stared at the walls, occasionally crying and hiccupping, wondering what was happening to my life.

Sometime later (without a clock I had no way of telling the passage of time), someone brought me a tray of food. It was a plain hamburger with a side of coleslaw. I had no appetite at all but knew I had to eat so choked about half down.

I'd just placed the tray with the uneaten food on the floor when a deputy came to the door. "Ms. Foster? Your attorneys are here. Sorry, but I have to cuff you. Would you hold out your hands, please?"

"Attorneys?" Burke had acted quickly!

After putting cuffs on me (they were heavier than I had anticipated), the deputy gently took my arm and guided me down a couple of hallways to the same interview room I'd been in just a month before. He ushered me into the room and closed the door.

To my surprise, I saw not only Burke but a short, squat, blond man in his mid-fifties with a perpetually serious expression. He was Connor Logan, a senior partner in our former firm and, in Burke's opinion, one of the best criminal attorneys in the state. Burke came over and gave me a quick hug before it was Connor's turn. Then Connor gestured for us all to sit. Despite having lived in the United States for more than half his life, he still spoke with a British accent.

I always wondered if, here in the Deep South, that accent worked for or against him and his clients in court.

"I'm sorry it took so long, El," Burke began. "Connor was the first call I made, and he was appalled at what I told him. He said he had a meeting he couldn't miss, but that I should come get him and we'd come up together."

"I know the Appalachian Circuit judge who will be hearing your case," Connor began. "We went to law school together. I called her from the road, and she already knew about your case. Seems the sheriff had already called her. Anyways, your arraignment is scheduled for three o'clock this afternoon."

He looked at his watch. "We have about an hour. Tell me what's going on. Start at what you think is the beginning."

I began with needing to pick up an herb order from Marie about a month ago. Connor interjected, "An *order?*"

I nodded, took a deep breath, and plunged in, knowing Burke – and probably Connor – wouldn't believe me.

"After I caught Asshole cheating on me, I found out I'm also a witch. That's a longer story than we have time for now, but while I was staying with my friends, I learned I'm pretty damned good at making magical potions."

I side-eyed Burke. "Rather than trying to find another secretarial job for after Burke retired, I decided to see if I could make a business of the potions. I did. When I moved up here, I found Marie's shop and, rather than drive back into Atlanta for the herbs I needed or order online and pay shipping, set up an arrangement with her for bulk orders."

Burke looked a little uncomfortable but stayed quiet. Connor just listened, making an occasional note on his legal pad during my recitation of events.

Once I'd gotten to present day, I looked directly at Connor. "I have *no idea* who this woman is, much less what her phone number is or where she lived. Like I said, I didn't even know Marie had a daughter. We weren't friends, just friend*ly*, you know?

"How in the hell did I send a text I don't remember to someone I don't know? I didn't even have a chance to look at my phone before Esme took it to El. All I know is I didn't do anything I'm accused of. And why are you so calm when I mention all the paranormal stuff? Burke certainly isn't."

Connor laughed. "First, who's Esme? Second, one of my sisters-in-law is a witch. My brother, and by extension, the rest of the family, has been living with magic and magical-type stuff for the last twenty-odd years."

Burke turned toward him. "Really? You never mentioned any of that. And I've known most of your family since you joined the firm."

Connor snorted. "And why would I bring that up in any conversation we might have had? Has no bearing on anything, really. Except in this case, it probably does. So, who's Esme?"

I eyed Burke again. "My familiar. She's a crow. She was waiting for me at the house. She took my cell phone off the counter right in front of the Inspector and took it over to El, who lives next door."

Connor just nodded. Burke looked even more uncomfortable. Connor said, "Spoofing a phone number is *really* easy these days, and I suspect that's what happened in this case. Someone is trying to frame you, although I have no idea why. From what I know, and what Burke told me on the way up here, you've lived a fairly normal, quiet life. Until the divorce and the reason for it, of course."

He patted his pocket. "I have your phone here. Your friend cornered us when we walked in, saying we looked like Atlanta attorneys and were we here to see you. Thankfully, Burke was with me because she said she knew his name. Otherwise, I think she'd have been less forthcoming. Her dog, by the way, looked rather menacing.

"What's your code? Let's take a look at it." He pulled out my phone.

"Zero-four-one-six-four-nine," I replied immediately. I trusted Connor as much as I trusted Burke.

Burke let out a guffaw. "My birthdate?"

"Would *you* have guessed it?" I replied smugly. "You're not supposed to have obvious codes like your own birthdate or Social Security number, but I needed one I could remember, so…"

He nodded, still chuckling. Connor, too, laughed as he unlocked my phone and tapped on the message icon.

"Last text on this phone was Saturday to your friend Ellen. So we know your phone has been spoofed. With your permission, I will release this into the Inspector's custody at the hearing. He'll probably say you deleted the text after sending it, but a forensic expert can refute that."

I nodded, then had a thought. "But what am I supposed to do without my cell phone? That's my only phone, including for the business. What if a customer calls or texts?"

Burke patted my hand. "We'll get you a new phone this afternoon and see if the judge will release your contacts off your old one, at least, while they examine it. But let's worry about getting you out of here and needing that phone, first."

Connor looked at his watch. "They'll be coming to get you in a couple of minutes. Before we part ways, please sign this retainer form."

I used the pen he handed me and scribbled my name in the spot indicated without reading. Like I said, I trusted them.

Connor put the pen back in his pocket and the form in his briefcase. "We'll meet you in the courtroom. It's going to be okay, Jo. Really."

Both men rose, and after Connor knocked on the door, the same deputy took me back to the holding cell. Within minutes, he returned. "Time to go."

Feeling humiliated, I was escorted via back hallways to a big courtroom. I saw El and Dave in the front row of seats, with Burke and Connor at one table and a younger man in a rumpled suit with Inspector Woods next to him at the other. Already sitting in the bench was a woman about my age, wearing a judge's robe, a stern expression, and reading glasses perched on her nose. Below her was a smaller desk with a court reporter ready to record. The deputy led me to Burke and Connor's table then retreated to stand next to the court reporter's desk.

The judge began with, "Mr. Logan. What brings you to my part of the state? I thought you confined yourself to Atlanta."

Connor smiled. "Your Honor, I'm here to defend a long-time friend. Friendship knows no jurisdictional lines."

The judge gave him a small smile back. "Very well." Then she looked down at the papers on her desk and back up at the prosecutor and Inspector Woods. "Gentlemen, I know this arraignment was hasty, but from what I see in these documents, your evidence is…it isn't even circumstantial. Are you certain you want to proceed?"

The younger man stood, cleared his throat, and addressed the judge. "Ms. Foster was requested to turn over her cell phone to Inspector Woods this morning. She refused. That, to Inspector Woods, suggested guilt."

Connor stood. "Your Honor, the Inspector had no warrant. Just handing over her phone which, by the way, is her only telephone *and* used for business, would have not only disrupted her livelihood but been an invasion of her privacy. Ms. Foster, as is her right, requested the Inspector return with a warrant. Instead of pursuing normal legal channels, he arrested her on the spot."

He held up my phone. "Ms. Foster is prepared to hand over her cell phone to the court, *provided* it undergoes a thorough forensic examination to prove she didn't send the text message she's accused of sending. You and I both know, and the Inspector should, that it's quite easy to spoof a telephone number these days. We want that proven.

"In addition, we would ask the court to order her provider to issue another phone and at least clone the contacts from this one so, while the wheels of justice turn, she can continue to work without interruption."

He walked up to the bench and placed my phone on it, told the judge what the unlock code was, then returned to the table.

The judge eyed the prosecutorial table. "I am very inclined to completely dismiss this charge, pending further investigation. You know better, Inspector Woods."

She thought for a moment then sat up a little straighter in her chair. "This court orders a complete forensic examination of the cell phone before me. It also orders Inspector Woods to take it to…" She looked at me. "…which provider?"

"Verizon," I replied.

"Verizon to clone *just* the contacts onto a new phone, which will be given to the defendant prior to her release from custody.

"It also orders the charge of malice murder to be held in abeyance until such time as further evidence comes to light. Mr. Woods, you will comply with my orders in an expedient fashion and inform both counsels of the forensic findings." She held out my phone to the Inspector, who walked to the bench with an evidence bag in his hand. He dropped my phone in it and returned to the table.

She looked back at me. "Ms. Foster, even though I am delaying the charges, that doesn't mean you're out of the woods. If your counsel can assure this court of your continued cooperation, I will release you on your own recognizance, provided you do not leave the state. Do I make myself clear?"

Tears started leaking out of the corners of my eyes. "You do, Your Honor. Thank you."

"Ms. Foster will definitely cooperate with the investigation," Connor said as he rose. "None of us like murder, and the best way to clear her name is to help find who actually committed the crime. She has no reason to leave the state…" He looked sideways at me, and I shook my head. "…so she'll be around. Inspector Woods should call *me*, however, if he has any further questions for my client."

"Of course," the judge said. "This court is dismissed." With a rap of her gavel, we all rose as she left.

El and Dave reached over the railing to give me a hug as the prosecutor and Inspector Woods gathered up their papers and walked past us out of the courtroom. "I knew it would go well," she said. "Coop and I will be out in the reception area. We'll take you home when they release you."

Connor gently pried me from El's arms. "It'll be an hour or more before you're released. Inspector Woods is going to have to hotfoot it to the nearest Verizon store and get you a new phone. Because of the judge's ruling, you won't be released until he returns with it.

"You'll have to sign some papers, one being an affidavit of your willingness to remain in the state. I know you know to read legal documents carefully, but I'll caution you again to do so just to ensure they didn't slip anything else in.

"For some reason, that Inspector has it in for you. I could see it in his eyes. Tread carefully, Jo, until this is all over. Don't answer even a seemingly innocuous question from him or anyone else without me present, understand?"

Burke put his hand on Connor's shoulder. "I know you're the criminal defense expert, but put me on as co-counsel. I'm retired and have more time to drive up here than you do. Cin and I don't have any travel plans in the next month, so it'll be easier all the way around."

Connor eyed him. "Your license still active?"

Burke grinned. "If I didn't keep it active, I couldn't go to the Bar meetings and schmooze with old friends. Of course it is."

Connor chuckled. "I should've known. Okay. Jo, we're off to go sign our own papers then heading back to Atlanta since you have a ride home. Call me or Burke anytime, and I do mean anytime, if you need us.

"My guess is that the forensic examination will take a week or more. I think they'll send it to the GBI lab over in Cleveland, which services this part of the state. I'll let you know what they find as soon as they tell me."

"I'm going to suggest an independent lab I know in Atlanta to Inspector Woods," Dave interjected. "They're faster than the GBI and do expert witnessing all the time. He may or may not take my suggestion, but it's worth a shot to clear this up faster. You willing to pay their fees so you don't have to wait on the GBI?"

Connor looked Dave up and down. "You're Jo's neighbor's boyfriend? Sergeant Anderson, I think?"

Dave smiled as he held out his hand. "Guilty. Also, retired from APD about fifteen years ago and still know my way around down there."

Connor shook his hand. "Jo is in good hands up here. Are you thinking about Electronic Experts down on Northside Drive?"

When Dave nodded, he blew out a breath. "Yeah, we'll pay the fees. The sooner this is over, the better."

He turned back to me. "I know it'll be tough, but try to relax about all this. You're innocent. We all know that. We just have to wait until the good Inspector figures shit out." He hugged me before turning to put his stack of papers in his briefcase.

Burke sidled past him to me. As he bent over for a hug, he whispered, "Don't worry about the money right now. We'll talk about it when it's all over."

My eyes widened. "What?" I whispered back. That was one thing I *had* been worried about. I knew how much Connor charged and was wondering if I had enough in savings to cover his bill.

"Like I said, when it's all over." With one more quick squeeze, he left with Connor. Once the two men were nearly out the door, the deputy, who'd been standing quietly near the wall, came over.

"Ms. Foster?" he said. "I need to take you back to start your release."

Dave put his hand on the deputy's shoulder. "Give her stuff back, Johnny, and bring her to my office. We'll do a full release once Will comes back with her phone."

"You sure, Sarge? Not SOP."

Dave eyed him. "I'm sure. You think I don't know how to do a release? Just bring the papers with her." He looked at me. "See you in a few."

It took about fifteen minutes to get back to the holding cell, the deputy to remove the cuffs, then bring me my bag of belongings. He told me it would take another thirty or so for the paperwork to arrive, and he'd get me then. Finally, he escorted me up two flights of stairs to Dave's office. After handing a sheaf of papers to Dave, he left.

El and Cooper were also there, Coop lying across her feet and appeared to be snoozing. El had a forbidding look on her face. "This bites big time. Why in the hell did Will arrest you in the first place?"

"Outside, El. Not in here," Dave admonished. "We'll wait until Will returns then complete the release. Once you're on the way home, you can theorize to your heart's content. In the meantime, are you hungry, Jo? I can order in some food."

I shook my head. "I ate part of an overcooked hamburger patty a few hours ago, and that didn't sit well. Still queasy."

"Understandable. But at least drink some water. The Verizon store isn't far, so it shouldn't take Will long to get the phone." He looked at his watch after handing me a bottle of water. "Probably just another fifteen minutes or so more."

We sat in silence. My brain was having a difficult time wrapping itself around the situation. What had I done to deserve all this? If karma existed, maybe I'd been a nasty person in a previous life and it was coming back to bite me in this one?

"You need to do that divination, girl," Esme's voice echoed in my head. *"It'll show you who's messing you up."*

"Yeah, yeah, heard you the first time," I remembered my surroundings and replied to her in my head. *"Can I have at least a couple hours after I get home to wallow?"*

"Moon's full tonight. Need to get it done."

I ignored her as she continued to rant on about the moon's phase and the need to do something I'd never done in my life – and something I was dubious about.

Nearly a half hour later, there was a brief knock on the jamb of Dave's office door, and Inspector Woods walked in. He thrust a box at Dave. "Here," he grumbled. "New phone."

Dave took it from his hand and eyed the man. "Will. There's a forensic technology firm in Atlanta that will be faster than the GBI Lab. I've spoken with Josephine's attorney, and he assured me they'll foot the bill. I'm not sure why you're targeting her, but the faster her innocence is proven, the better."

"I'm following *procedure*," the Inspector snarked. "I've already put her phone in a dispatch to the GBI. They'll prove she sent that text, and then we'll see who's innocent, won't we?"

With that pronouncement he nearly flounced out of Dave's office. Dave sighed as he handed me the box. I pulled the phone out, turned it on, and noted it was one model newer than my old one. I sighed as I figured I would bear the cost of the new phone and wondered how much it was going to increase my monthly bill.

They'd even cloned my password, which I would change as soon as I got home. A quick glance told me the only thing on it from my old phone were the contacts. I'd have to also spend time installing and configuring apps – and installing all the custom ringtones I had for my friends.

Dave sighed again. "I have *no* idea what's gotten into him. Will's been with the department for over ten years, and this is the first time he's ever gotten belligerent about a case."

He turned the pile of papers the deputy had given him toward me and handed me a pen. "Sign all these where indicated then El and Coop can take you home. I'm so sorry he's being a jerk. All we can do now is wait for the GBI."

I read each document carefully before signing. There were four: one acknowledging receipt of the new phone; one confirming I had turned my old phone over to them for the investigation; one certifying I had received all my property back upon release; and one promising to stay in the state until the case was resolved. Once I'd signed everything, Dave turned the pile back around and witnessed my signature.

"You're free to go, Jo," he said with a wry smile. He looked at El. "Take her home. She probably wants to shower this place off, and I wouldn't blame her."

El, who'd been quiet since her original complaint, stood, leaned over the desk, and gave him a kiss. "See you for dinner."

"Come on, Coop," she said, taking up his leash. He rose, and like the professional he was, trotted at her pace alongside her. Once outside the building, I saw Esme perched on the top of El's car. She bobbed her head once before flying off.

CHAPTER SIXTEEN

Fifteen minutes later, we were in my driveway. El put the car in park. "This has been a horrible day. Can we do anything for you? Instead of cooking, why don't you come over to my place for dinner. It probably isn't good for you to be alone right now."

I shook my head. "Thanks, but I think I *do* need to be alone. Esme said something about divination. Although I've never done that before, I want to try it. Maybe I can find out just what the hell is happening to me that way, since nothing mundane is making any sense right now.

"And Dave was right. I want a shower. A long, hot one. The holding cell was clean but…"

"I understand," she said as she leaned over to give me a hug. "Call if you need us. Day or night. You know we'll be right over."

"*I will help if I can,*" Coop intoned from the back seat. "*You are a nice lady, and this should not be happening to you.*"

I reached back to scratch his head. "Thanks, Coop. I appreciate that."

I had to walk around back to get into the house, and El pulled away as soon as I waved from the front window. I was thankful nothing untoward had happened at home because I'd been taken away without time to lock up. Hell, I was still wearing my slippers! My purse was still where I'd left it on the front table, with all my money and credit cards intact.

Instead of making a beeline for the shower, I went into the kitchen and poured myself a double gin and tonic. I didn't even feel bad that it wasn't quite five o'clock. I needed the drink.

As soon as I'd sat in my chair, Esme flew in and perched on the arm. *"Tough day, I know. But..."*

"Yeah, yeah," I interrupted. "Divination. You've been harping on that all damned day."

She gurgled her version of a laugh. *"Actually, I was going to say you needed to eat. I know humans need food to absorb alcohol. Getting drunk, or maybe sick, isn't going to help at this point."*

"Okay, *Mom*," I shot back. "Let me relax a little, shower, then worry about food. I'm not up to eating just yet."

"Fine," she spat then flew out her window. I could hear her grumbling to herself through our link, although I couldn't make out the words.

I pondered my situation while I drank. I couldn't *believe* this had happened, yet it had. Instead of wallowing as I'd said I would, I got angry. Angry to the point I felt my fingertips begin to tingle.

"Shit!" I cried as I hastily set my glass on the table, rushed to the kitchen, and held my hands over the stainless-steel sink where there was nothing flammable. My fingers still tingled, but the sparks were faint. I sighed in relief – I hadn't erupted into full-blown flares.

Esme was on the counter next to me in a heartbeat. *"Deep breaths. Calm."*

As I tried to get control of myself, she gurgle-laughed again. *"Despite being strong in Earth, looks like you've got a lot of Fire in you. Hmmm…"* she mused. *"Think we can put that to use in the divination."*

I glared at her. "Later, okay?"

I stood for a few more minutes, taking deep breaths and concentrating on slowing my heartrate. Once my fingers no longer tingled, I returned to my chair, picked up my drink, and drained the glass. Esme once again perched on the chair arm.

"I haven't gotten that mad since the night I caught Asshole. That was too close for comfort."

"But at least you're mad about it instead of crying. That's a good thing."

Although I wouldn't admit it, she'd been right about me needing to eat. Shower first, though.

I kept a selection of soaps on a shelf next to the bathroom sink. I grabbed the one I made just for myself, a purifying and calming blend of ylang ylang and peppermint. My shower was long enough to empty the tank. I relished the warmth of the water cascading over me and felt the refreshing sense of all the negativity of the day swirling down the drain with the water.

Once clean, I went to the kitchen. I still wasn't all that hungry, but thought I could choke down some pasta. So, spaghetti it was.

I'd just put the dishes in the dishwasher when I heard a car pull up. Wondering who the hell was visiting me now, after the day I'd had, I looked out the window to see Denise and Abby getting out of Abby's car.

I threw open the front door. "What are you two doing here?"

Denny ran up the stairs and enveloped me in a hug. "Oh, thank all the gods you're all right. We've been so worried!"

Abby hugged me in turn and, seeing the confused expression on my face, said, "Timmy had a vision of you in jail this morning and called me when he couldn't get hold of you. We've been texting for hours. You didn't respond to a single one."

Denise continued, "That worried us, so as soon as we got off work, we hit the road. We decided to come here, first, then to your neighbor, then to the police if we couldn't find you. But you're here. Was Timmy wrong?"

I pulled them into the house. "No, he wasn't. I *was* in jail for several hours today."

"*What?*" both women yelled as I pulled my new phone out of my pocket. I hadn't heard it chime, but sure enough, there was a missed call from Timmy and fifteen text messages between the two women. And three from customers, which I would deal with in the morning.

"Tell all!" Denise said.

"No, drink first then tell all," Abby corrected as she moved to the kitchen where I kept the booze. "We need it after all the worry and now? Even more so."

We settled in the living room, all three with glasses in hand as I related the events of the last ten hours.

"Holy shit," Abby exclaimed once I'd finished my tale. "Someone's got it in for you bad. Do you trust the cops?"

"Hell, no," I replied. "Dave, sure, only because he's El's boyfriend and seems a decent type, but this Inspector? Not in any universe. Even Connor noticed his glare while we were in the courtroom.

"Esme suggested divination. I was reluctant at first, but I think I need to use more magical means to figure out what's happening. Either of you ever done it?"

Denny shrugged. "Sure. Kinda standard operating procedure for witches when we need to know something we can't seem to find out by mundane means. Lots of different ways, though. We don't have enough time to teach you to read cards or runes, so…"

Esme chose that moment to come from wherever she was to perch on the arm of my chair.

"*Fire divination for her,*" she croaked. "*She'll excel at that once she gets the hang of it.*"

Abby eyed me. "Given your penchant for sparkly fingertips, she's probably right. Want us to help?"

I hoped my gratitude showed in my eyes. "Would you? I have no idea what I'm doing."

Abby directed the next question at Esme. "I know there's a full moon tonight, which will make it easier for her. When's moonrise?"

Esme cocked her head, thinking. *"In about a half hour. Enough time to teach her the basics then start the true divination once it's up."*

Abby nodded, then looked at me. "Okay, girl. First time is easiest with a real fire rather than the flame of a candle, so it's time to use that fireplace of yours. Thankfully, you have one so we don't have to worry about a firepit outside or going out into the chilly night air." She eyed my small stack of firewood. "That won't be enough wood. We need to gather more."

Denise smacked her on the arm. "I'm not going traipsing through woods in my scrubs in the dark. Give me thirty to go to Home Depot and pick up a couple of their bundles. You tell her how it works while I'm gone." She rose, grabbed the car keys Abby held out, and left.

Esme was still perched on my chair arm, watching Abby with interest. *"You teach often?"*

Abby smiled at my bird. "Not really. But I give lectures on herbal medicine frequently so I know how to couch information in terms novices will understand. *And* I've known Jo for years and know how she thinks."

Esme bobbed her head in a nod and stayed quiet.

Abby continued, "Okay, Jo. First, we're going to build a roaring fire. As big as this fireplace will handle. We need a *lot* of flame. Once you get the hang of this, you'll probably be able to do it with something as small as a lit candle, but until then, a lot of fire is easiest. A larger canvas on which to draw the picture, if you get my meaning.

"Then the actual doing. Remember how we practiced clearing your mind and focusing so you just gave me a static shock instead of setting me on fire?" I nodded. "You'll need to find that same clear-minded focus again. Once you're in that zone, you concentrate on what you need to know, in this case, who's fucking with your life. Then you stare at the flames and, eventually, a picture will emerge. Sometimes the answer is clear; sometimes it needs interpretation.

"It's not an immediate thing," she cautioned, "so don't give up after five minutes. Stay patient."

Esme snorted. *"Patience is not a word in this one's vocabulary."*

I glared down at her. "I'm learning!"

Abby smiled. "I know you don't like waiting for a damned thing, not even pizza delivery. But this time, yeah, you need to wait and let the vision unfold. It *will* come, I promise.

"In the meantime, I need a refill on my drink. How's your body handling the alcohol? You can be relaxed but not even tipsy for this. It can throw your visions off by a mile or more."

I looked at my glass, which was half full. "I think this ought to be my last. Not even thinking about what I'm about to do, but if I have any more, I won't sleep well, and I have a feeling tomorrow's going to be an even longer day than today."

"Smart girl," she replied as she went into the kitchen, returning a few minutes later with a full glass.

Denise returned a few minutes later with two plastic-wrapped bundles of wood in her arms. She dropped them into the basket on the hearth with a groan. "That shit's heavy. But it means the wood is solid so will burn well."

She pulled a penknife from the pocket of her scrubs and cut the plastic, handing it to me while saying, "I suck at building fires. Got any paper to get it started?"

I laughed for the first time that day. "If you looked, oh blind one, you'd see there's a small stack of newspapers folded behind the wood basket. On second thought, let me. I think I have more practice than you."

I tossed the plastic wrap into the bin then returned to build a fire. Yes, paper got it started faster, but I also had fatwood, or small pieces of pine that ignited quickly and burned longer than paper so the larger logs had time to catch. In about ten minutes, there was a nice fire going.

"Put a couple more logs on," Abby told me, eyeing the flames. "Remember, we need a lot of fire for this, not just a comfy, warming one."

Another ten minutes saw the flames shooting up toward the chimney. "Good," Abby said. "Now, sit on the floor in front of the fire. Not so close you're going to scorch yourself but close enough that it's almost your whole field of vision. Then do the rest. We'll wait."

I sat about three feet away from the hearth, closed my eyes, and started my calming exercises. I felt Esme on the floor next to me, leaning in a little so I could feel her weight. Strangely, it was comforting. As soon as my mind was blank, I opened my eyes, turned my attention to the flames, and silently asked, "Who is messing with my life?"

For what seemed an hour, all I saw was dancing flames. They were pretty but made no picture that I could tell. But slowly, I saw a face formed from flames. Remember that scene in *Harry Potter and the Goblet of Fire* where Sirius Black's face appeared in the fireplace to speak with Harry? It was sort of like that – a face made of flames but unmistakable in its features. When I recognized the face, I closed my eyes with a gasp. When I opened them again, it was simply a pretty fire in my fireplace.

Denise was crouched on the floor next to me before I could take another breath. "You saw something. What was it?"

I rubbed my eyes, trying to bring back some moisture to them after staring so long. Also, I wanted to erase that image from my mind.

"I...I..." I couldn't believe what I'd seen.

"*Spit it out, girl,*" Esme croaked. "*I saw it in your mind, but you need to tell them.*"

Abby was on my other side, looking intently at me. "Tell us."

I took a deep breath. "It was *Rob.* It was Asshole's face I saw."

Denise sat back on her haunches. "Wow. Are you sure your prejudices aren't influencing what you saw?"

"I don't know," I admitted. "I thought about him earlier tonight when I got so pissed my fingers started tingling, but I don't *think* I had him on my mind any further than that."

Abby pulled her phone out of her pocket. "Let's confirm."

A moment later, she was nearly yelling into her phone. "Go somewhere quiet so we can talk. This is an emergency."

Denise eyed her. "Who did you call?"

"Monica," she replied. At my quizzical look, she explained. "Monica is a bartender for Timmy and Chaz. She's the best seer we know."

Another minute and Abby was speaking again, explaining the situation and asking this Monica if she could do her own divination to confirm or deny what I'd seen without actually telling her details. It all seemed really vague, but apparently, it was enough. Abby hung up after saying, "Call me as *soon* as you can. Tell Timmy or Chaz or both to cover you for a half hour because it's for Jo. I'll make up your tips, okay?"

"And now, we wait," she said after pocketing her phone. "Let's try to relax, enjoying this lovely fire." We all sat and stared at the flames.

To pass the time (and so I didn't dwell on what I'd seen and fret about Monica's…whatever she did), I asked about her.

"She's in her mid-twenties and has had visions nearly all her life," Denise began. "I think they started when she was about five? Anyway, she's not a witch like we are but a true seer. Sometimes they come unbidden, like Timmy seeing you in jail this morning which, by the way, was unusual, but he does get them on occasion, and sometimes she can sit quietly and something will come to her.

"She works with Timmy and Chaz because her visions can come without warning, and she loses focus, stopping in the middle of whatever she's doing. It's weird, because she'll look like a statue, totally frozen in place, staring out into space. At their bar, all the regulars understand and just wait for her to come out of her trance. In a normal work situation, that wouldn't play.

"Also, she's got a phenomenal memory and can tell you what every customer she's ever served likes to drink. She makes damned good money that way."

After hearing that, I felt a little sorry for this Monica. I couldn't imagine losing awareness in the middle of doing *anything*. But Abby was probably reading my mind. "Don't feel sorry for her. She's now used to it and makes even better money than some of the best tarot readers in the city."

Twenty minutes later, Abby was yawning and my own eyelids were starting to droop. It had been one hell of a day and I had *visions* of crawling into my bed. Abby's ringtone ("Danse Macabre" by Saint-Saëns if you're wondering) pulled us all awake again.

Abby punched the button, greeted Monica then said, "I'm going to put you on speaker so we can all hear, okay?"

There was apparently an assent because she pushed another button and held the phone out between us.

One of the sexiest female voices I'd ever heard said, "Hi D. And…Jo, I'm assuming?"

Denise said hello, introduced me to Monica, then, "So, hon. You see anything?"

Monica blew out a breath and continued in a sultry voice that reminded me of Lauren Bacall. "I did. First, a woman, maybe your age? With graying black hair pulled into a short ponytail sat in a jail cell, crying. That morphed into a man about the same age, who had brown hair with gray at the temples and wore glasses – the kind without frames." We all looked pointedly at each other. That described my ex. "He looked…rumpled for lack of a better word. Like he hadn't slept well or maybe didn't care about his appearance.

He was arguing with a dishwater blonde female, maybe around my age? Who gave me the impression that she wasn't alive. Can't put my finger on why.

"Then I saw another man wearing a badge. He was clouded, so I couldn't see him or the badge clearly. When I see something cloudy like that, there's magic of some kind involved. Perhaps he's under a spell.

"After that, the vision got murky, like a foggy, dark night. Usually that means there's something else overarching the whole situation – probably also magical in nature. I couldn't see any paths, which is really weird. I can usually see *something* that will hint at how to solve a problem.

"That bothers me so I'm going to give it a day or so to perk then try again. I'll let you know if I get some clarity, okay?"

"Thanks so much," Abby said. "We owe you big time."

"No problem," Monica replied. "But I do need to get back to work. You know Chaz can't pour even a decent Scotch-and-water. See you two this weekend?"

"Probably. Kisses to Timmy and Chaz for letting you do this." Abby hung up.

"How in the hell did Rob…" I began. My fingertips started tingling again, and I took deep breaths to calm myself.

Abby stood. "Your descriptor of 'Asshole' for him was spot on. We know who the instigator is but need to think further on the whole situation. Also, we need to do some investigating. There's a witch involved, too, since Monica can't see through the murk. Who, and how Rob found them, is a very good question.

"We also need to work in the morning. C'mon, D, we need to go home and you're driving because I've been drinking."

They both hugged me. Denise hardest while saying, "Chin up, hon. We'll figure something out, and once we know who, other than Asshole, is behind it, they'll pay. I promise."

I hugged them back, nearly in tears. My friends were so damned wonderful!

Once their car had pulled out onto the road, I closed the screen on the fireplace, put my coffee together for the morning, and dragged myself into the bedroom. Esme flew on ahead of me and perched on the dresser, watching me get ready for bed.

"You did good tonight. I'm proud of you. And your friends are right. We will figure this out, and there will be hell to pay. Get some sleep."

She flew back out to the living room, and I heard her window flap bang as she left. (I had moved it from my bedroom not long after construction on the shop started because every time she came in or left, I was awakened by the banging of the flap.) As I settled myself in bed, I felt her settle down in her nest, too. It wasn't long before I fell asleep. I dreamed of jail cells, judges with forbidding faces, and nasty jailers.

CHAPTER SEVENTEEN

The following day, I tried to be normal. I replied to the text messages from my customers, filled a couple of orders and, because the boxes were small, stuck them in my mailbox rather than drive into the post office. But I couldn't get my predicament out of my mind. Why was Asshole trying to hurt me, and who was helping him?

Esme had gotten into the habit of perching on my desk next to the laptop, watching what I did on the screen. Over the previous few months, she had commented on the "new technology" and how much easier it was than all the handwritten work one of her previous humans had had to do. Online shopping was one of her favorite things to do. Every time I logged on to order a product I couldn't find in a local store, she stared at the screen.

And, like most crows, anything shiny, including the aluminum casing of the new coffeemaker I'd had to buy, caught her eye – even on a computer screen. I'd found bits of glass and one of those rings you get out of candy machines next to her seed bowl more than once. When I asked, she said they were gifts. I grinned and put them in a separate bowl to "display" them. I tried very hard not to giggle, even internally, at her idea of a present so I didn't insult her.

Today, however, she stared at me as I closed the laptop after sending the last invoice.

"You know," she began, *"the moon is full to the naked eye for three days, not just what astronomers can measure with their powerful instruments. Who cares if it's only ninety-seven percent full?"* She snorted. *"Modern witches and their science. Good for some things, but not helpful for others.*

"Anyway. You could do another divination tonight. If you can keep your mind on it rather than be freaked out by the first image you saw, you might see more."

I hated being a novice. I'd been out of school for over thirty years and *thought* I was done with studying. Learning how to be a witch during the time I'd lived with Denny and Abby had been excruciating. Esme, of course, heard all my thoughts.

"What did I say about never stopping learning?" she chided. *"There are plenty more aspects to being a witch than simply shocking someone with static or making good potions. Divination is another one. Even plain humans can do it.*

"You don't need *a full moon, but it does make it easier when you're new to the art of seeing. Once you get the hang of it, you should be able to divine during any phase of the moon. But for now, let's use the energy while we have it, hmmm?"*

She was right, I knew. Although not religious in the conventional sense, Mom had quoted the Christian Bible to me quite a bit while growing up. When I was older, I discovered her favorite phrase, "God helps those who help themselves," wasn't anywhere in that book, but it did make a great deal of sense. You couldn't rely on the gods (one or many, it didn't matter) to pay attention to little ol' you when there were people in the world much worse off. You had to take care of business on your own, hope the gods saw that and, eventually, pitched in.

I knew my phone would show I hadn't sent that text, but I also knew Inspector Woods wouldn't let up and would be continually looking for some new bit of evidence to prove my guilt. Monica thought he was under a spell of some kind, and that made sense, too. His attitude had done a one-eighty in less than a week, and if Dave thought he was nuts, there was something to it.

I blew out a breath. "Okay," I told her. "Maybe I *can* see something that will shed light on my problems. It won't hurt to try."

"Good girl. Moonrise is almost an hour later tonight. Usually, it helps to have a diary of sorts to record what you see immediately afterward. Especially if it's not immediately clear, like the face you saw. You'll want to re-read and ponder. So, got a spare notebook?"

I always marveled at her grasp of the English language and how it was employed in this modern age. *"I simply read your mind,"* she said. *"A picture with a word then how you apply that. Humans, most of the time, think that way. It's easy. Plus, I listened in once in a while to your teachers. English has evolved quite a bit since my first human. New words, new word usages, and all that."*

She knew I had a spare notebook – I was forever jotting notes and making lists, and when the stores had back-to-school sales, I picked up a handful dirt cheap. A couple of bucks' worth of notebooks lasted me until the next year's sale. I grabbed one from the shelf next to my desk and set it with the coffee carafe to take back into the house.

I spent the rest of the day cleaning. First, the shop then the house. Not that either was really messy or dirty but it kept me active, and my mind was free to think. I was in the middle of my second load of laundry when I had a thought. I called Burke.

"You doing okay?" were his first words.

"Best I can under the circumstances," I replied. "I called because I have a question."

"I'll answer if I can."

"Did something bad happen to Rob," I gritted my teeth at saying his name, "after the divorce was final? I think he's involved in all this, but I can't imagine why, unless it's revenge. Revenge for what, I have no idea, but it's a feeling I have." I tried very hard to keep the "woo-woo" out of the conversation. Burke had obviously been uncomfortable with it.

"No idea but I'm sure I can find out. Does this have to do with you being a witch?"

"Huh?"

He sort of growled. It was the sound he made when he was trying to process unexpected information, like a divorce respondent hiding an asset.

"Connor filled me in on all the witchy stuff during the drive home. He said he's even used his sister-in-law to help figure out a case when something isn't clear. I presume you did, uh, divination last night?"

Wow. He was taking this better than I'd anticipated. "I did. So did someone else Abby called to confirm what I'd seen because I might be prejudiced. My ex is involved somehow. I just don't know how or why. Thought I'd start with the 'why' then work on the 'how.'"

He growled again. "Let me do some digging. It'll probably be Friday before I can come up with anything. Thankfully, I still have favors owed to me. I'll call in a couple.

"In the meantime, keep your head down. Connor was right – that Inspector has it in for you. Don't antagonize him."

"Staying home and out of sight," I told him. "I have no plans to leave the house in the next week, except to go grocery shopping tomorrow."

"Can you get your neighbor to do that? I'd honestly prefer you stay completely out of the public eye."

"*No,*" I almost yelled. "I'm aware of Inspector Woods' attitude, but he can't prevent me from going to the damned store to feed myself!"

"Okay, then," Burke soothed. "But keep the GPS on your phone turned on. It'll provide tracking of your movements if he tries to pin something else on you."

I grunted. "Like that would do any good. He'd just say I left my phone at home. But yeah, I'll turn it on."

"Good. I'll call you when I know something about…Asshole, I think you prefer." He chuckled and hung up.

The moment I'd put my phone back in my pocket, it vibrated against my butt and chimed out UB40's "Red Red Wine." It was El.

"Hey," she said when I answered. "You better? Come to dinner tonight. I have a hard time cooking for one, and Dave's busy."

"Cooper will eat all the leftovers," I laughed at her. In the intervening months, I'd discovered El was an excellent cook, and her dog was of the same opinion.

"Yes, he would. But I'm making tacos, and he'd be farting all night if I gave him the extra."

"Taco Wednesday?"

She snorted. "No, Taco Tuesday a day late. I didn't feel like cooking when I got home last night – not even just to brown hamburger. Dave and I had takeout."

I wasn't going to argue with a free meal. "You're on. Six?"

"That'll work. See you then." We hung up, and I went back to my laundry.

"I know that woman likes her wine. You need to stay sober if you're going to…"

"Yeah, yeah. I know," I shot back as I unloaded the dryer into the basket so I could fold clothes in front of the television.

Shortly before six, I made my way through the woods to El's house. Now that the trees had almost completed their move, the path was fairly clear, but I still used the flashlight on my phone so I didn't trip over anything. Esme flew on ahead as if she'd been invited, too.

Cooper and the cat, Patches, greeted me at the deck door. As soon as El opened it, both raced inside ahead of me, and I felt a slight breeze ruffle my hair as Esme followed them in.

El just chuckled as I finally got to step into the house. "Seems Esme likes tacos, too. Does she eat everything you do like Coop does?"

"She'll take a bite of nearly everything if I let her. Crows are omnivorous, but she does have a somewhat discerning palate. I've discovered she doesn't like spicy food or some vegetables, like tomatoes. And nothing sour, either, like red wine vinegar salad dressing. Otherwise, I have to protect my plate. Still, she likes her seeds and probably eats bugs outside, too."

"I do eat bugs. Haven't you wondered why you don't have many mosquitos or gnats? But I have to eat a lot of them. Getting food from you means I don't have to work as hard."

El chuckled again and turned to look at Esme, who was perched on the mantel. "I've seen you in my garden, too. At least, I think it was you. I don't mind you eating bugs there, but don't eat any of my plants!"

El returned to the kitchen island where it was obvious she was chopping the ingredients for tacos. Seasoned ground beef sizzled in a pan on the stove. It smelled divine.

"Help yourself to a glass of wine." She gestured with her knife to an open bottle on the counter. "You know where the goblets are."

"Thanks, but water will do me fine," I replied as I retrieved a glass from the cupboard and filled it from a pitcher in the refrigerator. "I want to do some more divination tonight, and I'm told that's better done sober."

She finished her chopping and scooped the results into individual bowls. As she stirred the browning beef, she asked, "Divination?"

I remembered I hadn't told her about the previous night so got that story out of the way then said I wanted to try again tonight to see if I could figure anything more out.

"Your friends are pretty awesome if they drove all the way up here to check on you," she commented while pulling a foil-wrapped lump out of the oven. She opened it to reveal a pile of soft tortillas. Without a word, she handed me a plate and gestured to start fixing my dinner.

"They are. Denise has been my best friend since we were nine. I'm almost as close to Abby because she's just as cool as Denny. If there's something we wouldn't do for each other, I don't want to imagine what that is," I said as I helped myself to all the fixings.

Before I could turn toward the table, Esme landed on my shoulder and peered at my plate. "*Ew. Spices. And* tomatoes. *No thanks.*" She flew back to the mantel. I started laughing so hard I had to put my plate down before I dropped it.

"I'm going to remember that," I said as I sat and started putting my tacos together. "I'm going to fix tacos every day of the week. Maybe even a tomato and cucumber salad to go with them. You know, the kind you soak in vinegar."

El thumped her plate on the table. "Stop!" she cried, wiping tears from her eyes with a napkin. "If I keep laughing so hard, I won't be able to eat."

"So," El said, after calming down and before picking up her first taco. "Tell me about this divination stuff. Is it hard?"

Between bites, I told her what Abby had instructed me to do then how long it had taken me and what had happened when I saw Asshole's face in the fire. "Esme says I should try again tonight and try not to freak out at what I saw, in the hopes I'll see more. I get the feeling Inspector Woods won't give up trying to pin something on me, and I want to solve this if I can, to clear my name.

"The problem is, whatever I see wouldn't be admissible in court, so I have to do my own investigating. Abby and Denny said they'd do some of their own."

El chewed, obviously in thought. "You know," she said after swallowing, "you said this other lady said she thought magic was involved somehow. Paranormal investigating is what Cooper and I do. If there's some way we can help, especially since we're semi-official, I'd be happy to."

Coop lifted his head from El's knee where he'd been closely observing the movement of food from plate to mouth and addressed me. "*I am good at investigating. I can smell things humans can't. I can see things humans can't. I will help, too.*"

Patches piped up from her perch on the kitchen island where she, too, had been observing, "*I am small and can sneak into places he can't. I will help, too.*"

"Thanks," I told them all. "If I think you might be able to investigate, I'll tell you. At this point, I can use all the help I can get. I don't want to land in jail for something I didn't do!"

We finished eating, and I told El to go sit while I cleaned up. It was an ingrained habit from childhood – whoever cooked got out of cleaning up after a meal. I had done my fair share of washing dishes growing up and crowed when Asshole and I moved into an apartment with a dishwasher. Today, they were almost mandatory in any household, and I was grateful.

After the kitchen was clean, I went into the living room and gave El a hug. "Thanks for dinner," I told her. "But I need to go home and get ready for divination. You know, start a fire and all that."

She hugged me back. "Anytime. Like I said, I'm no good at cooking for one. And I like to cook. Well, most of the time. Call if we can help."

I let myself out the back and made my way home through the trees. They rustled as I walked, as if guiding me along my path, although I couldn't see anything outside the sphere of the flashlight. The moon wasn't yet up, and without the glow of city lights, it was *dark*.

Esme was already in the house, perched in her favorite spot on the mantel, when I finally made it home. "*You know, the trees and other plants are glad to have two magical people living so close to each other.*"

"How so?" I asked as I knelt to start a new fire, taking some fatwood and newspaper from the basket and arranging them on the firedogs with a couple of the logs Denny had purchased the night before. I made a mental note to clean out the fireplace in the morning. The ashes from two fires were about all this small fireplace could handle.

"*I heard you thinking about the trees rustling as you walked. They were acknowledging your presence. Seems nowadays only magical people care about the Earth. You two don't use chemicals detrimental to growing things. They like that.*"

"I don't think it's *just* magical people," I told her. "A lot of folks really do care and try just as hard to be nice to the Earth."

"*Maybe you're right. All I know is what I see in my surroundings. Especially over by the lake where it's mostly people building big houses with big yards; and driving big boats that spew oil and gasoline into the water. They don't seem to care about nature.*

"*You need a bigger fire. Like last night. Add more wood.*"

"I know," I groused. "I was waiting for this to catch good before adding more so I didn't smother it."

Finally, the fire was as big as I dared get it. I grabbed a glass of water and the notebook and a pen. I put those on the floor beside me before I settled into the same position as the previous night. Once again, I felt Esme lean against me after I'd closed my eyes and started the process of clearing my mind.

When I felt ready, I opened my eyes and looked into the fire, willing it to show me more about why my life was in such an uproar. I stared. And stared. I didn't want to blink and miss anything. Once again, it seemed an eternity before I saw something other than pretty flames.

The first image that manifested was once again Asshole's face. Then, the flames rearranged themselves to show another face – this one of an older man with a lot of wrinkles, bushy eyebrows, and what appeared to be a ducktail hairstyle. I almost laughed at the thought of an old man wearing a 'do from the 50s even today but caught myself.

That face transformed into Inspector Woods. Next to him I saw a clock…no wait, it was a watch. I saw a band coming off the top. Once again, the old man's face appeared then it was back to simply flames.

"Stop now and write down what you saw," Esme said. *"Because you saw him twice, the old man is important, and you need to describe him as thoroughly as possible before you forget."*

I blinked rapidly to clear the flicker of flames from my vision. Also, to get some moisture in my eyes. Staring really dried them out. I drained half the glass of water, then picked up the notebook and pen and described what I'd seen in as much detail as I could remember.

Once I'd gotten it all on paper, I re-read my words and pondered them. "So," I said to Esme, "if I'm interpreting all this correctly, and I don't know if I am, that old man has a lot to do with what's happening to me. I don't know anyone who looks like that, so why would he be involved?

"Then there's the image of Inspector Woods with a watch. Does that indicate time or something? Am I under a deadline of sorts?"

Esme was back on the mantel. She cocked her head as she looked down at me, still on the floor. "*It's possible. It's also possible your vision told you the watch is more important than that.*"

"What's more important than solving my problem as soon as possible?"

"*You're aware of magical amulets and such. And the seer said she thought the Inspector might be under a magical spell. Maybe the watch is an amulet that's affecting his judgement.* Something *obviously is. Otherwise, why would he have changed his attitude toward you?*

"*You should call your friends. They might be able to help with the interpretation.*"

I rose with a groan from the floor. I swear, it got farther and farther down each time I sat on it, or even crouched down to pick up something I'd dropped. I walked over to the kitchen counter where I'd placed my phone to check the time. Abby had told me, and I discovered all on my own, that magical energy would drain any batteries in the vicinity. One dead phone battery was all it took to convince me. Trial and error had taught me to put my phone at least six feet away from wherever I was working magic.

"Hang on," I protested. "Magic drains batteries. Watches have batteries. Wouldn't it have stopped working if someone had put a spell on it?"

Esme snorted. *"Modern humans! Watches didn't always have batteries, you know. I would suppose there are still some around that don't."*

I remembered Abby wore an antique watch – her grandmother's. She had to wind it every morning. "You're right," I acknowledged.

I looked at the time – it was nearly ten. I'd been at this for over two hours. No wonder my eyes were tired! "It's too late to call them tonight. They'll be in bed. I'll email Denny now. That way she can read it in the morning, ponder it during the day, and maybe call when she gets off work."

I grabbed my laptop and spent another thirty minutes typing an email, trying to be as thorough as possible in my explanations, including what Esme has said about the watch possibly being an amulet of some kind. Once I'd finished that, I gratefully made my way to bed.

CHAPTER EIGHTEEN

I was halfway through my first cup of coffee the next morning when Denise called.

She didn't bother with a greeting but began with, "Holy shit, girl! You saw a lot last night!"

I tried to get my brain working. "Um, was that a lot? And aren't you supposed to be either at work or on your way there?"

"I'm already at the clinic. I don't have a patient for fifteen minutes so we have a little time to talk. Abs and I read your email together during breakfast. Yes, that was a lot. Told *us* a lot, too.

"From your description, we're pretty sure we know who the witch involved is. He lives up in Woodstock and is a nasty piece of work – specializes in baneful magic. His personality matches his magic – we don't know anyone who likes him. He's good at what he does but isn't particularly strong. If he's behind all this, his spells are quite breakable.

"The question is, how did Asshole hook up with him? Also, how did your ex find out about magic in the first place? We need to do some asking around down here."

I gulped my coffee, trying to get enough caffeine in my system to jumpstart my thinking.

"Asshole, last I knew anyways, worked at a branch in Woodstock. Maybe they met there? As to how he found out about magic, I have no idea. It wasn't anything we discussed while married.

"What about the watch and what Esme said?"

"*That* is entirely possible. We've all agreed something happened to change the Inspector's attitude toward you. An amulet, charged with *really* nasty intentions, could do that. Do you remember if he wore the same watch both times you met with him?"

"I have no idea," I replied. "I don't normally check for that, you know? But…" I trailed off.

"What?"

"El and Cooper have offered to help if they can. Dave, too. They have access to the Inspector I don't. Maybe they can find something out."

"It's worth a shot. My buzzer just went off. I have to go to work. Text me if you come up with anything else. After work, we're going over to the Cozy Cauldron to start asking around about Mr. Johnstone. Someone might have heard about his latest endeavor."

My head was filled with about fifty shouty concerns, but the loudest one was worry for my friends. "If this guy is so bad, *please* don't get on his radar. I don't want anything to happen to the two of you."

Denny snorted. "No worries, hon. We're well-protected, and if he tries to mess with us, we can give better than we get. Gotta go. Talk with you later."

Esme flew through her door and landed on the table next to me. "*She has some good ideas. You need to call your neighbor with the giant. She can probably get in to see the Inspector, and the dog will be able to smell any magic.*"

"If he's wearing a spelled watch, why didn't *I* notice the magic? I should have, right?"

Esme made what I thought were meant to be soothing sounds, but they just came out as quiet caws. "*You were rather preoccupied at the time. Apparently, so was I, because I can normally detect it, too. No matter. We'll find out one way or another.*"

I drank two more cups of coffee before I felt human enough to start the day. After my shower and before I went out to the shop, I called El and told her about the previous night's divination and what Denny had said.

"That's interesting," she said. "Given Will's current attitude, I'm not sure he'll see us. But Dave certainly will and can somehow find out if he got a new watch.

"Let me call Dave. If Will did get a new watch, I'll contrive a reason to put me and Cooper in his path. If there's magic around, he'll smell it. Then we'll work on the next steps. Call you later."

I filled the thermal carafe with the rest of the coffee and dodged raindrops out to the shop. It was going to be a gloomy day, which perfectly fit my mood. That wasn't an ideal atmosphere, so I set my phone to the dance music channel that had come with my satellite television subscription. Within minutes, I was bouncing around the shop.

Grateful I didn't have to make any stock because I was certain my focus wouldn't be there, I busied myself with making up a batch of product labels and taking inventory on other packaging supplies. While I was doing that, the accountant called. I'd hired one to do the taxes because between the divorce and new business, they were more complicated than I thought I could handle on my own.

"Just one question," she said. "Do you want to electronically file? We can do that from here, but you'll still need to make a deposit next week."

I agreed with electronic filing (it saved me postage and I'd get my refund faster) and within minutes, my email pinged. Twice. The first had a copy of my return attached along with a form authorizing them to do the filing; the second had the forms to use for estimated tax deposits. I cringed at the amounts, but then reason took hold: they were based on the income *I* had calculated for the year. I just hadn't known at the time I'd have attorney fees to pay. I crossed my fingers that my annual income would be *more* than I had originally projected.

Esme landed on the desk next to my laptop and looked at me. *"You developed new products we know are good. I have a feeling those will take off. Don't be so preoccupied with money!"*

I sighed. "Without it, I have no place to live, no shop, no food, nothing. I know *you* don't pay attention to such things, but *I* have to. I can't just sleep in a nest high in a tree and catch bugs for food."

"Humans," she snorted then left. I sighed again. She'd been familiar to now three humans and still didn't understand how our economy worked.

While I was eating lunch, my phone pinged with a text. It was from El. Dave said Will got a new watch a week ago as a thank you gift for solving a robbery case at a jewelry store. Not that cops are supposed to accept gifts, but he did. Dave is writing him up, lol. Coop and I are going over this afternoon to try to run into him.

We were making progress! However, based on what I'd seen and heard about the Inspector, it was strange that he would accept a gift if it was against departmental policy.

"Hey Esme," I called. I concentrated to see where she was. If what I felt through our link was right, she was eating bird seed off the ground under someone's birdfeeder, along with some of her crow friends.

"*I'm eating,*" she groused. "*What?*"

"Is it possible to put *two* spells on an amulet?"

"*Yes. Why?*"

I giggled to myself. She had been so involved in eating, she hadn't paid attention to what I'd been thinking. Now I knew how to distract her!

"Because El said the Inspector *did* get a new watch, it was a gift, and he wasn't supposed to accept them. So, I was thinking, one spell to make him accept it, and one to change his perception of me?"

Her window flap banged, and she skidded to a halt on the table in front of me. Thankfully, her talons didn't leave gouges in the tabletop. "*That's an interesting thought. Two different coercion spells. Devious. I like it!*"

"Hey!" I exclaimed. "You're supposed to be on *my* side!"

She bumped me with the top of her head. *"I am. Doesn't mean I can't appreciate intricate magic."*

I sighed. I hoped my hunch was correct, but I was stuck until someone else confirmed or denied it. *Then* I'd probably need help to not only undo whatever spell was on the watch – if I could even get my hands on it – but extricate myself from the big legal trouble I was in. I went back out to the shop and started my shopping list for needed supplies.

The rest of the day passed uneventfully, without even a call from El.

The next morning, my phone rang just as I was crawling out of bed. I groaned. People calling me before I'd had two cups of coffee was getting old. The ringtone said it was Burke, and I answered eagerly, trying to sound awake as I padded into the kitchen.

"Did you find anything out?"

"I did," he began. "Your boy lost his job a month ago. Seems he sexually harassed one of the tellers at his branch, and she reported him. You know if the firing is for misconduct he can't draw unemployment.

"Also, he's apparently been living the high life since the divorce and is in deep financial trouble. He's two months behind on the mortgage payments, and his two credit cards are nearly maxed out.

"I couldn't find out anything more, but I spoke with Connor after my contact got back to me, and he suggested we hire a private investigator to follow Rob."

The business major in trouble financially? He'd really gone off the deep end. Except for hiding money from me, he'd been pretty frugal with spending while we were married.

"Listen," I said. "I did some more divination night before last. I got some more information. Not only is Asshole part of this…conspiracy, there's a witch involved, too. I spoke with Denise, and she and Abby think they know who the witch is based on my description of him. The guy lives in Woodstock, and Denny said his name is Mr. Johnstone." I finished by telling him about the Inspector's watch and everyone's thoughts there.

"Interesting. I'm in the non-magical world of law. My best idea is to wait until the forensic results on your phone come back. Without that text message, they have no case against you.

"That said, if there's something that can be done in the magical world, hiring a PI to find out if Rob knows this nasty witch might not be a bad idea. After that? I'd have to leave it up to you."

I slurped my coffee, again trying to jumpstart my brain. "Is there a way to find out if either man knew Marie's daughter? Why Asshole would be targeting me, I have no idea, but otherwise, why would someone spoof my number in a text to her? This is all rather convoluted."

"Let's let Connor do his attorney thing. He knows when someone's being set up and, after all his experience, can generally unravel the worst of tangles," Burke soothed. "I'll relay what you've told me, and since he knows about the magical world, can incorporate that into his investigation."

I told him to give my love to Cindy then hung up. While finally pouring my second cup of starter fluid, I thought about what he'd said about Asshole. After catching him in bed with his secretary, the sexual harassment didn't seem so far-fetched. But to potentially lose the condo *and* max out credit cards? That was totally out of character. At least, the character I thought I had once known.

Halfway through that second cup, my phone rang again. This time, it was El.

"I didn't wake you, did I?" she asked.

"No, but I'm only on my second cup. Speak in small words."

I could hear the smile in her voice. "Sorry I didn't call yesterday. We went to the sheriff's office yesterday afternoon as promised. Had to hang around for about an hour because he was out. *That* was tough because everyone wanted to know what we were doing there. I had to make up an excuse that Tyler – that's the sheriff – wanted me to report in on a case. Thankfully, he wasn't in, either, to confirm or deny my statement.

"Anyway, Will finally returned, and I *decided* I needed to see Dave just as Will walked past us. Dave's office is two doors down from Will's. Cooper, bless him, told me he was sorry in advance then proceeded to pull on his leash, prancing around the good Inspector, nearly knocking him off his feet.

"Once I..." She cleared her throat, "...got Coop back under control, Will threw a fit, saying he'd been against our involvement with the department in the first place, and my *damned dog* was a nuisance. He threatened to write me up in such a way I'd get fired. Dave, who heard the commotion in the hall, came out of his office and calmed Will down enough I don't think anything will come of it.

"After Will went in his office and closed the door, we went into Dave's office, where Cooper told me his antics were to ensure he got a good look at Will's watch. According to him, there's magic on it, but that was all he could tell me. Was that what you needed to know?"

At least that part of my divination was right. So it *was* being used as an amulet rather than, or maybe in addition to, telling me I was on a deadline. "It was. And thanks. I hope you're not in too much trouble. Seems his attitude isn't changed just toward me but everyone else, too."

She snorted. "I haven't interfered in any of his investigations. I only come in when the sheriff himself calls. So no, I won't be in any trouble. Tyler might tell me to keep Coop on a tighter leash when in the building is all.

"Question now is, if that watch is affecting his judgement, what's the next step? We can't exactly just take it off him."

"I have no idea," I replied. "I need to think on it some. And talk with my friends who might have ideas. They're a lot more experienced at all of this than I am. Thanks again. And thank Cooper for me."

After we'd hung up, Esme flew into the room. *"If it's an old watch, he won't wear it when bathing. I might be able to steal it."*

I was aghast. Stealing? She, naturally, heard my thoughts. *"Okay. Let's stay on your moral compass. Borrow? You can't see what spell is on it without having it in your possession, and I doubt he'd give it to you."*

"But," I stuttered. "You don't know where he lives. Even if you did, how would you get into his house? And he knows my familiar is a crow. What if he saw you? He'd immediately think of me."

"*Hmmm. Maybe you're right. I can find out where he lives, but to get it? Might be time to ask for some help.*"

"From whom?"

"*Lots of folks. Pixies, fairies, voles, and field mice come to mind. They're all small enough to get into the house and get the watch without being seen. Question is, what sort of payment would they want?*"

I had another thought. "We sort of assume there is a spell on it to make the Inspector accept the watch. Wouldn't it affect whoever got it? I mean, would they turn it over to me?"

"*Good thought. Best to ask pixies or fairies. They won't be affected by any human magic. Come to think of it, the fairies could remove any spell on it and leave it in place. That would be better.*"

I was dubious about this course of action but could honestly see no other alternatives. Until Inspector Woods was out from under that spell or those spells, he would continue to hound me – probably even once the GBI proved I didn't send that text message.

I sighed. "Okay. How do I find fairies, and how should I negotiate with them?"

Esme cocked her head in thought. "*Moon's still fairly bright, even though it is waning. There's a clan of them living in the woods behind your house. They're not so bad, as fairies go. Take a small bowl of honey out there after the moon rises. Your honey is organic, right? That will call them.*

"*After that? We'll have to see if they're willing to help and what they want in exchange. They can be tricky, so I'll be there to help. This afternoon, though, I'll follow him home from work.*"

"Yes, the honey I buy is organic. I suppose since they don't like chemicals on gardens or lawns, they don't like preservatives, either.

"I could ask El for another favor from Dave. He'd probably give up Inspector Woods' home address."

Esme moved her head back-and-forth in a 'no' motion. *"Human addresses mean nothing to anyone but humans. We rely on direction, smell, physical landmarks. If the fairies will help, they'll want* my *directions to his home, not yours."*

I still had my doubts but could see no other way. I *had* to get that watch off Inspector Woods – or get the spell or spells off it. Hopefully, once he was out from under magical coercion, he'd come to his senses and see I had nothing to do with either death. I agreed with Esme's plan then continued my wakeup process with another cup of coffee and social media.

After my shower, I went into the shop to play with soap formulations. Denny and Abby said the Calming soap was *too* calming – they wanted to fall asleep – and the Wake Up made Chaz jittery. I moved my laptop over to the counter so I could reference my database for herbs associated with each need.

Although I was trying to concentrate on the soap, Asshole's involvement in the current chaos that was my life kept popping into my mind. Then the fact that I was a *witch*, dammit, and should be able to exact my own revenge.

My eyes strayed to a master bottle of my Prosperity potion. It would only take a subtraction of one herb, an addition of another, and a minor change in the wording of my spell to make it an anti-prosperity potion. He was already in financial trouble. I could easily finish him off. *If* I could get near enough to dab the potion on him.

On the other hand, I made potions for protection. Why couldn't I protect myself?

"You're distracting yourself from the work at hand," Esme chided. *"You've got a good idea for a revenge spell, but wait for mundane law enforcement. If they don't succeed, you can.*

"Protecting yourself, though, is an excellent idea. Someone's messing with you personally. It's time to take care of that problem. After work.

"Now, go back to the soap." I grumbled about not needing her constant advice, especially when she wasn't anywhere nearby. *"I'm in one of the trees overlooking the shop. I can even see you through the window. Go back to work!"*

I somehow managed to put Asshole at the back of my mind and, as instructed, went back to the soap. It took all day to figure out new combinations of ingredients – ones that would do the intended job and still smell good. At least, to my nose. Once I thought I had a good recipe for each, I recorded them then made another test run. After that had hardened, I'd cut it into bars and send them down to Atlanta for opinions.

Around three, Esme announced she was off to follow the Inspector. When I said he probably didn't get off work for another couple of hours, she said it didn't matter. She'd be back before moonrise. Within minutes, I could tell through our link she was downtown – eating discarded food by the railroad tracks. Between her scavenging and seed bowl, she really would get fat.

"I heard that. Go back to your own work and leave me be."

I had just finished dinner when Esme banged through her door. This time, she didn't skid to a stop on the table but fluttered enough to land softly. *"Found him!"* she exclaimed.

"He *lives not far from here,*" she continued. "*I hung around a while to eavesdrop. He berated his wife and yelled at his kids almost the moment he got home. Seems the wizard didn't make his spell specific enough because he's being belligerent to everyone. By the way, the spell is still strong enough I could see it glowing through his shirt cuff.*

"*Anyway. I can tell the fairies where he lives. Some friends are keeping an eye on the place for me. One of his complaints was the mess under the bird feeder, which they were helpfully cleaning up.*"

CHAPTER NINETEEN

I still had a few hours before moonrise and had time to think about protecting myself. The more I thought about it, the more I wanted Asshole and the witch, whoever he was, to go through the same hell they'd been putting me through.

"Mirrors," Esme said. *"Reflect back what they've sent you."*

"But is – are the spells directed at me, or am I getting the result of them?"

"Doesn't matter. I don't know the wording of the second coercion spell, but your name is obviously in there somewhere. Otherwise, the inspector wouldn't be targeting you specifically."

I thought about what she said. I knew I was somehow being targeted, and it was time to re-focus that aim. I grabbed my makeup mirror from the bathroom and the smaller one I carried in my purse. I sat on the floor in the middle of the living room and placed the mirrors in front of me.

"Which way is Woodstock and which way is Atlanta from here? I need to face these mirrors properly." I knew Esme's sense of direction was perfect.

She hopped to where I was sitting and with her beak, moved the mirrors a few degrees left or right. She then fluttered to my lap and eyed her work.

"That'll do," she announced, stepping from my lap to the floor beside me.

I took a deep breath and centered myself. Esme leaned against my side, and once again, I felt comforted by her solid presence. Once I felt I was ready, I held my hands right behind each mirror. I took another breath and intoned,

"Nasty spells begone from me. Return to sender, effects to thee."

I repeated myself eight more times and felt the energy rise each time I did. After the ninth recitation, I pushed that energy in the direction the mirrors faced. The glitter of my energy was purple as it whooshed its way to wherever it was going. Purple. The color of justice. I grinned.

Esme cackled. *"That ought to do nicely. Serves 'em right, whatever happens to them."*

I thanked the Universe for its help then cleaned up after myself. A glance at the fireplace reminded me I needed to clean that out. With still a little time to kill before moonrise, I did so, leaving the bucket of ashes out on the deck to be dumped near the woods – when I could see properly.

Finally, almost to my bedtime, Esme announced it was time to go meet the fairies. I got the honey out of the cupboard and drizzled some into a custard cup until she told me it was enough. Then I put on boots and a light jacket, grabbed my phone, and headed outdoors.

Esme flew on ahead but guided me through our link. I used the flashlight function on my phone to ensure I didn't trip on anything. Once I'd reached a small clearing about fifty feet into the woods, she told me to put the dish of honey on the ground, back away about six feet, and sit, then turn off the light.

"*They don't like human light,*" she told me from a tree branch above my head. "*Stay quiet and don't fidget. They know you're here.*"

I sat on the cold ground for what seemed an hour but was probably only about fifteen minutes. My butt was feeling rather damp by the time I saw a twinkling light moving erratically through the trees toward me. It hovered at eye level about ten feet away and, peering into the darkness, I could see the light came off a small humanoid with wings.

I tried not to stare. He stood around eight inches tall, and his butterfly wings were nearly as wide. He was ethereally beautiful with sharply chiseled features, upward-slanted eyes, the proverbial pointed ear tips, a *very* toned body, and waist-length black hair. His clothing was nothing more than a loincloth, and I shivered with a perceived chill. In one hand he held a bow with an arrow already nocked.

Continuing to hover mid-air, he looked down at the dish of honey then back up at my face. Slowly, he moved his eyes from me up to the tree branch where Esme perched then back down to me.

"Why do you call us, human?" His voice was as musical as he was beautiful, with a bell-like tone impossible for any human to imitate. It was surprisingly deep for one so small.

"I came to ask for your help," I replied truthfully.

"*My* help or *our* help?"

Esme snorted from her branch. "*Your clan's, of course. I am insulted your matriarch would send a warrior to speak with a human already known to the clan. I know you've watched her these four months. She has been nothing but respectful in that time.*"

He angled his eyes back up. "Are you requesting our help as well?"

"*We speak as one, warrior. You know I am her familiar. Where is your matriarch that we might parlay?*"

Wow. So formal. I kept my mouth shut and let the expert do the talking for now.

He glanced once more at the dish of honey then back up to Esme. "I will return."

He flew back in the direction he'd come from, this time in a straight line. A few minutes later, four twinkling lights zoomed toward me, coming to a halt within a foot of the honey dish.

The warrior was back (arrow still nocked in bow), and he was accompanied by two similar to him without any visible weapons, as well as a female, slightly smaller in size but with a regal air about her. She was clad in a gown that reminded me of one Grace Kelly wore in *High Society*, all white, flowing fabric. I briefly wondered how she managed to not get her wings tangled up with the cloth when she flew – and how she got dressed with those wings in the way. To confirm she was *somebody*, there was a gold circlet across her brow, holding her silver-white hair in place.

One of the other males stepped in front of her, dipped his forefinger into the dish of honey then brought it to his mouth. He moaned, with pleasure I hoped, before turning back to the…matriarch, I guessed.

In a similar musical voice but not quite as deep as the first man, he said, "It is *good* honey. Local, as well."

He stepped back to her side, continuing to lick his finger. She nodded once, took a dipped finger of honey for herself and, in a very un-regal manner, sucked loudly. A second finger of honey later, she looked up at me.

"Your gift is accepted." As she spoke, the three men fluttered over, took the dish between them, and flew off with it.

Noticing my eyes follow the dish, she smiled. "Esme has told us of you, and how you are very new to this world. Odd, given how old you are for a human. No matter. They are taking your gift back to the clan for all to share. Do not worry – the vessel will be returned.

"Why have you called us?"

I cleared my throat. I knew this was *my* show. "I have come to ask for your help. There is a human under a baneful spell that I do not believe I – or any other nonmagical being – can remove."

I continued with my story, telling her of what had transpired in the human world, how it affected me, and what we believed about the watch. While I spoke, she never looked away but continued to lick her lips as if to get every single trace of honey.

Once I finished, she cocked her head then looked up at Esme. "Do you know where this *watch* with a baneful spell is?"

"I do. If we can come to an agreement, I can give you directions. At least to his dwelling. Once inside the dwelling, I know not."

The matriarch turned her attention back to me. "And what do you offer us for this service?"

Now came the hard part. I'd never been a haggler, and many flea market vendors were probably grateful for that. Esme had told me bargaining was normal and that if I paid their first asking price, I'd be thought a fool.

"What do you want?" I asked.

She thought a moment then smiled. "I like you. You have been kind to the land since moving here. Because I like you, I will make an easy bargain. A similar amount of honey every day for one of your years."

That was a *lot* of honey! I did some mental calculations – it was more than two gallons! I countered with, "A similar amount every day for one week."

We continued back and forth and finally settled on double the amount of honey once a month for a year. That was about a quart and a half and was doable, not only from a supply issue but it also wouldn't drain my wallet.

"Done," she said, smiling and holding out her hand. "I understand humans shake hands when a bargain is struck. We will do the same."

I took her small hand gently between my thumb and forefinger and we shook. She turned her attention back to Esme.

"So, crow, where do we go, and what is a *watch*?"

Esme gave her some convoluted instructions involving sun direction (east), stands of trees, human habitation, and smells. *"Once inside his dwelling, I do not know where it might be."*

I added my two cents. "Most humans take their watches off when they sleep or bathe. It will probably be on a table next to his bed, on a larger piece of furniture we call a dresser – it's to store clothes – or on a counter in the bathroom," I said. Then I turned my phone on and looked up an image of a watch. I found a good image of an analog one and turned the screen so the matriarch could see.

"This is a watch. His may not look like this, but it should give you an idea. A watch is a timepiece with bands so he can strap it on his wrist."

"The magic is still strong enough to be seen," Esme interjected. *"You should be able to home in on it when you get close."*

"Very well," the matriarch said then looked up at the moon. "There is still plenty of moonlight left this night. We will do as you ask. When we have completed this task, your vessel will be found on the railing outside your home. We will expect the first payment tomorrow. Then once each month as the moon starts to wane, yes?"

I nodded. "I will look for the dish when I get up in the morning and fill it before moonrise tomorrow night. *Thank you.*"

She said nothing more but flew off. I watched until I could no longer see her light then stood.

"You did well," Esme said. *"That was a good bargain for both sides. They* adore *honey, but the bees rarely let them have any, either in the wild or in hives built by humans. You get a nasty spell removed; they get a treat for a whole year."*

I turned the flashlight back on and made my way back to the house, feeling proud of myself for actually haggling rather than capitulating at the first offer. Again, Esme flew on ahead, stopping occasionally on a tree branch or the forest floor to ensure I went in the right direction. As soon as I got to my own yard, she bade me goodnight and flew off to her nest.

Once home, I made the morning's coffee then crawled into bed. I didn't fall asleep as fast as I'd thought I would, though, as worry about the next day's events crowded my head. What if the fairies couldn't remove the spell? And if they did, what then? Would Inspector Woods just automatically come to his senses and sheepishly go to the judge to drop the charges?

"Go to sleep. You're keeping me awake with all this worrying. Things will work out."

The following morning, I poured a cup of coffee then made a beeline for the deck. Sure enough, the custard cup was sitting on the railing, not only empty but apparently washed out, too. I breathed out a sigh of relief. That meant they'd been able to remove the spells from the watch. Esme landed on the railing next to it.

"Fairies are fastidious," she replied to my thoughts. *"They would not have returned a dirty dish that would attract insects."*

"So now what?" I asked as I took the dish and returned inside where it was warm. "Do I just sit on my hands and wait?"

"For the moment, yes. I am curious as to what the Inspector will do now that he's no longer under a coercion spell. Don't you have things to do in the shop?"

I nodded. As I already said, weekends meant nothing anymore. It might be a Saturday, but I had a potion order to fill and wanted to get the new soap samples down to Atlanta. I returned to my normal morning routine, which was drinking copious amounts of coffee while reading the news online and perusing social media.

I had just finished cutting the soap into bars when my phone rang with the theme to *The Golden Girls*. "Have we got news for you!" Denise exclaimed when I answered.

"Well?" I was impatient.

"We went to the Cauldron last night. Meant to do it Thursday, but we both were too tired after work.

"Anyway. Johnstone was there, sitting by himself in a corner with his drink as he always does. After we got seated at the bar and asked about him, Monica told us he was drinking top-shelf bourbon instead of the well stuff he normally drank. Seems he had either come into some money or was celebrating something.

"We told Monica what we thought was going on. She said she'd done some more divination, and he figured prominently in what she saw. So that all jives. Monica got Kaylee, his waitress, to subtly ask him about his celebration.

"Kaylee, for all her youth – I think she's *just* legal enough to work in a bar – is really good at getting people to talk. Monica says she'll make a fine therapist – or bartender – one day." Denise laughed.

"Thankfully, we were sitting on the side of the bar where we could observe without turning our heads and being obvious. Kaylee spent almost five minutes with him, even setting her tray on the table for a bit.

"When she came back to the waitress station, she and Monica spoke for another five minutes or so. I was about ready to go horn in on their conversation because I was getting antsy when Monica came back to us."

She took a breath. "Seems Johnstone had just completed a huge undertaking for a new client. Unlike most of his commissions, he said, this one netted him about four times what a regular one did. Hence his celebration. Kaylee said he sounded smug about it. Knowing what kind of a witch he is, she got the willies thinking about what he might have done.

"So, do you suppose this new client is Asshole?"

"Not sure," I replied, thinking about all she'd said. "Burke said Asshole is up to his eyeballs in debt – he's even behind on mortgage payments. *And* he got fired from his job for sexual harassment a month ago. Which is about the time all this shit started going down.

"I'm wondering not only how the two found each other but *why* I'm being targeted. I changed my will the week Burke filed the divorce papers so he wouldn't get a dime from me, no matter what. He knows that."

Denise cleared her throat. "It could be simple revenge, you know. Asshole had a nice life while you were married and your salary was paying the bills. Plenty of money to throw around, probably more than just the one girl on the side, things like that. The divorce put an end to that lifestyle."

"Burke said Connor is putting a tail on Asshole," I told her. "If we can put the two men together, that'll tell us something. But how do we get a court to recognize what's been done on a magical level?"

"We don't." I could hear her frown. "The mundane legal system will do what it's going to do without any not-normal information. But if anything your lawyers can turn up ties Johnstone into it, there's a whole magical community that will come down hard on him. He's already disliked, and if he's done something that nasty to one of our own, he'll pay for it. Trust me."

"I have something to tell you, too," I remembered before we hung up. I told her about the watch and my bargain with the fairies.

"You *bargained* with fairies?" she exclaimed. "Do you have no sense of self-preservation? They can be really nasty!"

"Hey," I retorted. "They were the only option to get into the Inspector's house *and* remove the coercion spell. Besides, according to Esme, this clan is relatively nice, as fairies go. They fixed El's ankle *and* her house last year after she killed the vampire wreaking havoc up here.

"And, also according to Esme, I made a good deal. The honey they wanted will only cost me around thirty dollars for the entire year."

"Don't get into the habit of working with them," she growled. "We can't bail you out if something goes wrong. Their magic is different than ours, and although they can negate human magic, the reverse doesn't hold true."

"I know," I soothed. "I have no intention of regularly working with any paranormal creature, humanoid or not."

"Still not happy here, but it's a done deal. Now we just wait for Monday to see if it had any effect."

"By the way," I said, changing the subject. "New soap samples will be in Monday's mail. Enough for you and the boys to try. Use it right away, will you? I'm anxious to get these products out."

"Will do." We said we loved each other then disconnected.

"I have a feeling human law enforcement will be able to bring your Asshole to justice," Esme said from her perch on top of one of the cabinets. *"And if nothing mundane happens to the witch from your spell, the magical community can take their revenge on him. Your friends said he's good but not strong. He won't be able to protect himself from a spell cast by thirteen stronger witches. Have no worries on that score."*

"I know," I sighed. "I just hate waiting." I turned back to packaging up the bars of soap.

"Patience, grasshopper, I believe is the phrase. I have faith." She flew out her door, and I was left alone with my thoughts.

CHAPTER TWENTY

The rest of the weekend passed uneventfully, if you discount my worrying about what Monday would bring. I couldn't seem to settle on anything or even focus on a book. I ended up watching old movies – most of which I knew by heart, which didn't help me stop fretting.

I was awake with the sun on Monday after a fitful night. Esme complained loudly several times that I was keeping her awake, but I couldn't turn my brain off enough to sleep soundly. I could tell I'd be drinking more coffee than usual.

After showering, I went to the shop but couldn't focus enough to make any product. Instead, I ended up playing a lot of solitaire on my computer, willing my phone to ring with some good news – for a change.

It wasn't until nearly three that Connor called. "I have some news for you!" he said.

"Hit me," I replied. "I could use *good* news."

"The GBI got to work faster than usual and the preliminary results on your phone came back an hour ago. I'll say that the Inspector sounded rather sheepish and I had a difficult time not saying, 'I told you so.' There's no evidence of the supposed text from you."

"That *is* good news, at least. But you sound like there's more?"

"There is, and it isn't the best of news. They found a tracking app on your phone."

"Huh? What does that mean?"

By the tone of his voice he was probably glaring at the phone. "Someone installed an app to track your movements. You didn't give anyone permission to track your phone, did you?"

"Hell no," I almost shouted. I started trembling, but this time it was with rage, not fright. Esme banged through her door, landed on the arm of my chair and leaned into me. I was surprised once again at how calming that was.

"Didn't think so and told the Inspector as much. This is a dark internet sort of app that won't appear anywhere the phone's user can see. The experts are still working on tracing where the information goes back to, but my guess is that app has been on your phone for quite some time *and* they'll track it back to your ex. Based on what you and Burke have told me, no one's had access to your phone without you knowing since you moved out of the condo. Rob is the most obvious suspect.

"At least with the new phone, we know it's clean. No one should be tracking you now.

"There's also the question of who spoofed your number and how. That's a police matter, and once they figure out which spoofing company sent the text, they'll have to get a warrant to find out who set up the account. My guess is they'll find it was Rob. Or maybe he had some help, and there's an accomplice. If all that turns out to be true, he really went off the deep end where you're concerned. A shame, really. He seemed like such a nice guy at the holiday parties."

He took a breath then continued, "The full report on your phone won't be produced for several days yet, maybe even a week, but as far as I'm concerned, you're off the hook for the murder. The charges probably won't be dropped until the official report hits the Inspector's desk, so keep your nose clean until all the formalities are observed.

"In the meantime, I've still got my guy tailing your ex. Burke told me of your concerns on the magical end of things, and we might turn up something useful there. So far, he's been mostly hanging out at the condo, but if he's gone as nuts as we think, he'll go somewhere else eventually. I'll let you know what we find."

I heaved a sigh of relief. "I can't tell you how much I appreciate all this, Connor. It's a huge weight off my shoulders, knowing it's actually been proven I didn't send that text."

He chuckled. "Just doin' my job, as they say. Honestly? Your case isn't as complicated as some others I've handled. The main thing was the forensic tests on your phone. And now we've found out someone's been tracking you, there's a lot the police will do I don't have to. First, they have a murder to solve. Second, although tracking someone's phone without their permission isn't illegal in Georgia, I think we can make a case for stalking, which is. I've already told him you'll want to press charges on that score once they figure out who's on the other end of the app. Your Inspector has his hands full."

I thanked him again and disconnected. While it was good news they'd proven I didn't send the text, I was still at sea as to *why*. And if it was Asshole, how had he found out about magic and gotten a witch involved? Then there was the tracking app. Just thinking about that made my blood boil all over again.

"Good news!" Esme crowed, both figuratively and literally. *"You're off the hook for all the nasty stuff. Now it's just a question of finding out who and why. The police can do that."* She flew back out her door.

I decided to call it a day. I'd not gotten anything productive done and didn't see another couple of hours playing solitaire would help, so closed up the shop and went back into the house.

Three more days passed with no word from anyone. I only had a couple of orders to get out, so spent the rest of the time reading up on how to more effectively market my business. I didn't want to start selling direct, but I needed to increase sales. There had to be a way to get more shops to carry my products – or generate more sales from my current customers. This was the least enjoyable part of owning a business as far as I was concerned.

Finally, my phone rang late Friday afternoon. It was my generic ringtone, and there was no number on the Caller ID, so I answered with a tentative, "Hello?"

"Ms. Foster?" A female voice, and not one I recognized. "Is this Josephine Foster?"

"Yes, this is Josephine Foster."

"My name is Wanda, and I got your number from Monica Adams who got it from Denise Randall."

She didn't give me a last name, which I found a little suspicious. "What can I do for you?"

"I think it's more what I can do for you. I dated Harvey Johnstone. At least, I did up until a few weeks ago. I overheard Denise talking with Monica at the Cozy Cauldron last week about Harvey, and I think I can help you."

I put my book down, now intrigued. "How?"

She sighed. "You know Harvey's into baneful magic, right?"

"Yes. So I've heard. Don't know the guy myself."

"About a month ago, we were at dinner, and he was distracted. There was a look of glee on his face. I asked him what was on his mind.

"Normally, he doesn't share much of what he does with anyone, but that night, he told me he'd met a man who needed him to cause major trouble for his ex-wife. That sort of magic is right up Harvey's alley, and he was eager to prove just how much trouble he could cause with magic.

"He didn't go into any specifics but it seemed like it wasn't going to be just a normal hex to cause someone to lose a job or something like that. It sounded much worse."

She went quiet, then continued before I could see if we'd been disconnected. "A few days later, I was over at his house, and he was still cackling about what he was going to do. I got worried. I don't mind a small hex here or there, but when I hear the word, 'death,' come out of someone's mouth, well, that's a bit too far, don't you think?"

"I'm listening," I said to keep her talking.

"While he was in the bathroom that night, I went into his workroom and found his notes. He keeps his notes on whatever he's working on at the moment right out on his bench. They included your name, someone named Robert Schmidt, and two women with the last name Rice. There were also notes on poisons readily available around here plus a few other scary things like coercion spells.

"He caught me looking over those papers and hit the roof. I told him what it looked like he was doing went beyond the bounds, and I wanted nothing to do with anyone who would go so far and I was through with him. He shrugged and told me it was my loss because this would bring in a lot of money he could buy me gifts with. Then he threatened that if I told anyone what I'd seen, I'd pay for it.

"I'm stronger than he is, so I wasn't worried. I just threw up my heavy-duty protection spell, grabbed my purse, and left. I tried to put it out of my mind until I overheard that conversation."

"Why didn't you tell anyone what you'd seen?" I asked. "With those notes, even the mundane police would have been able to do something."

"But would they?" she countered. "And, knowing Harvey, he probably burnt the notes as soon as I left. There wouldn't have been anything for the police to find – if they actually believed my story and bothered to search his house."

This, at least, tied Asshole to the Johnstone character. I thanked her for the information, hung up, and mulled over what she'd said. I tried viewing the caller information on my phone, but it didn't come up, so she had truly blocked her number.

Then I called Connor, who was in a meeting. I turned to Burke. Someone had to know what I'd just learned. Although the fairies had, theoretically, removed any spell off Inspector Woods' watch, I wasn't certain I was ready to speak with him – about anything.

"I already know about your phone," Burke said. "So this call can't be about that."

"It isn't." I proceeded to tell him what this Wanda had told me.

"Interesting," he commented after I'd finished. "No last name. And she apparently blocked her phone number from you. No matter. If she's needed, someone down at this bar of yours will be able to tell us who she is.

"I'll pass along what you've told me to Connor. I'm playing golf with him and a couple of others from the firm tomorrow. Don't know if there's anything to be made of it, but if there is, he'll know. Chin up, Jo. Everything is starting to come together."

I had just disconnected when El called. "Dinner tonight?" she asked. "Dave has an event going on over at the school, so it's just me and the furry kids. Anne's coming, too. We can have a hen party. Come about six?"

"I'm always up for free food," I laughed. "See you in a couple of hours."

At the appointed time, I walked through the woods to El's. It was still light enough I could see my way without any artificial light. The trees had continued moving in their inch-at-a-time manner, but the path was now quite obvious.

"I don't know if you can understand me as well as you can El, but the path is now wide enough," I said out loud as I reached the clearing that was El's yard. "If you want, you can stop."

"Because of their roots, they will have to continue moving for another week or so. Otherwise, they'll just have to do it again in a few years," Esme said. I saw her perched on El's deck railing. *"The fairies are directing this, remember? They know how wide the path has to be to accommodate your large feet."*

"Yeah, yeah. I know. Humans are huge and destructive at times," I shot back. I climbed the stairs to the deck, and as I opened the door to let myself in, Esme flew past me. I heard El laugh and call a greeting to my bird as she landed on her favorite spot – the fireplace mantel.

"She really does go everywhere you do, doesn't she?" Anne asked after we'd said hello to each other.

"Not really," I replied. "I think she came with tonight because there's food involved. We have this irritating mental link, so she knows what I'm thinking all the time. She's been a peanut gallery from several miles away."

"Peanut gallery? Well. I never!" Esme huffed, pausing in her grooming long enough to glare at me. El giggled again then translated for Anne as she handed each of us a glass of wine.

"Dinner in about a half hour," she told us, sitting across from me with her own glass of wine. "I got involved in a book and forgot to start it on time."

I had learned we were all avid readers, so the discussion turned to books. I loved fantasy in all its forms, El liked historical fiction, and Anne would read any bestseller out there, regardless of genre. By the time El announced that dinner was ready, I had already added a couple of titles to my to-be-read list.

Dinner was, as always, delicious. El made a chicken-and-rice dish that used the drippings from the chicken to make a gravy with white wine. I started to question giving the furry (and feathered) kids their own plates after we'd eaten, but she assured me the alcohol cooked off and it was perfectly safe. Good thing. All three plates were cleaned within minutes.

Anne and I cleaned up the kitchen, then we all retired back to the living room with another glass of wine. Esme resumed grooming her feathers on the mantel, Cooper lay on the floor next to El, and Patches disappeared – probably into her bedroom, El told us.

"So, how's the investigation coming?" Anne asked. "I had to fly home for a few days and returned to El telling me you'd been arrested for murder? How the hell did they think *you* did it?"

I hadn't had a chance to fill El in on recent developments so recounted what had happened over the last couple of weeks for Anne's benefit with El interjecting her part of the story, then the last few days for both of them. Anne's eyes widened with each revelation.

"Holy shit, girl." She gulped her wine. "You're awfully calm for someone who's been accused of murder *and* found out the ex is involved. And some ne'er-do-well witch, too?

I grimaced then took a drink of my wine. "I'm much calmer since they've proved I didn't send that text message. Now I'm more pissed than upset. I have to wait on mundane law enforcement to do their thing and completely clear my name.

"Asshole…," Anne's guffaw interrupted me. "…yeah, that's the name I use for the ex… thought me catching him with his secretary was bad? Between me, Denny, and Abby, he'll regret this.

The hex my friends put on him is nothing compared to what I'm going to do to him."

El cleared her throat. "Based on what you've said, and what Dave has said, your ex is going to wind up in the pokey once Will completes his investigation. That witch, though? I doubt they can implicate him. Unless *his* phone is the other end of that tracking app."

"What hex?" Anne asked. I told her about the spell my friends had done to make Asshole impotent. She laughed so hard she had to wipe a couple of tears from her eyes. "Oh. My. God. I'd never have thought of something like that. I think I'd like your friends."

I smiled. "You probably would. They're good people."

"So you've got something up your sleeve?" El asked.

"Not specifically," I admitted. "I'm still pretty new to this magic stuff. But I've gotten damned good at potions, and I can think of several modifications to ones I already make to make his life more miserable than it already is – like making him homeless. But I'd like to see what law enforcement does first. His ending up in jail for a bunch of years would satisfy me.

"That witch, though? I did a spell last night that should reflect whatever he's sending my way back to him. Asshole, too, if you want to know the truth. Hopefully, that means getting mundane law enforcement on his tail. If not, my friends are cooking up a spell, although I don't know exactly what."

Anne leaned forward. "You know I'm not a witch, but if there's any way I can help, you know I will. Framing you for *murder*, for god's sake, goes way over the top. I could probably find a ghost or two willing to haunt these guys for a while."

I laughed. "This Johnstone fellow probably knows how to ward off a haunting. Based on what I know of him, he'd probably cause harm to the ghost rather than just banishing it. I wouldn't want that. But thanks. I appreciate the vote of confidence."

We changed subjects, thank goodness, and Anne told me something of her traveling life. I had already been clued into Anne's lifestyle and, although it sounded interesting, wasn't for me. I was most definitely a homebody. Then she surprised both of us.

"You know, I'm thinking about settling permanently in this area."

El choked on her wine. "You're *what?*"

Anne smiled at her. "You know I've been here for over a year." El nodded. "There's a reason. Chet and I have gotten rather serious."

El stared at her. "Who's Chet?" I asked.

"He owns the bookstore in town," El supplied before Anne could answer. "They've been seeing each other for almost a year. But I didn't think it was *that* serious!"

"It is, and it isn't," Anne said. "I think we're both too set in our ways to, like, move in together. First, I've never lived with anyone since leaving home. Second, I don't want to live in his apartment – over the store," she informed me. "And he doesn't want to live in the RV. On the other hand, neither of us wants to see anyone else.

"Plus," she grinned, "I really like the area. And I'm kind of tired of securing all my belongings, driving somewhere else, then making it all comfortable again. I've seen most of the country over the last few years and I think it's time to make a permanent stop."

El drained her wineglass, got up to get the bottle, and refilled all our glasses before sitting again. "Are you going to permanently rent your spot, then, or look for somewhere else?"

"I've already spoken to the resort owners, and although I really like where I am, don't like their terms for a permanent rental. I'm looking for land somewhere close, though. I'd like to be near the lake if I can."

"Anne likes to swim. A lot. Even when I think the water is too cold," El told me. Then she turned to Anne. "But the lake is almost fully developed. And any lots around it are probably going to be sky-high."

Esme, of course, had been following the conversation by listening in on my thoughts. "*I could probably fly over the area and find a good place,*" she volunteered.

I stared. This was so unlike my familiar. "*Hey. I can be nice to others.*"

Before I could open my mouth, El translated what my bird had said for Anne's benefit. Anne looked up at the mantel. "I appreciate that, Esme, but I have to find a lot *for sale*. Not just a vacant one."

Esme gave the crow equivalent of a shrug. "*Don't say I didn't offer.*"

After the necessary translation from El, Anne added, "Joshua is already looking for me. He hears *everything* from humans and ghosts in the area and will find out if someone wants to sell. Plus, he knows the lakefront like the back of his hand and will know if a lot is suitable for parking my RV without me having to go take a look. I'm not really in any hurry."

We finished our wine then Anne stood. "I need to go. If I stay any longer, I'll have more wine and won't be able to drive home. Bear would never forgive me if I missed feeding time."

El and I stood, too. Anne hugged El, thanking her for the dinner and wine. Then she turned and hugged me. "You *know* I'll help if I can. Anytime. You need a ghost? I'll find you one!"

With a wave, she picked up her purse and left. Shortly, we heard her car start, and tires crunched on the gravel as she drove away.

El poured another glass of wine, gesturing with the bottle toward me. "More?"

"I don't have to drive, so sure," I smiled as I held out my glass.

"Her news was…unexpected," El said. "I knew she and Chet *really* liked each other, but I didn't think it was serious enough to make her want to park permanently. I'm glad for her. She's never been married. Never even had a long-term relationship as far as I know."

"Good for her. As long as it's *right*," I said.

"Seems to be. What about you? Any prospects?"

I laughed, a wry chuckle. "*No.* And I don't want anyone right now. After spending most of my adult life with Asshole, I'm happy being single."

She nodded. "I can see how you might be. I like the relationship I have with Dave. A couple of nights or maybe a full day a week with him seems to satisfy my need for company. Otherwise, it's just me and the furry kids. I like it that way. Especially after the hectic life I led being Thomas' wife."

She had told me of her socialite-wife life before her husband's death. It sounded entirely too people-y for my taste. Not to mention all the politicking she'd had to do. However, she had two children, of whom she was quite proud, come out of that life. I liked them. I could also like being an aunt more than a mother, I thought, but I kept that idea to myself.

Finally, it was time to make my way back to my own house. I thanked El for dinner, wine, and conversation, and let myself – and Esme – out the deck door. Four glasses of wine had left me more than a little tipsy, and I might have weaved and stumbled a bit as I walked the path home.

"See. This is why they need to make the path wider," Esme chortled from somewhere in the trees.

"Yeah, yeah. Huge human," I grumbled. It took me longer than normal to put the morning's coffee together (I may have miscounted the number of scoops of grounds) before I fell into bed.

CHAPTER TWENTY-ONE

After taking one of Abby's hangover remedies (I *still* hadn't been able to make one on my own) I managed to get the yard mowed on Saturday before rain set in. Not being much of an outdoorsy person anyway, I was okay with that and spent the rest of the weekend curled up on the sofa with a couple of good books. Esme even stayed in the house most of the time, claiming although water rolled off her feathers, she got tired of raindrops in her eyes.

It was still wet and gloomy Monday morning when I dodged the raindrops out to the shop. I'd gotten a text from Timmy telling me the new soap was wonderful – just the right amount of energy. Abby had texted her approval of the new Calming formula. I spent a couple of hours writing a newsletter to subscribers letting them know about the new recipes and updating the website to reflect the changes. Then it was time to make some stock.

I'd just gotten to the point of infusing my spell into the liquid soap when my phone rang. It was Connor.

"I have good news," he said. "I got the paperwork from Inspector Woods dropping the charges against you. You're a completely free woman!"

I sagged against the counter in relief. "Hallelujah!" I cried. Then had a sobering thought. "But what about that tracking app on my phone?"

Connor almost laughed but stopped himself. "I don't know what happened, but the good Inspector has come to his senses. I called him after I got the official email. He says he's *very* concerned about someone setting you up. The judge issued a warrant to get the name behind the account with the spoofing company.

"They're still trying to figure out where the tracking app goes back to. It appears to be a burner phone and, although not impossible, that will be a little more difficult to trace. They're working on it.

"In the meantime, I think my work is mostly done. Unless you want me to continue having my guy follow your ex. Thus far, he hasn't gone anywhere but the condo and a couple of strip clubs where he didn't interact with anyone but the waitresses and dancers."

"Nah, but thanks," I replied. "I know Burke told you about the male witch we know is involved. I think I'm going to wait to see what Inspector Woods comes up with before I do anything else."

Another sobering thought hit me. "Send me your bill. I'll get it paid immediately." It would probably drain what was left of my savings but needed to be done.

"I can't send you a bill because it's already been paid," he said.

"*What?*"

"Working in family law, you probably wouldn't know, but the firm has funds escrowed to cover fees in criminal cases where the accused can't really afford us and the partners deem the cause worthwhile. It's our version of Legal Aid. Every partner here knows you, and once I told them you'd started your own business after leaving us – without saying exactly what that business was – they all agreed to cover your case. Including the private investigator.

"You are loved, Jo," he soothed. "I would've taken your case *pro bono* and paid the investigator myself had it been necessary. We all know there's no way you could've committed such a crime, and it was my pleasure to help you through all this."

I sniffled. Loudly. "Please thank everyone profusely for me. This is such a weight off my mind!"

He laughed, this time in all sincerity. "Burke already did. On the way back to Atlanta that first day, he was the one who said the escrow ought to pay your fees after your twenty-five years of loyal service to the firm. Once I told him everyone had agreed, he sent a bottle of whiskey to each partner. Well, a bottle of rum to Marcia. You know she hates whiskey.

"Anyways," he cleared his throat. "I'm still your attorney of record and will stay so until I've been told the murder *and* illegal tapping of your phone have been resolved. While Inspector Woods seems to be back on the right track, I still don't want you interacting with him personally. Who knows if he'll change his mind? Therefore, he still has to communicate through me. I'll let you know if and when he contacts me."

By this time, tears were streaming down my cheeks. I honestly couldn't believe my good fortune! Not only had the firm covered the expenses, Burke had spent a lot of money on that booze – he didn't believe in the cheap stuff, and there were, last I knew, fifteen partners in the firm.

Through the tears, I thanked him again. I promised to let him know of any developments on my end then we disconnected.

Immediately, I sent a group text to all the people who had supported me over the last couple of weeks: Denny, Abby, Chaz, Timmy, El, and Anne. Just got word from my attorney. Charges against me have been dropped! They're still working on all the problems with my phone. But I'm off the hook!

Almost before I could take a breath, there was a pawing at the shop door, and I heard a baritone voice say, "*Open up!*"

I opened the door to find Coop, panting and tongue lolling. A moment later, El came running through the trees. She cleared the three steps up to deck level and barreled into me, hugging me so hard I had a difficult time breathing.

Then she backed away, leaned over, and put her hands on her knees, panting almost as much as the dog.

"I…shouldn't…have run," she said between gasps. "Too…damned old. But I wanted…to be the first to congratulate you."

"Geezus, woman," I cried. "There was no rush. I don't want to be the death of you! Come inside and sit. Catch your breath while I get you a glass of water."

They both followed me inside the shop where El plopped onto the only chair and Coop collapsed at her feet. I got her a glass of water from the tap and looking around, couldn't find anything to use as a bowl for Coop. I ran back into the house to get one of my mixing bowls and once I had filled that, he lapped up about half of it.

"The soap!" I heard Esme exclaim from her spot on top of one of the cupboards. I hadn't heard her come in but she was right. I turned to find one cauldron a complete mess. In my exhilaration over Connor's news I'd forgotten what I'd been working on and it had started to burn.

"Dammit," I cried, putting on my oven mitts to pull the pot off the heat. "That's twenty bars wasted."

"Probably worth it, though," El said. "At least, I'd think so given the news you just got. Tell you what, salvage what you can and sell it to me. Even without the magic, I like your stuff."

"It's not going to even smell right," I told her. "The whole batch is going to stink because of the burning. No, I'll just scrape it out and dump it. It'll degrade in the compost pile."

El laughed. "You're going to have a really clean compost pile, then!"

"I need to let it cool before I can clean that out. So, why did you feel a need to *run* over here?"

She finished her water and handed me the glass, which I set on the counter to be carried back into the house and dishwasher. "Like I said, I wanted to be the first to congratulate you. And ask what you're going to do next. Will can only work on the mundane stuff. You said there's a witch involved, and I assume you'll go after him, right?"

I nodded. "But not until the mundane investigation is complete. I need to know exactly who was involved and how far. After that? Like I said, Denny and Abby are cooking up something.

"Until then, I'm going back to my life. Now I don't have to worry about being in jail for twenty years for a murder I didn't commit, I can concentrate. I haven't really been able to make much in the way of stock because my focus has been shot to hell for two weeks. I've got a business to run."

"I've been thinking a lot about your situation, and I have some ideas," El said. "Both the murder and your business."

I eyed her. "Okay. I'm stopped until the mess cools. Let's go in the house where it's more comfortable, and you can lay your ideas on me."

I shut the shop down, and we all went back into the house. Coop immediately lay on the floor in the living room in front of the cold fireplace. Seemed even without the heat, it was his favorite place, no matter the house he was in. Esme, as was her custom, banged through her door and took up position on the mantel.

I started another pot of coffee, and while it perked, told El of the firm paying my legal fees.

"You have some damned good friends there," she said. "I've never heard of such a thing and was all ready to lend you some money to pay their bill. I know you're almost living on a shoestring and was worried you couldn't afford it. Based on what you've said, they're not the cheapest firm in the city."

"It probably would have drained the rest of my savings," I admitted. "But now I don't have to worry about that either. I do appreciate the thought, though." Privately, I knew I wouldn't have taken her offer. Borrowing money from a friend, and one I'd just met, was a sure way to kill the relationship.

Coffee cups in hand, we sat in the much more comfortable chairs in the living room.

"Okay. Your ideas?"

"First, the murder," she began. "Coop has a *fantastic* nose. If you can get something of your ex's with his scent, like a piece of clothing, then the address for that witch, he can sniff out whether your ex has been there. That would just be more evidence to tie them together, even if it wouldn't be admissible in court."

Coop raised his head. *"I have a very good nose. Better than any human. I will help."*

I shook my head. "Thanks, you two, but I can't get anything of his without seeing him. Which I'm not going to do. Connor said at least one of the phones on the other end of the tracking app is a burner. Maybe they'll trace it back to Johnstone. Who knows? But I'm leaving that in mundane hands for now. Next?"

"Second, I'm bored shitless," she said with a wry smile. "The garden only takes a couple of hours a week, and the jobs from Tyler are only once a month or so. I can only read so much before I get bored of that, too. I don't want a j-o-b, but I need something more to do.

"In my previous life working with several charities, it was all *marketing.* Selling the idea of the charity to potential donors, mostly. I can't tell you how many cups of coffee or tea I drank, or fucking banquets I organized, all to *sell* the *idea* of the charity to raise money.

"You need to *sell the idea* of your business and its products. That's selling *you*, which means *marketing.* Let me take over the marketing of your business. I don't know a damned thing about magic, but I know your products – at least the soaps – work. I can market something I believe in. I'm good at it."

My jaw dropped. It was good my mouth wasn't that large because it probably would have hit the floor and bruised my chin. "I…" I stuttered. "I don't know what to say. Wait. Yes, I do. I can't afford to pay you. I can barely afford to pay myself!"

She smiled. "I don't want or need your money. I *need* to fill hours, or I'm going to go stir crazy. I haven't found anything else to do that interests me.

"Between me and my kid, I think we can raise your visibility quite a bit. Sam's been bugging me ever since Christmas. Your business – especially the magical aspect of it – piqued her interest. She likes a challenge, and so do I. A small business like yours in a niche market is definitely a challenge."

"Take the offered help," Esme advised. *"I have a good feeling about this."*

Honestly? So did I. El was one of those outgoing people. From the little I'd seen, she was comfortable speaking with complete strangers about nearly anything, whereas I wanted to stay in my little shop, not interacting with anyone – not even my familiar, if I could've managed it.

Esme snorted. El looked up at her. "Something, Esme?"

"The introvert is wishing I wasn't around. Too bad. She's stuck with me."

El grinned then looked back at me. "Well? What do you think?"

I took a deep breath then held out my hand. "Trial period of three months?"

"Six," she replied. "Takes a while to build momentum."

"Deal," I said, shaking her hand. "But if it takes off, you have to let me pay you somehow. I'd feel guilty otherwise."

She rubbed her hands in glee. "As much soap as I and Sam can use. Maybe Jason, too, but except for the wakeup stuff, I don't think you have one that smells *manly* enough. Maybe you ought to work on a recipe for that?"

I thought that would be, like the amount of honey I would have to pay to the fairies, a really good bargain. *No one* used hundreds of bars of soap.

"So," I said, draining my coffee. "Where do we begin?"

We spent the next two hours going through a full pot of coffee and a couple of sandwiches while discussing my social media accounts and some of her suggestions – including a monthly newsletter. I cringed at that one. Although I knew a regular newsletter was a good idea (all the marketing gurus said you needed to have one), I had no idea what to say so frequently and usually only sent one when I had some news.

"No worries," El assured me. "Sam and I can come up with topics, ask you questions about them, then put it together based on your responses."

Coop whined that he needed to go out, and El decided she'd muddled my brain enough for one day. "Give us a few days to come up with a plan," she said as she hugged me goodbye. "You have no idea how excited I am about a new project!"

Once they'd left, I went back to the shop to clean up the mess. Although El was right in that it was excusable because of the good news, I was still pissed about the loss of product *and* the effort it would take to get everything cleaned up before I could start a new batch.

An hour later, I finally had a clean cauldron. Then, reminding myself I had two of them, in addition to making a new batch of soap, I started a potion I was running low on. I was about to infuse the magic into it when my phone started singing "Friends in Low Places." It was Chaz.

Leaving it sitting on the desk, I hit the "answer" button with my pinky. Without even a greeting, I said, "Call me back in ten minutes. Got a batch of potions going," and disconnected.

I had to re-focus because my thoughts had turned to wondering why Chaz had called, but I finally got in the right frame of mind. I grinned as I saw the light blue glitter swirl into the mixture I stirred. This potion was to induce calm, and I *knew* it was going to be a good one.

I'd just managed to clap the lid on the pot when Chaz called again. This time I wasn't as brusque when answering.

"Hang on. I need to set the timer." I switched over to the clock function of my phone and set it for three hours. Returning to the call, I said, "Hey, what's up?" as I stirred the soap. His low chuckle echoed down the line. "The Atlanta grapevine is working overtime today. I have some news I think you'll enjoy."

"Oh?"

"Your, uh, buddy, Harvey Johnstone, was arrested last night by Woodstock police, theoretically to be extradited to California."

"For what?"

His chuckle had turned into a full-blown laugh by now. "Fraud! I don't know all the details – yet – but my guess is someone hired him for some magical work, and it didn't go as promised. Cali has more of a grasp of the magical world than Georgia does, and they have some laws on the books addressing it.

"Anyway, he's out of the picture for a while if what I'm hearing is correct. At least a year, maybe more in jail if convicted, and I doubt they'd have gone to the trouble of extraditing him if it wasn't a biggie and they had the receipts to prove it."

I smiled a nasty smile. My spell was working! "That *is* good news! One down, I think, one to go."

"I presume you're talking about your ex. Any more news on that front?"

"None since I texted you this morning. My guess is it'll be a while yet, before I hear anything else. They have to do more tracing on stuff related to my phone. That takes time."

"Of course. Keeping fingers and toes crossed it resolves quickly. It's time to open so gotta run. Thought you'd want to hear the news, though!"

"You're right! Thanks for letting me know. Kisses to you and Timmy."

"Kisses from both of us back!" He disconnected.

"Based on what I've heard about that blackguard, serves him right." Esme had an opinion about everything.

"Like Chaz said, it must be something big if they actually paid to extradite him. They don't normally do that for much less than murder, I think. Doesn't matter. He can't do much from jail."

"He can with just his intent, you know."

"I know, but not much if he's not very strong. And Wanda, whoever she is, said he had a full workroom, meaning he relied on more than just his intent to get things done."

CHAPTER TWENTY-TWO

I spent the remaining hours before the potion was ready pouring the soap into molds then puttering. I watered the plants and moved a couple to give them better light now that it was spring. I took note of my soap stock and put in another order for the melt-and-pour base I used. Now I didn't have to worry about paying an attorney's bill, I felt more comfortable with my financial situation and didn't mind increasing my inventory.

I was about to start the first strain of the potion when there was a knock at the shop door. I opened it to find Inspector Woods standing there, hands in his pockets and a sheepish look on his face.

"May I come in?" he asked.

"You're supposed to be talking with my attorney, not me," I shot.

"This has nothing to do with the case and everything, I think, to do with, uh, magic. I came to ask for your help."

Curious, I let him in then picked up my phone, found and started the 'record' function. I returned to pouring the potion into the straining apparatus. "You can talk while I finish this. It can't wait. And just so you know, I'm recording our entire conversation. If you say one word about the case, I'll turn it over to my attorney in a heartbeat."

"I understand. But honestly, I know you have an attorney and wouldn't violate that."

"So. What do you want?"

He leaned against the desk opposite me. "I assume you know I was reprimanded for accepting a gift."

"I'd heard that," I replied.

"I've never done anything like that before, and all of a sudden last week, I wondered at my own actions. I woke up one morning feeling like I'd just come out of some sort of brain fog.

"Although I continued to do my job, and that included clearing you once the phone tests came back, I still chewed on what had happened to me. I must have had some look on my face that Dave noticed because he asked this morning what was bothering me.

"When I told him about my concerns about my own actions, he sat me down and told me about the watch and the magical spells you thought had been placed on it. As you can see..." He held up his wrist, which didn't have a watch on it. "...I took it off. I only want facts influencing my judgement.

"I tried returning the watch to the person who had sent it to me, but they assured me they hadn't. That convinced me what Dave said was true. That I was under some sort of a magical spell."

Although I had my back to him, I could tell he'd not taken his eyes off me during his recitation. Without turning, I asked, "And you want my help how?"

He might have moaned a little. "I don't *ever* want to be influenced by magic again. Is there something you can do that will prevent, uh, spells, from, uh, controlling me?"

I turned to eye him. "You want me to do magic to prevent magic from affecting you?"

"Can you?"

Several loud caws reverberated through the shop. Esme was laughing. Inspector Woods startled, then when he realized she was up on the cupboard where he'd seen her before, relaxed a little.

"The good Inspector is finally figuring some things out."

"I can. Do you want an amulet, like a bracelet or even that watch, or do you want to drink a potion?"

He screwed up his face. "I think I'd rather wear something, if you don't mind."

"Okay. How about that watch? I'll need that, a piece of your hair, and two days."

"But isn't the watch what got me into trouble in the first place?"

"To be honest with you, I paid fairies to remove the spells from it. It's safe to wear now."

His eyes bugged. "*Fairies?* They're real, too? And how…"

"Yes, they're real. And I'm not going to tell you everything that happened. You'll just have to take my word that the watch is clean. So, do you want me to use that or another item?"

He gulped then nodded. "The watch is in the car. I'll be right back."

He left, and Esme laughed again. *"He's not comfortable with this. But it's a good idea. Even Gargantua's woman says paranormal incidents are more frequent than they used to be. This probably won't be the last time someone tries to influence him.*

"How are you going to spell the watch?"

"Smoke," I replied immediately. "It's the only thing that will take hold without affecting the functioning of the watch. I mean, if he's going to wear one, it might as well work, right?"

"Good girl!"

I didn't have a chance to admonish her about the "girl" comment before the Inspector returned. He held the watch by its strap between his thumb and forefinger and at arm's length, as if it would bite.

I grabbed a ziplock bag from the shelf and, taking the watch from him, put it in the bag. "Now I need a piece of your hair."

"Why?"

"To personalize the spell to you, dummy. You want the magic to be strong, don't you? A generic protection spell will work, yes, but if I make it specific, it'll be more effective."

He gulped again then ran his fingers through his hair, coming up with a couple of strands. I took them from him and put them into the bag with the watch.

"Oh," I had a thought. "You don't use any hair product, do you?"

"No. Why?"

"Chemicals. They interfere with magic. If you did, I'd need some hair from right after you shower."

"Oh. Well, I don't."

"Okay then. Come back when you get off work Wednesday. I'll have it ready for you."

"And payment?"

"None necessary." I grinned at him. "I don't want anyone else to go through what I have the last couple of weeks. Consider it my contribution to proper law enforcement or something."

He nodded, left with an "until Wednesday," and after deleting the recording from my phone, I turned back to Esme.

"You should have demanded some sort of payment from him."

"It's a nickel's worth of herbs and an hour or so of my time. Not to mention goodwill and all that. I really don't want anyone else going through the bullshit I've been subjected to. It won't hurt to have him in my debt. He might come in handy in the future."

My stomach growled, letting me know it was dinner time. Checking the progress of the strain, I decided I didn't want to wait for it to finish so put a cover over the top and shut down the shop for the night.

The following day was the most normal I'd had in weeks. I finished the potion I'd been working on and made two more batches of soap. In between, I filled a couple of orders and got those out to the mailbox. By day's end, I felt a sense of accomplishment and was calm enough I could turn my attention to Inspector Woods' amulet.

Esme, naturally, had followed me into the house, and after dinner, she perched on the mantel, eyeing the watch I'd taken out of its plastic bag.

"You can't use it," she pronounced gravely. *"Not only did the fairies remove the original spells, they put another one on it."*

I looked at her in alarm. "What?"

"You can't see it? No, I suppose not because it's not human magic. I can't tell what it's supposed to do. Just that there's fairy magic on it. Because I don't know the intent, I don't know if your magic will work with it.

"You should probably figure some else out."

I stared at the watch. She was right. I couldn't see any magic on it. I could probably weave a bracelet for him, but to be honest, couldn't see him wearing one. And I'd told the Inspector I was going to use that particular watch. He'd get suspicious if I didn't, and I really didn't want to explain about different magics. I turned to her.

"Can I ask them what they did? Will that indebt me further?"

"Don't know. Probably won't hurt to ask, though."

I sighed. "Do I need to wait until moonrise? Do I need to take more honey?"

She shook her head back and forth. *"No to both questions. Not to mention I don't think you want to wait until moonrise. It's not until after you go to bed tonight."*

"But why did I need to wait until moonrise the last time?"

"Because it would be easier for you to find your way to that clearing. Now that you know where it is, moonlight isn't as necessary."

With another sigh, I put on a jacket, grabbed my phone, and headed toward the trees. When I got to the woods' edge, I activated the flashlight app and aimed it at the ground ahead of me. I didn't want to step on anything I shouldn't and anger the fairies. With Esme murmuring directions in my head, I made my way to the little clearing and, as before, turned off the flashlight and sat on the still-cold ground.

"Your show," Esme told me. *"No need to yell. They're not far and can hear you."*

I nodded in acknowledgement. "Matriarch," I called softly. "May I speak with you a moment?"

I tried not to fidget as my butt chilled. If this was going to be a regular occurrence, I would need to remember to bring a blanket with me – at least until the middle of summer when the ground beneath the trees would finally warm up.

It took about ten minutes, but finally, I saw a single twinkling light zipping my way from farther in the woods. It came to a halt a few feet away and I saw the same warrior (I thought) hovering in the air. Although he had a bow in his hand, there was no arrow nocked in the string. *That* was a relief!

"What do you want?" he asked.

"I have a question for your matriarch. At least, I think it's for her. Whoever removed the spells from the watch a couple of weeks ago."

He nodded. "It was she." Turning back toward the woods, he let out a low whistle that sounded very much like the call of a wood thrush, which was out of place at this time of the evening. A moment later, three more lights zipped my way and, as before, it was the matriarch and her two…guards, I guessed. Just as before, her dress was gauzy and flowing, but this time, it was the green of newly-formed leaves.

In her melodious voice, she asked the same question. "What do you want?"

I took a deep breath. "That watch you removed spells from a couple of weeks ago? Esme tells me there is another spell on it, fairy magic.

"The man who was affected by that watch has asked me to give him an amulet to protect him from other harmful spells. The watch would be ideal for such. Esme says she doesn't know the intent of the fairy spell, so doesn't know if my spell would work.

"I wanted to ask what the spell was, and whether I should pursue another course of action for that man."

I had assumed the circlet on her brow inferred royalty of some sort, and to me, that meant dignity, even aloofness. That assumption had been somewhat dimmed by her loudly sucking honey off her finger, and I was further disabused of my notions when she grinned like a madwoman then cackled.

"The spells on that – watch you called it? Were clumsy and starting to dissipate. The magic was leaking all over everything in its vicinity. That dwelling was such an unhappy place! So sad when a witch cannot focus their intentions well. No matter. It took but a moment to undo them.

"You told me you were being affected by that magic. Rather than risk someone reapplying their spells and further harming you, which would negate the *intention* of our bargain, not just the letter, I decided to ensure the watch couldn't be used that way again. No human magic can override ours, so it was simple to apply a blocking spell.

"Your familiar is correct that you would not be able to use it as an amulet for your magic. But I will make another bargain with you."

I think I visibly cringed. *Another* bargain with fairies? She noticed my discomfort and giggled. She actually *giggled!* Then she sobered.

"I know our reputation. Indeed, it is probably justified. But we like you and the woman with the dog and, so far, see no reason to be mischievous where you are concerned. For *one* more vessel of honey, I will fix the watch so it repels *all* magic, human or otherwise."

I blew out a breath. I could afford a couple more ounces of honey.

"She is being quite generous," Esme opined. *"I'd take that bargain were I you."*

The matriarch looked up at the branch Esme perched on. "Indeed, familiar. I *am* being generous. As I said, we like these two humans. The dog isn't bad, either. You?" she raised her eyebrow. "We have not yet decided."

Esme snorted. *"We have known each other my entire life. I'm not changing. Doubt you are, either. Shall we agree to coexist as peacefully as possible?"*

I wondered what had transpired between the two but kept my mouth shut. There would be time enough later to delve into the relationship between a crow and fairy. And also to wonder just how old these fairies were. Instead, I drew the matriarch's attention back to me.

"I agree to your offer – one more vessel of honey for a repelling spell on the watch. Are you able to return with me to the house? The watch is there, and I can give you the honey immediately."

She nodded then stuck out her tiny hand. "Agreed. And yes, we can accompany you now."

Once again, I took her hand between my thumb and forefinger before gently shaking it. Then rose – with a groan. I had stiffened during my twenty minutes of sitting on the cold ground in the chill night air. The matriarch looked at me with pity but was quiet.

Thirty minutes later, two of the men accompanying the matriarch had flown off with the custard cup of honey I'd placed on the deck railing (I, too, had been generous and filled it almost to the brim) and the matriarch had removed her previous spell before applying another. I still couldn't see the fairy magic, but Esme assured me the color of the magic had changed. Not that either of us knew what the spell's intent was, but I had to trust the matriarch.

"It was a pleasure doing business with you," the matriarch said before she flew off into the night, her remaining guard with her. "Call if we can be of assistance in the future."

"*Hopefully not,*" Esme groused. Privately, I agreed with her. Based on what both Esme and Denise had said, *doing business* with fairies got you into trouble more often than not. But I didn't voice that opinion. Instead, I just nodded at the matriarch before putting the watch on the counter in the shop where it would be ready for the Inspector's visit the following day.

Once back inside for good, I made a cup of hot chocolate and curled up on the sofa, wrapped in a blanket. I hadn't yet dispelled the chill that had permeated my bones. It might be late April, but mountain nights were still *cold* to my southern born-and-raised body.

"*So,*" Esme said. "*Bad witch taken care of, amulet taken care of. Now what?*"

"We wait," I replied, almost burning my mouth as I gulped the hot beverage in an attempt to warm up. "Now that Inspector Woods isn't under any coercion, I think it won't be long before this whole fiasco comes to an end. The techy folks will find evidence pointing to someone, and mundane law enforcement can take it from there. I should be completely in the clear."

"*And if it points back to your ex?*"

I shrugged. "I'll wait to see what happens. Jail time would suit me. If he doesn't get that, I'll figure out a way to get revenge. To be honest, he's already dug himself a pretty deep hole if what Burke said is true. It wouldn't take much to completely bury him at this point.

"If it is Asshole, I still don't understand why. If he was going to try to hurt me, it would have been better to do it *during* the divorce proceedings when it would be possible to get more money. Now that the divorce is finalized, it makes no sense. No sense at all."

"*Your friend said he might be trying to get revenge for you messing up his lifestyle. It could be as simple as that. Although, as I said, I don't understand a lot of the way humans think.*"

I grimaced. "Neither do I sometimes. On to another matter. What's with you and the fairy matriarch? Seems you don't like each other much."

Esme sighed. *"We had a…disagreement…not long after I was first fledged. Had to do with my human at that time. Leave it at that."*

"Hey," I said, "You know everything about me. Shouldn't the reverse also be true?"

"Not necessarily. Suffice it to say they were messing with my human. I saw to it they stopped. Leave it be."

She was as stubborn as I was, and I knew I wouldn't get anything more out of her – at least not at the moment. I'd learn what went on at some point, though. I finished the rest of my hot chocolate and yawned while telling her, "I'm going to bed."

True to prediction, Connor called the following morning with the news that the tracking app on my phone had been traced to not only Asshole's personal phone but a burner they also connected to his name. Someone had stupidly left the phone on, and they triangulated the signal to Johnstone's house. Given he was already under arrest for fraud, this added more layers to the evolving story – and immediately connected the two men.

"As I told you, I'd already told Inspector Woods you'd want to press stalking charges on the tracking app," he informed me. "Can you meet me at the Sheriff's Office at two tomorrow to file the paperwork?"

"I think the Inspector is due here later this afternoon," I told him. "He's supposed to come by to get an amulet from me. Perhaps I can save you a trip and ask him to bring the paperwork with him?"

"An amulet, you say? He really is starting to accept magic. If you're comfortable signing the complaint without me there, then yes. It should be fairly straightforward. I'll call him back and tell him you told me you two were meeting this afternoon and to bring the complaint with him."

I had a thought. "Have they said more about the spoofing call?"

"Not yet. That takes more time since they had to get a warrant and serve it on the spoofing company then wait for that company to respond. Those companies drag everything out as long as they can, whereas mobile service providers are fairly quick to provide whatever information law enforcement wants once the techies provide their proof.

"Must run. Have a client meeting. Call me if you see *anything* out of the ordinary before signing the complaint." After I agreed, Connor disconnected.

"Sounds like everything is coming together nicely," Esme commented. I nodded then went back to reading the marketing plan El had emailed me that morning. It sounded like a lot of work, and I felt guilty that I was getting so much done for virtually nothing.

Esme was listening in, of course. *"She sounded quite excited about her proposal and didn't want much in the way of payment. If she's okay with it all, you should be, too."*

CHAPTER TWENTY-THREE

True to his word, Inspector Woods knocked on the shop door shortly after five. I had just cleaned up from cutting a batch of soap, and he leaned over the counter to inhale the aroma of the twenty bars sitting there, ready for packaging.

"Those smell wonderful!" he told me. "My wife would love the lavender-scented ones. How much for a couple of bars?"

I smiled. "I don't retail, but I'm happy to give her, not you, a couple as a gift. I should warn you, though, they're not just scented. They're infused with magic, too."

He eyed me. "To do what?"

"The lavender ones are infused with a calming intention. Just enough to get rid of the stress one might feel after a difficult day."

He chuckled. "She'll like that even more. She has to keep up with not only me and my demanding job but two small boys, too."

I smiled again. I already knew he had little ones but wasn't about to tell him how I knew. "Then let me wrap two for you. It'll only take a minute.

"While I do that, put this on." I handed him the watch then got my packaging supplies out. It only took a couple of minutes, but I had my back to him while doing so.

"He hasn't put the watch on. He's turning it this way and that, looking as if the magic might be obvious to a human." I heard Esme's gurgling laugh.

When I turned to hand him the wrapped soap, he was still holding the watch by its strap and staring at it.

"Well? Aren't you going to put it on?" I asked.

"How do I know this will do that job? Or that it won't affect me in some way?"

I glared. "You don't. You'll just have to take my word for it. But it's not going to do you a damned bit of good if you just hold it. Put it on!"

He sighed then strapped it to his wrist. "Should I feel any different?"

I just shook my head then asked, "Don't you have some papers for me to sign?"

He looked a little sheepish. "I don't. I didn't have time to get them put together before coming over. Can you come to my office mid-morning tomorrow to do that?

"Also, I have a problem I hope you can help with. I got the answer from the spoofing company early this afternoon. That, too, traces back to your ex's personal phone. All that is enough to justify bringing him in for questioning related to the younger Ms. Rice's death. Since he lives in Atlanta, I've had to coordinate with Atlanta PD. They tried to pick him up for me, but although his phone pinged as being at the condo, he wasn't. His car isn't in the parking garage, either. Do you have any idea where he might have gone?"

Asshole had really gotten himself into big-time trouble, and I wondered again at what had caused him to – probably – turn to a life of crime. It didn't take but a moment for me to reply. "His folks live in Florida, and if you ask them, their darling son can do no wrong. I suspect he ran home to Mom."

"Damn. Sorry. I can't bring him back from there for just a misdemeanor or even for questioning. But on the off chance I can find a way, do you remember their address?"

How could I not? More than twenty years of sending cards on birthdays and their anniversary and traveling to spend Christmas and other special days with them had etched it in my memory. I grabbed a piece of scratch paper and quickly wrote their names and address then handed it to him.

"Thanks," he said. "Is there anywhere else you can think of?"

I shook my head. "He didn't really have any close friends. At least, not anyone I think would hide him from the police if he is indeed guilty of something. Most of the people we socialized with when we were married were work colleagues – either his or mine. He didn't like my friends, so I saw them separately.

"He's not the outdoorsy type, so I don't think he'd take to the woods like the Atlanta bomber did. Hell, he probably doesn't even know how to light a campfire. He wasn't even ever a Boy Scout."

The Inspector nodded, making a few notes in the notebook he'd pulled out of his jacket pocket. Once he'd finished writing, he put it back in his pocket, then looked at me.

"Thanks for that," he said. "I was extremely unpleasant to you for a couple of weeks, and even though I now know I was under some sort of spell, I still apologize. Your cooperation has been most helpful.

"Now, I need to run so my wife doesn't think I got *really* caught up at work. Although I'm used to eating reheated dinner, it's nice if I don't have to, you know?

"Shall we say around ten tomorrow for the stalking complaint? I should be able to get it drawn up by then." He held out his hand, which I shook while agreeing to the time then handed him the bars of soap.

"One last question," I said before he could leave. "What sort of penalties is my ex facing for all this?"

"Stalking – first offense, anyway – is up to a year in jail and a thousand-dollar fine. That I know I can prove. However, if this all ties together like I think it's going to, that will be the least of his worries. Malice murder, or abetting the same, can carry twenty years to life. I can't say how involved he is until I have all the pieces, though. See you tomorrow morning." He smiled before leaving the shop.

"Based on the cop shows you watch on television, he's being more forthcoming than he should to a civilian. He seems a decent sort."

I nodded my head in agreement. "Now he's not under any sort of spell, I kind of like him. He doesn't – now – discount magic and its effects, and he probably *is* telling me more than he should. Maybe he's making up for arresting me?"

Although my stomach was starting to grumble, I finished wrapping the soap and storing it until needed. Then I headed into the house to make dinner. I read until bedtime, and in what seemed the first night in weeks, fell asleep quickly with no bad dreams.

The next morning, I woke up with an idea. I *really* wanted my ex to pay for anything illegal – or immoral – he'd done. The crap I'd been through in the last few weeks was more than anyone should have to endure. But Inspector Woods said he couldn't bring Asshole back from Florida – if that was where he was. What if my ex was back in Georgia? Maybe even in Atlanta? I was a *witch*, dammit, and should be able to do something to help the cops.

"What are you thinking?" Esme flew in her door and landed on the table next to my chair. Her voice sounded like she'd just woken up so, apparently, hadn't read *all* my thoughts.

"I'm ninety-nine percent certain Asshole is with his parents. He always clung to them when times got tough before, so I doubt anything has changed. I think I can lure him back to Atlanta using a drawing spell. Once there, the police ought to be able to pick him up for questioning."

"But you'd need a personal item for that. And you said you didn't have anything."

"I never got around to throwing away my key to the condo. If he hasn't changed the lock, I should be able to get in and look. He's a slob, so I'm pretty sure his razor won't be clean, or there will be dirty clothing about."

"*Hmmm. Might be a plan.*" She sounded doubtful. I asked about the tone of her voice.

"*I'm sure your spell would work. I'm concerned, though, about you getting into the condo. What if you're seen? Since you no longer own it, wouldn't that be considered illegal?*"

I hadn't considered that, but she had a point. On the other hand, if he'd been responsible (at least in part) for all the bullshit I'd had to endure the last few weeks, I wanted him to pay. The more I thought about it, the more I was willing to risk getting caught if it meant *he* got what was coming to him.

Esme reminded me I needed to go see the Inspector that morning. I inhaled another cup of coffee before showering and getting ready to leave. I transferred my wallet and a few other necessities from my purse to a large tote bag. I also put spell ingredients into it before slinging it over my shoulder and heading out.

Once at the Sheriff's Office, I had to wait for Inspector Woods to retrieve me from the reception area. He led me to his office, where he placed several pages on his desk so they faced me. Then he set a pen on top of them. "Read then sign at the bottom."

I took my time reading, knowing Connor would thrash me if I hadn't. It all seemed straightforward, detailing the forensic tests on my phone and how the GBI had traced the tracking app back to two phones registered in my ex's name. It also mentioned the date our divorce was final and that the app was still in use after that.

I read all four pages through twice before signing at the bottom of the last page. Inspector Woods witnessed my signature then said, "I'll file this yet today and once filed, a copy will go down to Atlanta, just in case your ex returns. I've put a BOLO – be on the lookout –

on his car with instruction that he is wanted for questioning in a murder case. A misdemeanor – the stalking charge – wouldn't get quite as much attention. Hopefully, someone will see him driving somewhere."

I nodded in understanding. We shook hands, and as I climbed back in my car, wondered if road atlases were still available. A map was crucial to the spell I intended to bring Asshole back where Inspector Woods could reach him. A quick search on my phone told me they were and I could even pick one up at Walmart – there were several on my route. I smiled to myself before heading to the four-lane on my way to Atlanta.

Once at the condo building, I had a spell of déjà vu. I had lived there for nearly twenty years, and my heart hurt for a moment, remembering how happy I'd been in that place – once upon a time. Then I remembered my cozy cabin in the woods, my love for the business of making potions and soaps, Esme, and my very cool new neighbor. I was happier now than I'd been in a very long time – if one discounted the bullshit my ex was putting me through. I sucked in a breath and hit the elevator button.

Once off the elevator, I pulled a pair of latex gloves from the tote and put them on before heading down the hall. I wasn't certain if anyone would dust for prints but wanted to ensure mine weren't anywhere anyone would think of to look. I knew the security cameras would show me entering and leaving the building, and one could reasonably surmise my destination but that, I hoped, was as far as they would get.

My key easily opened the door to the condo. I didn't think Asshole would have changed the lock, and I was right. But I wasn't prepared for what I saw when entering. Instead of the clean condo I had left nearly two years earlier, it looked not only like a tornado had hit, but the occupant had no care for hygiene. The remains of microwave dinners and dirty glasses littered every available horizontal surface, and dust covered those. As I walked toward the bathroom, the smell of unwashed linens and clothing assaulted my nose. I knew my ex was a slob from the day we moved in together – I had always quietly grumbled as I picked up after him – but this went beyond the pale.

However, that would probably make my job easier. As Abby had found, his razor was sitting on the edge of the sink, not even rinsed but clogged with hair and remnants of shaving cream. The shower drain was covered in hair and soap residue. I cringed, wondering how *anyone* could live like that.

"Suck it up, buttercup. You have a job to do." Esme, as always, was in my head even from one hundred miles away.

Reasoning the hair off his head would be easier to deal with than tiny pieces of beard from his razor, I picked up a clog from the shower drain then rinsed it off in the sink. It was a large clump, and I hadn't even taken all of it. Was he balding? I almost died laughing at the thought. He'd always been so proud of his thick head of hair.

I took the clump of hair to the kitchen where I blotted it dry on one of the last sheets of paper towels. Then from the tote bag, I pulled the atlas and a small jar of sugar. It was difficult to find a clear space to work, and I ended up sitting in the middle of the living room floor.

I opened the atlas to the map of the interstate system. I divided the clump of hair into two, placing one on top of the town where his parents lived and the other atop the city of Atlanta. It took a few minutes to center myself amid all the chaos of a filthy condominium I desperately wanted to clean, but I finally managed to block out my disgust and focus.

Although Esme wasn't physically present, I could feel her weight leaning against me, as she had done before. I startled at that, which pulled me out of the moment.

"How...?" I began.

"*My magic,*" came the reply. "*I'm adding it to yours. Now, focus!*"

I wiggled a little in my cross-legged position then closed my eyes and re-centered myself. Finally, I opened my eyes and stared at the map. While sprinkling a line of sugar from the hair in Florida along the route one would drive between the two points and ending at the hair on Atlanta, I intoned,

"Atlanta is home, for which you yearn. To that place you must return."

I repeated myself eight more times then pushed my will out with both my hands and a breath. Again, the color of my magic was purple. When I felt it leave my perception, I tore the page from the atlas and folded it so the hair and sugar stayed inside. I climbed to my feet – again with a groan – then picked up after myself, putting all my supplies back into the tote. Looking around to ensure I'd left nothing behind, I left the condo, re-locking the door behind me. While waiting for the elevator to arrive, I pulled off the latex gloves and put them in the tote as well.

I felt a strong sense of satisfaction on the drive back to the mountains. I might even have giggled a bit. Asshole would get his comeuppance; of that I was certain. How long it would take, I had no idea. But he *would* face a day of reckoning soon.

I spent a very pleasant weekend. After mowing the yard again (I couldn't wait until I could afford a service), I paid some attention to my plants, did a little cleaning, then watched television or read.

Mid-morning Tuesday, my phone rang. Surprised to see "Fannin County" on the display, I answered cautiously.

"I thought I'd let you know APD picked up your ex this morning," Inspector Woods said. "He's being transported back up here as we speak, so I'll be able to charge him with stalking *and* question him about Ms. Rice's murder. If he tells me anything of interest, I'll keep you informed."

I grinned, although he couldn't see it. My spell had worked as intended, and more quickly than I'd thought. "Thanks, Inspector. I do appreciate the information."

After disconnecting, I did a little happy dance around the shop. It looked like my life would be back to normal fairly soon. I wanted to share my happiness with *someone* so called El and gave her the good news. Esme grumbled in my mind about not being "someone."

After I'd told her what the inspector had said, El laughed. A good, long belly laugh. Once she'd gotten her breath back, she said, "It's about damned time they got him. Did Will mention that nasty witch? The one you said was being extradited back to California?"

"No. I guess that'll depend on what Asshole says, if anything. I have a hunch he'll spill whatever beans he's got. I don't think he's strong enough to keep his mouth shut if the Inspector is a tough interrogator."

I could hear the grin in El's voice. "I've never watched him, but from what Dave says, Will *always* gets what he needs. One way or another. I would guess that within the week, he'll have this case wrapped up tighter than a drum.

"This calls for a celebration. Taco Tuesday at my house?"

We agreed I'd be at her house around six. I went back to filling a few orders. Although it had only been a week since El and Sam had taken over the marketing of my company, I thought I'd seen a small uptick in sales. One of the potion orders I was shipping out was to a new customer.

I had followed what they posted for me on social media with interest, trying to learn from the experts. It had mostly been informational – about the magical properties of the herbs I used. But there were a couple about me and my love for what I did, which made a difference in how my products turned out. There were no "buy my stuff" posts although, occasionally, they put in a link to my online store. Apparently, those sorts of posts worked.

That night, over a second glass of El's excellent wine, she mused about how the Atlanta police had apprehended my ex when they thought he'd left town. I grinned into my glass.

"Did you do something?" she asked.

"I might have used a drawing spell to bring him back."

Her eyes widened. "You did? How does that work?"

I explained how I was fairly certain he'd run home to Mom, getting hair from his filthy condo, and how the drawing spell worked, without going into any detail.

"You *broke* into his condo?"

"Did not *break* in. Had a key, and it still worked. Not my fault if he's so stupid he didn't change the lock after the divorce."

She sat back in her chair and took a gulp of her wine. "What if you'd been caught?"

"Don't know. Like I said, I still had a key. I guess they could charge me with trespassing. It was a chance I was willing to take. I want my name completely cleared and whoever put me through a month of hell to pay."

She took another swig. "You've got some balls, girl, I'll give you that."

"*She was doing what she thought she needed to. I support her,*" Cooper's deep voice rumbled. He was lying in front of the fireplace watching our conversation.

"*She was in no danger,*" Esme added from her perch on the mantel. "*I was watching the outside of the building to ensure there were no police around.*"

I turned to her in amazement. "You were? I thought you had stayed up here."

She groomed her chest feathers in seeming nonchalance. "*You needed another set of eyes. Just in case. Mine were the best ones.*"

I was flabbergasted. I had no idea she'd followed me into the city.

Our conversation turned to lighter notes of El planting her garden for the season. She informed me she'd added a fourth tomato plant, and I had better like them because she was certain she'd have more than she could use.

"I love tomatoes," she told me. "But I can only use so much pasta sauce and ketchup."

"So why did you plant a fourth?"

"Because Dave likes fresh tomatoes and asked me to put in another. I just don't think he realizes how many fruit a single plant will produce."

I let out a laugh. I'd grown a single tomato plant on the condo balcony one year. Asshole didn't like them, I couldn't eat them all, and I ended up bringing basketfuls into the office so they didn't go to waste. That was the last year I'd grown any vegetables at all.

After a third glass of wine, I decided it was time to head home. Between the wine and the knowledge my life would soon be back to normal, I felt light as I wended my way down the path the trees had created. Once again, I vocalized my thanks to both the trees and fairies for making the trip between the two houses easier.

CHAPTER TWENTY-FOUR

A week later, there was a knock at the shop door. I opened it and was surprised to see Inspector Woods standing there. "May I come in?" he asked.

I ushered him in and, once again, saw him eye my coffee cup with interest. Chuckling, I silently poured him a cup and handed it over as I said, "What can I do for you?"

He took a drink then set his cup down on the desk and looked at me. "I came to tell you your ex confessed to nearly everything. Thanks to him, we now have Mr. Johnstone in custody here on the charge of malice murder, which trumps California's fraud case. Your ex is not only charged with stalking you but also as an accessory to one murder."

I almost choked on my coffee. "What?"

He sighed and sat in the office chair before taking up his coffee again. "It is probably the most convoluted murder case I've ever been involved with, and I worked in Chicago for four years.

"It's a long story. Do you have time?"

I didn't have anything on the stove so nodded. "Let's go into the house where it's more comfortable for both of us since I only have one chair out here."

I grabbed the carafe before leading him into the house. I told him to go sit in the living room as I set the thermos on the counter then started another pot of coffee. Esme banged through her door and flew to the mantel. Inspector Woods was staring at her as I joined him.

"Does she have free rein?" he asked.

"Pretty much," I grumbled. "It was either give her the freedom to come and go as she pleased or listen to her complaints all the time. Not to mention getting up constantly to open and close a window."

"*I am a familiar. Of* course *I get to come and go as I please.*" The peanut gallery had spoken.

He swallowed once then nodded. "Okay. The story of the murders. And yes, both Rice women were murdered.

"Your ex-husband met the younger Ms. Rice at a strip club in Atlanta about six months ago. She was a dancer; he was a customer. They started a relationship. Apparently, she and her mother didn't see eye-to-eye about her choice of an occupation. From what I can gather, their arguments were so bad the younger Ms. Rice wanted her mother dead.

"Mr. Johnstone was a customer of the bank where Mr. Schmidt worked, and they, too, struck up a friendship. Mr. Johnstone made no secret about his, uh, magical leanings and to keep his girlfriend happy, Mr. Schmidt introduced the two in the hopes Mr. Johnstone could help the girl out.

"At the same time, your ex was very upset about the changes the divorce made to his financial situation. Although he knew he wouldn't benefit if something happened to you, he wanted you hurt. Did you know he tried to find your house and, even with the tracking app, couldn't? He said although it told him he was at the correct location, there was no driveway."

I laughed. And silently thanked Chaz. "A friend put up wards the day I moved in. They're designed to keep anyone with bad intentions from finding my house," I told him. Then I wondered about that – the Inspector hadn't had the best of intentions the day he arrested me. I'd chew on that later.

"Wow. Magic will do that, huh?" He looked intrigued. "Anyway. The three of them concocted a plan to poison the elder Ms. Rice and pin it on you. Your ex knew you were into herbs, so the younger Ms. Rice looked at her mother's business records and found your name, thereby making their scheme easy, they thought. Mr. Johnstone made the poison, although your ex didn't know the particulars, and the younger Ms. Rice was to administer it when told the tracking app said you were headed to the store. I guess they were lucky you actually went there instead of somewhere else in the vicinity that day."

He drained his cup and asked for a refill, which I got for him as I replenished my own supply of caffeine. I told him to continue talking as I did so.

"When you weren't arrested for Marie Rice's murder, your ex figured they needed to do something else. By this time, both older men had tired of Katherine Rice's whining. She had apparently even threatened to tell the police Mr. Johnstone had poisoned her mother. So they decided to get rid of both of you. That's where the spoofing text came in. Although he hasn't confessed, I believe it was Mr. Johnstone who over-inflated Katherine's tires and instructed your ex when to send the text. We've been able to track the burner phone found at his home to within a mile of her house that evening.

"Both men are in jail; both have been denied bond as they are deemed flight risks. Your ex was indeed in Florida. Local traffic cameras picked up his license plate a half mile from the address you gave me for his parents. Why he decided to return to Atlanta, I'll never know, but I certainly am glad he did." I inwardly chortled. I'd never tell!

"I believe your ex will testify to everything in exchange for a lighter sentence. He honestly thought they'd never be caught and is now scared shitless – excuse my language – about prison."

"Will I need to testify at their trials?" I asked. I didn't really want to but would if called.

"I don't think so. We have the forensic evidence from your phone, and Mr. Schmidt confessed to his part and what he knew of the others' roles. You didn't know Mr. Johnstone at all, and I have your statement as to what you saw the morning you found Marie Rice."

He stood and handed me his now-empty cup. "I am truly sorry for everything you've been through the last couple of months. I know it's been hard. But without your knowledge of magic, I don't think I could have solved this. Actually, I don't think I *would* have because of the watch. Which, by the way, was also Mr. Johnstone's doing, according to Mr. Schmidt.

"Also, I wanted to tell you my wife loves the soap you gave her and wants to know where she can purchase it when she runs out."

I smiled at that. "Nowhere local now that Marie's shop is closed. She was probably going to carry at least some of it. Closest place would be The Unicorn's Hut in Woodstock. While I think about it, do you know what will happen to Marie's store? I really hate driving into Atlanta for my herbs or ordering them online and paying exorbitant shipping."

He shook his head. "From what I understand, despite their disagreements, Katherine was her heir, and *she* had no will. So unless they can find another relative, Marie's assets will go to the state. At some point, the store will get sold along with the building, I guess. But that will take months. Sorry."

I sighed. It was back to fighting Atlanta traffic again. *Unless*, I mused, I could convince Denny or Abby to do my shopping for me?

"You could always grow your own. Or convince your neighbor to do it."

I nearly replied aloud then remembering the Inspector's presence, thought back, *"You know I can't grow that much and some of them, like myrrh, won't grow here at all. No, it's better to buy. Besides, I hope I get busy enough in the shop I won't have time to pay attention to a large garden."*

Inspector Woods must have spoken and I missed it because he said, "Ms. Foster?"

"Sorry," I replied sheepishly. "Esme. Did you say something?"

He looked at me oddly. "That is *so* weird. Yes, I asked if you had any other questions I might answer."

"Not that I can think of. I am truly flabbergasted my ex would go to such lengths. I never thought of him as *that* vindictive. But it is what it is, and he'll get what's coming to him."

He nodded, shook my hand, and left. I blew out a breath I hadn't been aware I was holding. Then I noticed I had two coffee cups and went into the kitchen to put the empty one in the dishwasher.

"So. It is done. You did well, grasshopper, with your drawing spell."

I turned to her. "Where are you learning all these idioms? I know *I* don't watch that much television."

She snorted. *"You did when you were younger. I have a good memory, you know!"*

I snorted back.

Two days later, I was in the courtroom for Asshole's second arraignment, El at my side. We sat three rows back from the prosecutor's table. I noticed my former in-laws sitting in the row immediately behind the defense table. They, thankfully, didn't see me. Before the judge entered the room, the ex was looking around and spotted me. He screamed, "You bitch!" and tried to jump over the railing between the attorney's table and the spectator seating. The bailiff caught him, holding him firmly.

That didn't stop the ex. "You ruined my life! I'll get you for this!" he yelled at me, spittle flying out of his mouth as he continued to rant.

The former in-laws saw who he was yelling at and glared. I gave them a flat look back. Then his mother started crying – again, if her red eyes were any indication.

"Calm," Esme said. She didn't need to do so. I was fine although a little flabbergasted at Rob's outburst. A smug smile may have crossed my lips, though, as I watched two sheriff's deputies forcefully re-seat him in his chair and put him in leg shackles. All the while, his head was turned toward me and he muttered. Unpleasant things, I'm sure. His attorney stared at him then tried to calm him down.

"Has he gone completely bonkers?" El whispered to me.

"Looks like. I mean, *I* didn't ruin his life, he did," I whispered back.

"All rise," the bailiff said. As we all stood, the same judge I'd seen a month earlier entered the room. "The Honorable Mary Carpenter presiding."

"You may be seated," she said as she sat. The bailiff went over to her and whispered in her ear. Her eyebrows raised as she looked at Asshole. Then she banged the gavel and intoned, "This court is in session.

"Robert Alan Schmidt, you have been charged with stalking and accessory to malice murder. Based on what I was just told, I am going to add disorderly conduct and making terroristic threats to those charges. How do you plead?"

Asshole's attorney cleared his throat. "Your Honor, in light of recent events, I would ask for a psychiatric examination of my client."

"I am *innocent!*" my ex yelled. "It's all her fault!" he jerked his thumb back toward me. "I don't need a shrink!"

The judge banged her gavel again. "Mr. Schmidt. I asked you a simple question. I believe you answered 'not guilty.' Is that correct? A 'yes' or 'no' will suffice."

Asshole's eyes went wild, and his face got even redder. "This is such a boatload of shit. I didn't do a damned thing," he shouted to no one in particular.

Judge Carpenter banged her gavel yet again. *"Mr. Schmidt.* Control yourself!" She looked at the defense attorney. "I will grant your request, Mr. Houseman. Defendant is remanded to state custody without bail. He will be examined by a state psychiatrist within thirty days to determine whether he is fit to stand trial. We will reconvene in forty-five days. Next case!" Her gavel hit the sound block one final time.

It still took two deputies to escort Asshole from the courtroom. Normally, they'd just have gestured the prisoner in the direction of the door that led to the cells, and the perp would shuffle along. Of course, my ex wasn't that meek. After his attorney whispered in his ear, he became belligerent, started toward me even though he was hand- and leg-cuffed, and the deputies ended up nearly dragging him through the door. "I'll get you!" he growled while looking over his shoulder at me.

"Wow," El blew out a breath. "Good thing he didn't make bail. I think you'd be in some trouble if he had."

"I'd just be stuck at home behind Chaz's awesome wards, is all," I replied. "Asshole told Inspector Woods he'd tried to find my house and couldn't. But that's a moot point. I don't think he'll be going anywhere for quite a while. The man has truly become deranged, so probably a mental institution instead of jail. Either way, I don't have to concern myself for ten or more years.

"Come on. Let's go get some coffee."

El preceded me, but before I could even get to the courtroom door, a hand grabbing my arm stopped me. "What did you do to my son?" his father snarled.

I wrenched my arm away, said, "Not a damned thing," and continued out the door with my head held high.

He wouldn't be deterred, though, and followed closely. As soon as we were in the hall, he grabbed my arm again. "I know you're a witch. Rob told me. You must have done *something* to him. He was always a sweet boy until you divorced him."

This time, after pulling away once again, I rounded on him. "Alan. *Mister* Schmidt. I caught your son *in flagrante delicto* with his secretary in *our* bed. He was *not* a sweet boy until the divorce, although you wouldn't believe that, would you? As to my being a witch, yes, I am. But I cannot influence someone's mind." I didn't tell him others obviously could.

To my surprise, Dave appeared in front of us, El at his side, both with a concerned look on their faces. "Is there a problem, Ms. Foster?" Dave asked.

"Thank you, Sergeant Anderson, but Mr. Schmidt here was just leaving."

To his credit, Mr. Schmidt took one look at Dave's uniform and glared at me once again before taking his wife's arm and heading toward the elevator.

"Who was that?" Dave asked.

"The ex-in-laws," I told him. "Still thinking their little boy can do no wrong and whatever happened is obviously someone else's fault." I shook my head. "Whatever crazy has materialized in Asshole's brain has *got* to be related to them coddling him his entire life.

"After all that, I need a drink but it's too early so coffee will have to do. Who's coming with?"

El smiled and raised her hand. "Me. The shop two blocks down not only has great coffee but awesome pastries." She stood on her tiptoes and kissed Dave. "See you tonight."

"Come with me," Dave said. "I'll take you out the back way just in case those two are hanging around out front. Based on what I've seen and heard, you did good getting out of that marriage, Jo."

I nodded in agreement. "Why were you up here anyway, Dave?" I asked as he escorted us down a side hall.

"Curiosity, mostly," he grinned. "I had a few minutes so was listening to the proceedings from behind the judge's door. Once she tabled the case, I came out for a quick kiss before going back to work. Two kisses, actually," he said as he leaned down to kiss El before punching a code into a keypad next to a door.

"They're so cute together," I thought as I followed them down a drab, utilitarian hallway. I was glad my new friend was happy.

"I believe you are, too," Esme said.

I thought for a minute. I was, actually. Discounting the events of the last month-plus, life was good. I had a business I loved that would provide me with a good living thanks to El and Sam's marketing efforts, I was growing into my power as a witch, had a cozy house in the woods, and *good* friends. Who could ask for more?

"You have an awesome familiar, too."

I snorted. There was that, too.

ALSO BY DEBORAH J. "DJ" MARTIN

<u>Nonfiction</u>

Herbs: Medicinal, Magical, Marvelous!

A Green Witch's Formulary

Baneful! 95 of the World's Worst Herbs

A Green Witch's Cupboard

<u>Fiction</u>

Ogre's Assistant Series:

Stressed!

Upheaval!

Transformation!

Immortal Spirit

Blue Ridge Series:

Reinventing Herself

ABOUT THE AUTHOR

A semi-retired accountant, Master Herbalist, author, and witch, Deborah J. "DJ" Martin abandoned frozen Minnesota many moons ago and now lives in the woods of the southern Appalachian Mountains with her husband, four cats, and numerous woodland creatures. If you can't find DJ in the garden or visiting her grandchildren, check Facebook (@authordjmartin), Twitter (@authordjmartin), or her website http://www.authordjmartin.com.

If you want to keep up with DJ and the happenings in the mountains, you can subscribe to her quarterly newsletter here: https://www.subscribepage.com/authordjmartin. You'll also get a free story!

The best way to get word out about books is through *you*, the reader. If you like this book (or any other author's, for that matter), please leave a review wherever you bought it, on Goodreads, or on social media. It helps. Thank you!

www.ingramcontent.com/pod-product-compliance
Lightning Source LLC
Chambersburg PA
CBHW072055190726

48294CB00005B/1539